Also by Will Thomas

Some Danger Involved
To Kingdom Come
The Limehouse Text

THE HELLFIRE CONSPIRACY

Will Thomas

A Touchstone Book
Published by Simon & Schuster
New York London Toronto Sydney

TOUCHSTONE
A Division of Simon & Schuster, Inc.
1230 Avenue of the Americas
New York, NY 10020

First Touchstone hardcover edition July 2007

TOUCHSTONE and colophon are registered trademarks of Simon & Schuster, Inc.

For information about special discounts for bulk purchases, please contact Simon & Schuster Special Sales at 1-800-456-6798 or business@simonandschuster.com.

Designed by Melissa Isriprashad

Manufactured in the United States of America

10 9 8 7 6 5 4 3 2 1

Library of Congress Cataloging-in-Publication Data

Thomas, Will.
The hellfire conspiracy : a novel / Will Thomas.
   p. cm.
"A Touchstone book"—T.p. verso.
   1. Barker, Cyrus (Fictitious character)—Fiction. 2. Private investigators—England—London—Fiction. 3. Great Britain—History—Victoria, 1837–1901—Fiction. 4. London (England)—Fiction. I. Title.
PS3620.H644H45 2007
813'.6—dc22

ISBN-13: 978-1-4165-4805-8
ISBN-10:   1-4165-4805-X

In memory of my father, Charles C. Thomas,
who taught me how a man should act and set the bar high

THE HELLFIRE CONSPIRACY

1

IRECOGNIZED THE SOUND, THOUGH I HAD NEVER heard it before. I was in the middle of the agency's account books, totaling figures, when it came. The window was open because it was warm in our chambers, and outside, the horse traffic in Whitehall Street was heavy. Inside, Cyrus Barker was at his desk answering correspondence, while Jenkins, our clerk was having a low conversation with a prospective client in the outer office. The agency had been doing well; we were busy and would no doubt be busier still. It was shortly after one o'clock on Friday, the twenty-sixth of June, 1885, and when I heard it, I thought to myself, *That's the sound of a saber being drawn.*

Barker's pen rolled off the edge of his desk and fell to the floor, and I heard the whisper of the revolver, holstered beneath his chair, clearing leather. I was not as well prepared. For one thing, the account book was in my lap, and for another, my pistol was tucked away in one of the drawers of my roll-topped desk. By the time I'd dropped the book to the floor and had my hand on the pull of the drawer, Jenkins was already backing slowly into our chambers.

"Visitor, Mr. B.," he stated with as much *sangfroid* as one can muster with the point of a saber thrust against the Adam's apple.

"Thank you, Jenkins," the Guv stated with the same aplomb. "Won't you come in, sir?"

Our visitor came into the room, spurs jingling and eyes resolute. He was a sight in his gleaming helmet and breastplate— one of Her Majesty's Life Guards, her personal troops, the most highly trained soldiers in England, if not the world. Their parade grounds were just down Whitehall Street, but I had never seen one without a horse under him. Needless to say, we'd never had one in our offices before, taking a sword to a harmless clerk.

"He says I don't have an *appointment*," the man snapped. "Why does everybody need a bloody appointment these days?"

It's strange what goes through one's mind during a dangerous situation. In a moment, the fellow could be gutting our clerk and then my employer would be sure to shoot the man dead, but all I could do was stare in fascination at the officer's mustache. It was a deep, fiery red, waxed in the shape of a "W," and it quivered when he shouted.

"It is not necessary that you have an appointment," Barker said, setting his pistol on his desk. "But it is necessary that you cease threatening my clerk. Put away your saber, before you do someone harm."

The point of the saber came out from under the knot of Jenkins's tie, wavered in the air for a moment as if seeing what other mischief it could find, and then the major thrust it back into its scabbard with a loud snick of metal against metal. His features suddenly went slack and his epauletted shoulders slumped forward.

"He's going," Barker warned. Just then the officer's knees gave out, and I caught him, or tried to. He was six foot to my five four and outweighed me by at least three stone. His weight pressed me down until I lay on the Oriental rug with him splayed across me. He hadn't quite fainted. I still saw the gleam of his eyes under the shadow of his helmet, but he was obviously in a state of shock.

"Jenkins," our employer said as he came around the desk, "fetch the brandy."

"Right, sir," the clerk said, moving quickly to one of the back rooms of our chambers. It was the fastest I'd seen him move before three o'clock in the afternoon. He was generally feeling the effects of the previous night's liquor in the mornings, but it was remarkable how having one's tie pared with a saber will bring out the latent industry in one's character.

By the time Jenkins got back, we'd managed to get the slack-limbed soldier into the visitor's chair. His face grew as red as his tunic, and we feared under the circumstances he might break down. Barker looked at me from behind his black spectacles and his brows disappeared behind them in a frown. I believe we were thinking the same thing, which was that neither of us knew if his uniform contained such a thing as a handkerchief. We tugged them from our own breast pockets and proffered them simultaneously, but he shook his head, refusing both.

It is in a man's nature when faced with an emotional crisis to prepare for flight. If the person in crisis is a child, he feels he cannot possibly help the tot as well as its mother; if a woman, that he has blundered yet again and is not only unequal to repairing the situation but also probably could not even correctly diagnose the problem. But, if the emotional person is another man, it is the worst possible catastrophe. The societal fabric has been rent. A man would rather be shot by a firing squad than to break down in front of his fellows, and to witness such a breakdown is almost as bad a breach of decorum as to break down oneself.

The guardsman sat for a moment with his head in his hands, breathing heavily, and I feared he might pass out again. My employer, for once, was at something of a loss, looking away and drumming a finger on his blotter while waiting for the man to gain his composure. Jenkins stood beside us, holding the small snifter of brandy. If someone wasn't going to drink it soon, I would. Barker kept it strictly for medicinal purposes, but all this was getting on my nerves.

"Get hold of yourself, man!" my employer suddenly bellowed, and we all jumped. It did the trick. A soldier is accustomed to taking orders. When he jumped, he was as slack as a rag doll, but when he landed in his chair again, he was every inch a guardsman. He sat ramrod straight, and nothing but the redness of his stony face left evidence that anything had occurred.

"Good. Now say it out plain. Speak up, now!"

It took the man a moment to compose himself before he finally got it out. "She's gone, sir! They've taken my daughter, Gwendolyn."

"Who has?"

"I don't know, sir. White slavers, I think. She's been abducted."

"I see. How old is your daughter?"

The guardsman frowned. "Eleven. No, twelve. Her birthday was in April. We got her a tea set. The little kind, you know. And a doll. It's still at home, but she isn't."

"From where was she abducted?" Barker questioned, trying to keep him calm.

"The East End," he stated. "Hypatia—that's my wife—volunteers in the East End once or twice a month. Says it does her soul good to help the poor, and she has made friends there. She takes our daughter along, says it is good for her to see how the other half lives. What was she thinking? She had no business taking Gwendolyn to the East End. Anyone could see how dangerous it is. She—she—"

"Drink!"

As if it were an automatic response ordered from the baser parts of the brain, the major took the glass from Jenkins and emptied its contents down his throat. He gave a shudder afterward, as the heat from the alcohol rose up his throat, and he absently wiped his lips with the back of his gloved hand.

"What is your name, sir?"

The man seemed to consider it, but the words took a moment to sink below the surface. "What? Oh, sorry. It is DeVere. Major Trevor DeVere."

"Very well, Major DeVere. From where in the East End was she abducted, specifically?" Barker had retrieved his pen and opened his notebook, but he was tapping the pen against his blotter impatiently. So far the major had not been very coherent, but I gave him the benefit of the doubt that he would be of more use on the battlefield. He had a missing daughter, after all.

"Bethnal Green, at the corner of Green Street and Globe Road."

My employer had a cabman's knowledge of London streets as well as a statistician's grasp of crime. "That area has its share of criminal activity, but it is not quite the Black Hole of Calcutta. Do you know for certain she was taken? Perhaps she just met a local girl and is off playing in the street somewhere."

DeVere shook his head until his helmet rattled. "No, sir. The children don't play in the streets there anymore. Their mothers won't let them. Hypatia says they are afraid the white slavers will take their children and sell them to brothels in France or seraglios in Araby."

"I believe your wife has been reading too many sensational newspapers," the Guv pronounced.

"No, sir," the major responded. "I spoke to a family this morning who'd had their daughter taken. Poor family but respectable. The girl had been their pride and joy and just twelve. She's been gone close on to a year now. And now the monsters have my Gwendolyn. I'll kill them, I will. I'll track them down and skewer every last one of them if it is the last thing I do in this life!"

"Let us do the tracking," Barker said. "We are experienced man hunters, after all. When was your daughter last seen?"

"About nine o'clock this morning."

"And what does she look like?"

"Beautiful, sir. Long blond hair, blue eyes. She's small for her age and has a smile that goes straight to the heart."

Barker cleared his throat. "For what agency does your wife work?"

"The Charity Organization Society."

"Obviously you have been on parade. How did you learn of your daughter's disappearance?"

"Hypatia sent a telegram."

"And what did you do then?"

"I rode off to Bethnal Green, of course. I questioned Hypatia and all the staff. Then I spent an hour riding about the area. After that, I thought to tell Scotland Yard, so I rode back here. A fine lot of good that did me. They claimed Gwendolyn must be missing for twenty-four hours before they would lift a finger! Damned incompetence!"

"Their hands are tied by regulations, Major. You must not blame them. What brought you to my door?"

"Well, sir, I thought if the official detectives won't do it, perhaps a private one will."

"Why did you choose me, if I may ask it?"

"Your door had the shiniest plaque."

Barker and I looked over at Jenkins, who favored us with a smug smile. Five years developing a reputation as one of the best private enquiry agents in London and many pounds sterling outlaid for advertisements in *The Times,* and someone came to his door on the strength of the shine of the brass.

"Very well, sir. I shall accept your case and begin searching for your daughter. Have you brought a retaining fee?"

"Uh, no, sir," the major said, abashed. "I didn't think of it. I don't carry money in my tunic."

"Then Mr. Llewelyn here shall collect it later." Barker cleared his throat. "Major, most guardsmen do not ride independently about the city in full regalia. Did you have leave to hunt for your daughter or have you in fact deserted your post?"

DeVere lowered his head. "I did rather ride off, I'm afraid. I shall be in a spot of trouble when I get back."

"Then I suggest you cross the street to your barracks, take your medicine like a man, and leave the case in my hands. I cannot believe Her Majesty's army would be so callous as to demote you under the present circumstances, though you had better prepare yourself for a sharp reprimand."

Major DeVere slowly rose to his feet. "You are correct, of course, Mr. Barker. I must return to my duties."

"Yes, but you look a fright. I have a mirror and comb in one of my back rooms. Come this way."

Barker led him down the passage to one of the rooms behind his chambers, and Jenkins followed, leaving me alone to think. It seemed to me I'd read something in the newspapers about the white slave trade, girls forced into prostitution and boys into hard labor in mines and foundries. I'd seen women in the East End, pursuing their occupation boldly in the light of day, but it had never occurred to me that they might not have come to the work willingly or were below the legal age of consent, which was thirteen years.

DeVere came back into the room. Barker was tugging at the bottom of the fellow's tunic as Jenkins brushed his shoulders. I got the absurd notion we were all seeing him off to a dance instead of a reprimand. His face was still red, but his mustache was combed.

"When shall you call upon me?" the major asked anxiously.

"Immediately, if she is found. Otherwise, tomorrow."

DeVere clanked out, sword swinging and the rowels of his spurs clanking at the expense of our floor. We crossed to the window and watched him mount a gray gelding unsteadily before turning toward the direction of his barracks.

"Do you think she has really been abducted?" I asked.

"I scarce can say," Barker answered. "The newspapers are full of dire warnings, but I have never heard of those who traffic in white slavery brought to the dock. But, come. Every minute we waste increases the odds that we won't recover Gwendolyn DeVere alive."

2

WE WERE IN A HANSOM ON OUR WAY TO THE EAST End. Normally, my employer sat back and viewed the town. Just as a physician monitors a patient's health by counting his heartbeat at the wrist, Barker watches the faces and actions of passersby and infers London's health thereby. He was in a hurry now, however, and had offered the driver a double fare if he got us to Bethnal Green within twenty minutes. He was perched forward in the cab with his arms thrown over the doors, beating on them to some tune in his head.

"Blast this traffic," he complained. "London is becoming far too crowded. It is not healthy for millions of people to be pent up within just a few square miles."

He said that, but I knew he loved cities. He needs to be in the thick of things where important events are occurring. I could no more picture him in some bucolic lane than I could a London tram.

"To tell the truth, I didn't believe the white slave trade really exists, sir," I called out over the clatter of the horse and the creaking of the cab. "I thought I read somewhere that it is a myth!"

"It's no myth," Barker bawled in his low, harsh voice. "Hundreds of girls go missing in England each year, couriered to Belgium or France and bound for brothels on the Continent."

"Girls this age? She is but twelve."

"Aye, this age. They traffic in maidens exclusively, and it is a lucrative trade."

"Then why does not the government put a stop to it?" I demanded.

"You want the truth, lad? Because the girls are poor. Their fathers expect no help from the government. The major, however, is middle class. He feels the cost of the government is square upon his own shoulders and that is why he is angry that Scotland Yard would not help him. But it will, it will. No middle-class girl can go missing in this town, mark my words, Thomas."

I felt the jolt as the brake was engaged and the wheels slid to a stop at the curb. Barker bolted out with a jiggle of springs while I passed the driver the double fare through the trapdoor above me. I stepped down to the pavement and looked around at the site of Miss DeVere's disappearance.

Bethnal Green is not as infamous as Whitechapel, its sister to the west, nor does it have the exotic reputation of Limehouse to the south, but it is fully the equal of both in terms of squalor. The Green gathers about itself a tattered and musty shawl of respectability and the illusion that it is a nice, safe place to raise a family. Tens of thousands of parents have done so, after all, moving here from small villages or larger towns. They came looking for work in the great capital and thereby condemned themselves and their children to this bland, seedy quarter, choking daily on the reek of factories and dust of dung-covered streets. It was an economic trap that, once sprung, secured them for generations to come, never to breathe fresh air or to wander in country meadows.

There was nothing green in Green Street where the Charity Organization Society stood, and no birds twittered overhead, though underfoot thin and molting pigeons pecked in vain among the rubble of shattered paving stones for sustenance. All the people I saw here had what Shakespeare called a lean and hungry look. It was a natural place for charity work but not one I would have let a wife of mine go into, and certainly not a child. The Charity Organization was housed in an old mansion that must have seen many guises over the years. Now a hoarding stood over the door that announced its name to those who could read. There were a handful of idlers in front of the building, reminding me of a Doré illustration I'd seen of the East End, all charcoal-gray beggars and rubbish-strewn streets.

Once inside, we passed through a hall containing more idlers, into what had once been a ballroom but which now contained several desks. There was an attempt at gentility here, with a recent coat of paint on the old walls and vases of flowers here and there, but the atmosphere was depressing all the same. A pair of young women listened to a litany of troubles from a stout applicant for aid, while a doctor investigated the state of a few juveniles' throats.

"I beg your pardon," Barker said, stepping up to the two young women. "Might we see Mrs. DeVere?"

"Are you the police?" one of them asked sharply. She was an attractive girl with black hair, dark eyes, and olive skin. Her companion, I noted, was equally pretty.

"We are private enquiry agents engaged by Major De-Vere," my employer supplied, doffing his hat.

Both women were small, and Barker towered over them. He is a capital fellow and one cannot fault his tailor, but though he was doing his best to diminish himself in this largely feminine environment, his appearance was formidable.

"I will take you to the director," the girl said. "Please come this way."

It seemed natural to me that the organization must have a man at the helm to steer it, but as is often the case, I was wrong. The director, it turned out, was also a woman.

"Thank you, Miss Levy," she said, after our guide had entered and explained our appearance. "I am Octavia Hill. Won't you gentlemen come in?"

"Cyrus Barker at your service, madam. This is my assistant, Thomas Llewelyn."

Miss Hill was a handsome woman in her late thirties, who might have sat for a Renaissance painting of the Virgin Mary. There was nothing at all about her in the way of artifice, and I doubted that anything could ruffle her air of solemn grace and caring. She seemed capable of attracting idealistic young maidens to her work.

"I am glad you have come," she said. "I have been trying to comfort Mrs. DeVere."

Hypatia DeVere was in great distress, as one would expect. She sat in a chair in front of Miss Hill's desk, bowed down. Much of her blond hair had escaped its chignon, her eyelids had swollen from much weeping, and her slender neck had given up all effort to hold her head erect. There is a point beyond which one cares nothing about one's appearance before strangers, and she had flown past it earlier that day.

"Hypatia, these gentlemen have come to speak to you."

"Police?" the woman asked huskily, wiping a tear from the end of her sharp nose with a handkerchief and pushing a strand of hair out of her face before giving up on it.

"We are private enquiry agents, madam, hired by your husband."

"Trevor hired you," she murmured almost to herself. She cleared her throat and then looked at us through pale, watery eyes. "Was he . . . well? He was agitated when he left."

Barker must have thought it best to reassure her. "He was quite well, yes. He explained the situation to us, secured our services, and returned to his duties."

"Good," she said, hiccupping into her handkerchief. "I'm sorry. This has been rather a strain. But surely Gwendolyn has just wandered off, and this fear of white slavers is merely a f-fantasy."

"It is imperative that we start searching immediately," Barker said. "Does anyone recall young Miss DeVere speaking to anyone today, either a girl or boy her own age or an adult?"

"No, sir," Miss Hill stated firmly. "Gwendolyn preferred to read or amuse herself than to play with the local children."

"Has she ever wandered off by herself?"

"Once with a girl named Ona," her mother said shakily.

"Can you tell me what Miss DeVere was wearing?"

"A blue sailor dress with a white collar. It has a stripe around it, very pretty. She was wearing black hose today and high boots of brown patent leather. I wanted her to wear the black boots, but she said they pinched."

"Thank you, ladies. We must not tarry any further." Barker looked over at the distraught woman. "Do you have a photograph of your daughter that I might borrow, Mrs. DeVere?"

"Not here, I'm afraid."

"What about Mrs. Carrick?" Miss Hill asked. She turned to my employer. "We have a volunteer whose husband is a photographer. I believe Gwendolyn was in the photograph he took of us all just weeks ago."

"It would be most helpful to see what she looks like," Barker said.

Octavia Hill came around her desk and opened the door. "Rose!" she called.

I hoped it was Miss Levy's attractive friend, and felt a jolt of disappointment when a plain-looking, dowdily dressed woman answered the summons.

"Rose, these gentlemen are detectives searching for Miss DeVere. Do you recall if Gwendolyn was in the photograph that your husband took a few weeks ago?"

I looked at Barker. It was on the tip of his tongue to correct her, preferring to be called a private enquiry agent. He swallowed it back.

"I believe she was, miss. I developed it myself."

"Would it be possible for you to take Mr. Barker and his assistant to the emporium to get the photograph? It would aid them in their search."

"Certainly, Miss Hill. Come this way, gentlemen."

The woman turned and led us between the rows of desks in the outer room. She had narrow shoulders and, though she was in her twenties, already had the look of a matron. I passed some of the more winning young ladies on my way out and suppressed a sigh.

"Do you really think the girl has been taken?" she asked as we stepped outside.

"Don't you?" Barker countered.

"I couldn't say. To tell the truth, I don't know her very well. I'm in and out all day. I heard she run—er, ran away once or twice."

"Mrs. DeVere said she had merely gone exploring."

"Did she?" Mrs. Carrick asked. Her dark brows gave the remark a skeptical look. "She dotes on the girl. Turn here, gentlemen."

We turned north on Cambridge Road, passing the Bethnal Green Church.

"You think she might have run away?" Barker pursued.

"I didn't say that, did I?"

Rose Carrick was of average height for a woman, five foot one or two, but she kept both Barker and myself working hard to keep up with her. Barker let out those long limbs of his, while I bobbed along behind.

"What exactly do you do at the organization, Mrs. Carrick?"

"I deliver charity cases to their destination. It's not easy work. Sometimes it is old men that are going barmy to the lunatic asylum or boys and girls to orphanages. I've been kicked so many times I have permanent bruises on my ankles. But I get them there every time." She stopped abruptly. "The emporium is up near Victoria Park. Come!"

She doubled her speed again, if such a thing were possible. I began to feel sorry for the barmy old men she escorted. Finally, in the Old Ford Road, she turned and led us to her husband's shop.

CARRICK'S FAMILY PHOTOGRAPHIC EMPORIUM was stated on the placard above a set of bow windows. The windows advertised PORTRAITS, POSTAL CARDS, AND CARTES DE VISITE on one side and REASONABLE RATES upon the other. It was a cut above the other shops in the street and looked relatively new. Mrs. Carrick opened the door for us and stepped inside, the bell on the door ringing as we entered.

"Stephen!" she called.

From within the next room a baby cried. I thought perhaps it was their child, but a harried-looking man in his shirtsleeves stepped out from behind a beaded curtain.

"Hallo, darling. I've got a real wailer this time. Can't get the little chap to calm down." He raised his brows when he saw us. "Who are these gentlemen?"

"They are detectives. You remember Mrs. DeVere? Her daughter, Gwendolyn, has gone missing."

"Good heavens. Is it . . . slavers?"

"We don't know, Mr. Carrick," my employer answered. "We have only just been hired. Cyrus Barker, at your service."

"Stephen," his wife said, "was the girl in the picture you took of the C.O.S.?"

"I think so. It should be in the display book there."

There was a large counter in the middle of the room, and Mrs. Carrick moved behind it and began flipping through an album of photographs.

The wailing in the next room reached a crescendo.

Carrick and his wife looked through the photographs, leaving me to form impressions. I had seldom seen a more mismatched couple than the Carricks. Next to her plainness, her husband was a regular Apollo. He could have been a stage actor, so well built and favored as he was, while his wife looked like a charwoman beside him. Yet they genuinely seemed to care for each other. It left me wondering over the vagaries of love and attraction.

"Here it is!" Rose Carrick cried triumphantly, pulling a photograph from the fittings of the album. "And she's right there, as I said she was."

Gwendolyn DeVere was at the end of a large group of people standing formally in front of the Charity Organization Society. Miss Hill was in the center, flanked by Miss Levy and her friend on one side, and Mrs. DeVere and Mrs. Carrick on the other. They were accompanied by wealthy-looking men and women whom I took to be donors. There, at the far right end, looking forlorn and out of place, was the missing girl, Gwendolyn DeVere.

She was a pretty little thing. Her father had described her hair as blond, and she was Nordic looking, like her mother. Her shoulders were slumped and her face solemn, leaving me to hope that the parents had better photographs of the girl at home. I myself would have hated to leave this one image to posterity.

"How well do you gentlemen know Bethnal Green?" Carrick asked.

"I have had several cases that brought me here but none that centered in the area. I don't believe my assistant has been here at all."

"Perhaps I could give you a brief tour of the area."

"But you're photographing a child," Mrs. Carrick objected.

"Why don't you take him, dear? I'm afraid I can't do a

thing with him. You know you're much better with babies than I." Carrick kissed her on the cheek and reached for a bowler hat and a stick on the stand by the door. "Thanks, love. Won't be a tick."

He herded us out the front door and lit a cigarette once he was in the street, sucking in the smoke like it was fresh air. The child inside was still in full cry.

"Liberation," Carrick pronounced. "Come this way, gentlemen."

3

"SHALL WE HEAD NORTH, SIRS? BETHNAL GREEN is roughly triangular, bordered on the north by Victoria Park, on the south by the Mile End Workhouse, and on the west by the old Jewish burial ground. The gasworks is only a few streets away from here."

Carrick led us up Cambridge Road. "This district was in its heyday at the end of the last century, when the famous boxer Daniel Mendoza lived here," he said between puffs. "This used to be the center of the silk-weaving trade. Things went to seed after trade with China opened up, and the old place has become rather run-down. Land is cheap here, and plenty of young families have moved to the Green. The Tower Hamlets Council is making an attempt at renovation. It seemed the perfect place to open a photographic emporium."

"You strike me as an educated man, Mr. Carrick," Barker noted. "You've had some time at university."

"Not much gets by you, does it, Mr. Barker? Yes, I had a year or two at Christ Church in the seventies, under Dodgson. It was he that awakened my interest in photography.

My father thought it all a waste of time, however, and cut me off. I've been fending for myself ever since."

I could understand Carrick's tale of woe. If anything, my own was even worse. Oxford could be an uncommonly hard place if one does not conform to its standards.

Carrick pointed out the market gardens, the Jewish cemetery, and other sites around the area. Finally, we made our way back up to the Old Ford Road and the emporium.

"How shall you gentlemen proceed?" Carrick asked. "I mean, if Miss DeVere really has been taken by someone."

"For now," Barker said, "we are like spies in the land of Canaan, getting the lay of the land."

"Then I hope, sirs, for both your sakes, that you do not encounter any giants. Best of luck finding little Miss DeVere."

"Impressions?" Barker asked, after Carrick had returned to his emporium.

"They're an unusual couple," I stated, "but then, Bethnal Green probably doesn't have the sort of standards Kensington does. His story is not much different from my own."

"Who is Dodgson?"

"He's a mathematician and an author. I've heard he has an interest in photography."

"What sort of thing has he written?"

"You're jesting, aren't you? He writes as Lewis Carroll. *Alice in Wonderland*?"

"Never heard of it."

"It's a book for children."

"There you are, then. I haven't any."

"What shall we do now, sir?" I asked, hoping he would suggest a café or tearoom. I needed a restorative and a good rest before venturing out again.

"We've searched the perimeter, now we must search all the streets in between."

"That will take hours," I said.

"Yes, it will. We'd best not dawdle."

"What are we looking for, sir?" I dared ask. "She's not going to suddenly appear in the street; and if she's been taken by someone, they've got her drugged or tied up and hidden away somewhere."

"I'll admit that walking these streets tonight is more for the DeVeres' benefit than my own. It lets them see that we are working. I can as easily think and plan while I am walking as I can in my office, so no harm is being done."

"But harm *is* being done. I'm sorry sir. This is just so maddening. I can't believe someone would actually take and sell a child into slavery. There has to be a special place in hell for such people."

"There is," Barker said. "Matthew eighteen-six says, 'But whoso shall offend one of these little ones which believe in me, it were better for him that a millstone were hanged about his neck, and he were drowned in the depth of the sea.'"

"How do you know she hasn't been spirited out of the area already?"

"I don't," he admitted. "It is an arbitrary boundary, but one must look somewhere."

"For all we know, she could be on her way to Brighton or Dover."

Barker frowned and then thumped me soundly on the shoulder. "Ha! Good lad. Come."

He led me into Brady Street, where he stopped in front of a telegraph office.

"I'm going to send a telegram or two. You stay outside and keep your eyes open for a street arab. If you find one, tell him I want Soho Vic in the Green. Got it?"

"Yes, sir."

He went in, and I leaned against the doorframe, out of sight of passersby. I'd never caught a street boy before, but it couldn't be too different from catching trout barehanded as I had as a child in the rivers of Gwent. All one had to do was be inconspicuous, pounce at the last moment, and hold on for dear life.

It took ten minutes before I spotted one. I saw him running along, watching citizens for a bulging pocket or a hanging chain. He passed me unknowingly, and I stepped out and seized him fast by the back of his oversized waistcoat.

"Take your bleedin' mitts off, you toff," he demanded, struggling in my grip.

"Barker sent me," I said, letting him go. He ran around the corner, but a moment later he came back again.

"Why didn't you say so?" he asked.

He was a villainous-looking tyke, malnourished as they all were, his hair untouched by any brush.

"The Guv wants Soho Vic. He'll be in the Green all night. A girl's gone missing."

"'E's in the West End. Gimme cab fare and I'll get 'im 'ere that much sooner."

"No cabman would give you a ride, and if he would, you'd still pocket it and hop one from the back for free. The district might be green, but I'm not."

He muttered a string of foul words before catching the coin I tossed.

"There's a bob for your troubles. Now off with you. You're wasting daylight."

Five minutes later, we were walking down Whitechapel Road, heading toward the heart of the quarter. Barker stepped into a doorway, filled and lit his pipe, and then we pressed on.

"Bethnal Green," he explained as we walked, "is the factory of the East End. The product of that factory is children. You'll seldom find a family here that does not have more than three of them. The average age of marriage here is sixteen, and young girls are not encouraged to live at home after that and drain the family's resources. After marriage, the new husband goes off to grind his life away in one of the local factories, while his bride stays in their new flat and scrimps every penny. A child is expected once a year for the next five years. For the successful families, the young boys grow up and learn a trade or help support the family and the next generation of girls are out the door at sixteen. All members of the family shall work together for one another's benefit, so that the parents can enjoy some degree of comfort in their later years. As for the unsuccessful, which includes the majority, there are coal-and-blanket charities like the C.O.S. and the Salvation Army. These families shatter and each goes his own way. The average age of death here is the lowest in London."

"That is terrible, sir."

"Aye. Commingled with this family atmosphere is every kind of vice you can imagine. The bawdy houses are studded all through the Green, like currants in a scone. Whitechapel wears its evil openly, but while Bethnal Green has an air of respectability, it is no less vice ridden. Small wonder the constables walk their beat here in pairs. Turn here."

We walked northward. It seemed like every other road and possibly better than most. I saw a cab pull up and disgorge a gentleman, who passed into some sort of private club.

"We are in the most disreputable area in all of London. I've always wondered why God does not destroy it with fire and brimstone, as he did Sodom. Even Vic's boys avoid it."

We headed into Cambridge Road and soon saw Green Street again. As we neared it, we passed a building covered in turrets until it fairly bristled into the sky.

"What is this, an annex to the church across the street?" I asked. It looked very old and somewhat ecclesiastic.

"It is the Lunatic Asylum. The district grew up and around this building and the church. Ah, look. There is the C.O.S."

"Shall we stop in and see if anything has changed?" I asked.

"No, we shall return here in the morning. Before then, I wish to acquaint myself with every street in the area."

Six o'clock passed, and seven o'clock, and still Barker called no break. Would we not eat? I wanted to save Gwendolyn DeVere as much as he, but my body was crying for food and my energy was flagging. We laced the streets of Bethnal Green as if it were an old boot, and still he would not stop. Seven thirty stretched into eight o'clock. Was he fasting? I'd been raised a good Methodist, and watched my mother fast on rare occasions, but I had never done it myself. I wasn't certain I could, but I did not want to be found wanting by my employer. So I said nothing, though my stomach rumbled and twisted in discomfort. Finally, at eight thirty, according to my watch, I could be silent no more.

"Sir, are we going to have dinner tonight?" I asked.

As it turned out, I picked the worst street in London to say it. Barker stepped up to a vendor just beginning to pack up and ordered one of whatever it was they sold.

"We're shuttin' down for the night, sir," the man said. "I can't guarantee they be as 'ot as they was."

"No matter," Barker said. Apparently it wasn't, to him.

"Very well, sir, but I won't charge you. You can help yourself to what's left."

The Guv turned and put dinner in my hand, a lump wrapped in soiled newspaper. I opened it and found a potato that had been roasted in bacon grease. Then he handed me a drink, a tin cup of lukewarm tea. It was connected to the stand by a stout chain. Goodness knows how many people had drunk from that cup since it had last been washed. The night before, we had dined on pheasant and lobster and a rare bottle of wine, for our butler, Jacob Maccabee, was attempting to establish a wine selection in his room. *Such is life,* I told myself. Philosophy always goes well with poor food. I bit the potato once, twice, three times, then washed it down with the stewed tea. The author George MacDonald said that a potato is enough of a meal for any man. *A Scotsman, perhaps,* I thought. I offered the rest to my employer and when he refused, I tossed it into the gutter.

The sun had vanished like the light of a spent match. Bethnal Green was not Mayfair; such light as there was brought out the fallen women displaying their cheap finery, attracted to the light the way a candle draws moths. Barker showed them the photograph and questioned them as readily as anyone else in the district, though it brought nothing but ribald comments from their lips.

There was a flash of ghostly white at my elbow and a more corporeal clatter of hooves on cobblestones, and before I could do anything, Major DeVere had sprung from his horse. He was in mufti.

"Anything?" he asked.

"We have secured a photograph of your daughter," Barker replied, "and have been questioning people. We have been taking each street systematically, but nothing has turned up so far."

"She's really gone. I can't believe it," DeVere said, shaking his head. "My girl in the hands of filthy white slavers. I mean, some part of me still clung to the hope she was off playing somewhere and would return in my absence."

"I'm sorry, sir."

"Just keep looking."

"We must stop at midnight in order to be ready to search again at eight."

"Very well, carry on," he stated like the officer that he was. He climbed back onto his gelding and rode off.

"There goes a soul in torment," I said, watching the ghost horse as it disappeared into the night. Barker made no comment. I turned to see he was not there to make one. Somehow between the time the major had jumped onto his steed and ridden off, my employer had disappeared.

"Oy!" Barker suddenly bellowed down one of the passages at a pair of shadowy figures. He plunged into an alley off Globe Road so narrow his shoulders nearly scraped on both sides. We shot out of the alleyway into the next thoroughfare, narrowly avoiding being run down by a cart, then plunged into another across the street. I could make out some movement ahead of us but no more than that. The Guv was advancing swiftly, however, and in a minute or two he seized his quarry.

"Got you!" Barker said, lighting a match against the rough brick. Our quarry were two large women in their late fifties, perhaps, so unattractive as to conjure the word "hags" in my mind. "Why, it's Mum Alice. And surely this cannot be Dirty Annie. I thought you were both in the stir."

The first began to mewl a sort of answer to my employer, but her moniker was due to an unfortunate disfigurement that made her nearly unintelligible. The explanation was taken up by her friend, who was so porcine it was a wonder to me how she had traversed the alleyway. Her hair hung long, gray, and greasy down her back, and the dress she wore looked like a tent.

"Alice just got out of Holloway Prison a month ago, yer worship, and I left work'ouse Tuesday last."

"How are you mudlarks getting by? Still doing the kinchin lay?"

Kinchin lay? I wondered. I wasn't familiar with a great deal of thieve's cant, but a lay was a crime, a dodge, some sort of trick to be played at someone else's expense.

"No, sir, 'pon my honor. We learnt our lesson, hain't we, Alice? Just scrapin' by like. Doin' some rag pickin'. Caught a few rats for the ratman, enough for a pint and a pasty twixt the two of us, but we hain't made so much as a farthing today."

Barker lit another match and held the photograph up to the light. "A child has gone missing today. Girl, twelve years of age, blue sailor dress, white collar with a stripe around it. Black hose and petticoats. Brown patent leather boots. The peelers will be checking every fence and pawnshop in the East End."

Annie put out a pudgy hand. "Oh, stop, yer worship, please. You're making me mouth water. Sounds like Rowes of Bond Street. Very high priced. Couldn't ask for better."

"I want you ladies to know if any of these articles should appear in the area, I'll be laying for both of you unless you find them first. Am I getting through to you?"

"Yes, yer worship," Annie said, her voice high and trembling with fear. Alice had begun to mewl again.

"You girls hear of any slavers in the area?"

"No, no," Annie said, and Alice shook her head emphatically. "If they're here, they keep to themselves. They ain't local—not permanent, anyways."

"Off with you, then. Give them sixpence and not a farthing more, Thomas."

Both hags scuttled forward and circled me. I could smell the rank odor and see the dirt that gave Annie her sobriquet. I slipped a sixpence into her hand and wished I could wash my own.

"Find some gainful employment," Barker ordered, "or I'll find it for you. I'm watching you."

"Yes, sir," they said, shuffling off. "Fank you, yer worship!"

We emerged again in the opposite direction into the welcome light of a gas lamp.

"What is a kinchin lay?" I asked.

"It's stealing the clothing off children. It's the first thing I thought of when I heard Miss DeVere had gone missing. The child is not usually hurt and generally comes home crying and embarrassed. If such a thing had happened to Miss DeVere, however, she would have returned by now, surely."

"I'd never realized how easy it was for a child to go missing," I said aloud, as we returned to Globe Road and resumed our search. "Bethnal Green's got to have one of the highest populations per square mile in all England. Hundreds of eyes are watching one every day. Surely, if a child disappeared, someone would be able to say, 'I saw her on Friday morning at ten on Green Street.'"

"One would think such would be the case, lad, but the sheer population means the average citizen on the street might see hundreds of individuals in a single hour. I want you to think of this, too: the disappearance of Miss DeVere is a tragedy, and I fear no good will come of it, but suppose the child had been poor. Would our dragnet be put out then? Would any official notice have occurred if ten were missing, or twenty?"

"'Ello, gents," Soho Vic said as we came out of the alleyway. He was leaning nonchalantly against the side of a building, picking his teeth with a splinter of wood, looking as sloppy and mismatched as only a street urchin can. "What gives, Push?"

"We would consult, Vic," Barker stated. He always treated Vic like an adult, rather than the species of vermin he was. I'll grant that on occasion he was useful.

He shrugged his slender shoulders. "Step in my or-fice, then."

"I need your lads here in the Green for a week or so, if you're willing," the Guv continued. "A girl has gone missing, a West End girl, and we believe slavers are about."

"Got it. Anyfing in p'tic'ler we'se lookin' for?"

Barker showed him the photograph. "The young lady and any signs of white slavery. Keep a watch on her father, who will be searching for his daughter on a gray horse. Oh, and I suppose it wouldn't hurt to watch our backs as well."

"It'll cost you," Vic warned. "Yer talkin' an even dozen."

"Then it will cost me," Barker said philosophically.

"Right. I'll get on it. 'Night, sir. 'Night, Ugly."

The latter was for my benefit. Someday he would be eighteen years of age and I was going to treat myself to a hard one right on the point of his chin. I'd half a mind to take a leaf from Barker's book and consider him an adult already.

We plodded along through the gaslit streets. The few lamps had been put here as a deterrent to crime, but this only pushed it into the dark alleyways on either side. The faces of the few people we passed were sunk in the shadow of their hats, save for the chalky white tips of their noses. Everyone was anonymous, which was good for the criminals and bad for the solitary bobby trying to protect people on his beat.

By eleven o'clock I had run out of energy and was going on sheer endurance. I toddled along beside my employer, trying to keep my eyes open. It was a bad feeling to know that for all our efforts, we had failed to locate Gwendolyn DeVere. Failure is not a word Cyrus Barker takes lightly.

When the Bow bells finally rang twelve, I nearly fell to the pavement. We had paced these streets for over ten hours.

"Right," Barker said with finality. "Let us find a cab, then."

His harsh whistle summoning a cab to Mile End Road was the sweetest sound I had heard all evening. I scrambled up into the cab when it arrived and propped myself in the corner. I would need all the sleep I could get; knowing Barker, we would start all the earlier in the morning. I let the steady clop and jingle of the horse, taking us away from this terrible district, lull me to sleep, a London lullaby.

4

THE NEXT MORNING I WAS DOWN IN THE KITCHEN
having a *pain au chocolat* and a cup of coffee while waiting
for our chef, Etienne, to prepare my omelet. I was still half
asleep and ruminating on how different life was here from
the harsh reality of Bethnal Green, but a mile away. Then
out in the garden I saw that Barker's ward, Bok Fu Ying,
had arrived and was speaking with her guardian while in
the act of attaching a leash to Harm's collar. My employer's dog was rarely leashed. Washing down the last of
the bun with my coffee, I went out the back door to see
what was going on.

"Where is he going?" I asked, for it was obvious she was
taking him somewhere.

"We are going to Yorkshire, where he have union with a
lady Pekingese," she explained. As always, the girl wore a
jet-black mourning dress and a heavy veil.

"It is time to go to the office, Thomas," Barker said. He
tries to curtail any conversation between us, claiming that I
am susceptible to female charms. I wished her and her
charge a safe journey and followed my employer.

A note was waiting upon our arrival at Whitehall. There was now a telephone set in Scotland Yard, but old habits die hard. Barker took the message from the salver Jenkins presented and read it.

"A child's body has been found in the sewers of Bethnal Green," he announced. "We had better look into it. Come."

The day had started badly and was getting steadily worse. I had not yet prepared myself to see a corpse. Viewing corpses was one of my least-favorite parts of private enquiry work. Children are like fireworks, energy bursting forth in every direction. To see one lying still, never to rise again, is hard. I am no sentimentalist, but if they, with all their energy, can be brought so low, what hope is there for the rest of us?

"How did Scotland Yard know we are investigating Miss DeVere's disappearance?" I asked.

"I rang Terry Poole last night, but it looks like Swanson's handling the case."

In Grafton Street, a grate had been pulled out of the gutter and a tall ladder set at an angle in the hole. A constable guarded the ladder as if all Bethnal Green were waiting for him to leave so they could steal it. Barker identified himself and was just about to take hold of it when a head popped out of the hole like a badger from its sett, and soon a pair of wide shoulders squeezed out of it as well.

"Barker," the man stated in greeting. He wore a tan mackintosh, with greasy spots where it had rubbed against tunnel walls, and a bowler hat. He and the Guv were of like size and shape. He even had the same Scottish accent, but that was not surprising. Detective work, both public and private, was an occupation that seemed to attract Scots. In fact, so many were in Scotland Yard that some jested they had taken up the work when the Scottish kings the street was named for had died out.

"Swanson," Barker responded. "Bad business, this. Is it Gwendolyn DeVere, do you think?"

"That's for the coroner to decide. I'm just here to drag out the body and fill out the forms."

"Who found the body?" my employer asked.

"A lunger, crawling after pennies and such in the sewers. Thought it was old clothes when she first came upon it. Her scream must've echoed for miles through the tunnels. You after having a gander?"

"I've seen both sewers and dead bodies before, unless there is something else of interest."

The inspector gave a grim smile. "Not unless you are a connoisseur of sewer pipe."

"The body, man. Tell me about the body."

"I've got two men bringing it up in a tarp. She's a'most the right size as the DeVere girl, but, no, it ain't her. The body is too decomposed. Must've been down there a fortnight, at least."

We stepped back as the first constable's helmet appeared out of the hole. The second constable was pale as death and wobbly on the ladder. They set the burden down on the pavement and moved away. Without preamble, Barker lifted the tarp. The little face inside was bloated, the eyes swollen, the mouth set in a rictus. The stench of decay hit me then, and the hand of the grave clutched me about the throat. For a second, I thought I would be ill. But the feeling passed, which in itself was alarming. How dulled was my soul becoming to this work?

Cyrus Barker removed his hat and then gently laid a hand upon the little corpse. Inspector Swanson and I watched his lips move in prayer, and in unison we removed our own bowlers. Then slowly the Guv shook his head.

"I'm sorry 'twas not the child you were searching for, Cyrus."

"Perhaps it's a blessing, Donald, and the girl lives yet. You'll send word after the postmortem, will you not?"

"Aye, I will." Swanson turned his head, looking between the two of us. "Oh, bloody hell," he muttered. "This is just what I need. Here comes Stead."

"The newspaper editor?" Barker asked.

"The gadfly, you mean. The commissioner would rather have him behind bars than any criminal alive. No photographs, Stead!"

I dared glance over my shoulder. Stead was young for the editor of a newspaper as widely subscribed to as the *Pall Mall Gazette*, not yet forty, I should say. He was of average build, with curly hair and a short, thick beard, and he looked a perfect fireball of energy. He had been directing a young companion to set up a large tripod and camera. Stead had been the first to print photographs of people in his newspaper but had raised the ire of the British government a number of times. Surely, he could never put such a tragic sight as this corpse into his newspaper.

"What have we here, then?" he said, skirting Barker and bending over the body. "Oh, my word, it is a child. Who could have done such a thing? Do you know how she died, Swanson?"

"Won't know until the postmortem, Stead, you know that," the inspector said peremptorily. "We just brought her up and have no statement to make."

"She is clad only in a chemise and bloomers. Another piece of humanity lost in the machinations of the slave trade."

"It is just like you, Stead," Swanson said, "to start editorializing before you get the facts. There is no proof that this girl was a victim of the trade. In fact, there is evidence to the contrary. The whole purpose of their operation would be to get a girl safely and in one piece to France, or wherever it is they send her."

Cyrus Barker, who up until that moment had neither spoken nor moved, knelt down, pulled the handkerchief from his pocket, and delicately wiped the sewer muck from the thin neck of the little corpse. The throat was a battleground of bruises and pale, graying flesh.

"Strangled," he pronounced. "Two-handed, by the look of it. I'll hazard a guess that the neck bones are snapped—the child is so small." He set the handkerchief in a ball on the cobblestones beside her.

"We haven't met before. William T. Stead," the newspaperman said, putting out a hand. "And you are?"

Barker looked at the hand warily, as if it were a cobra about to strike, then took it in his own. "Cyrus Barker. Private enquiry agent."

Stead repeated the name for the benefit of his photographer, who had taken out a notebook and was now scribbling it down.

"It isn't often the Yard works with private agents," the editor noted. "How did you become involved in this case?"

"He's not," Swanson spoke up, anxious to take control of the situation. "Mr. Barker is investigating a child's disappearance in the area. I called him in because I thought this might be the child in question, but it is obvious this one has been dead for some time."

"Barker. Barker . . ." Stead snapped his fingers. "You're the chap who advertises in our rival *The Times.*"

"I hardly call *The Times* the *Pall Mall Gazette*'s rival, Mr. Stead," Barker said drily.

"Touché, Mr. Barker," he responded, flashing a strong set of teeth. "'*A touch, a touch, I do confess.*'"

"Hamlet, act five, scene two," Barker murmured.

"Very good, sir. An educated detective. Truly a rarity."

I thought Barker was going to correct him and say that he was a private enquiry agent, but instead he said modestly, "Self-educated, I'm afraid. My assistant, Thomas Llewelyn, is the Oxonian."

I thought it politic to follow the photographer's example and take notes, so I merely tipped my hat to him, and took out my notebook.

"Marvel upon marvel. It's a wonder that the Yard has not snapped up such talent. Actually, no, I suppose it isn't."

"All right, Stead, move along," Swanson ordered. "We don't have time for idle chitchat. This corpse must go to the morgue."

We all stepped back as the mortuary cart was wheeled down the street toward us by a constable. The lifting of the body released a fresh wave of effluvia, and Stead turned away with a grunt. He handed my employer a card.

"I should like to interview you for an article sometime," he said.

"I decline to speak about myself, sir, but if it relates to a case and is a matter of public record, certainly. I do not approve of all you do but appreciate the campaign you ran to get Gordon relief in Khartoum, though it proved too late for Gordon himself."

"The man deserved better than the shabby treatment Gladstone's government gave him."

"Is it usual for an editor of your prominence to stalk the streets of the East End?" Barker asked. "Surely you have men for that."

"Oh, gaggles of them," he replied, "but this is a personal crusade. Scotland Yard wishes to sweep the issue of the white slave trade under the carpet, as does Parliament. It is not a pretty subject, you see, and they think it better to avoid it. However, I intend to send the facts into every library, public house, and parlor in London and to force Parliament to pass a law against it, no matter what the cost."

"That is quite a crusade," Barker said. "But, then, if my history serves me, all the crusades ultimately ended in defeat."

"That is true," the newspaperman admitted, "but they must have been glorious battles nonetheless. I hope we shall speak again, Mr. Barker. You are more of a surprise to me today than that poor wretched body pulled from the sewer. Come, Ronald."

"Odd johnny," I noted as they left. "Do you think he really tries to do it all for the public good, or is he merely selling newspapers?"

"An editor not concerned with the public good is a churl, lad, but one not concerned with selling newspapers is a fool."

"You would do well to avoid him," Swanson warned. "He's got a bee in his bonnet over this slave trade business. Bloody socialist."

We bid our adieus to the inspector, and as we walked away, Barker gave me a nudge on the elbow.

"What is it?" I asked.

"Follow the sewer."

I looked down beneath my feet. I didn't have a knowledge of the sewer plan of London, as I'm sure Barker had, but I could tell which way the pipes went: north and south. I saw what he was thinking. A good rainstorm would have washed the body into the Thames if it had not been discovered. Whoever found it would have assumed the child had fallen into the river. "And just where would such a body, collected from the river, have been taken?" he asked.

"Wapping," I said.

"Aye," Barker grunted. "The Thames Police."

"You think there is a connection between the two girls?"

"I don't believe in coincidence. One child is lost and another is found. As far as I'm concerned, it is worth an immediate inquiry."

5

A TWENTY-MINUTE WALK BROUGHT US TO THE odd little police station perched upon the docks of Wapping Old Stairs. We were soon seated at a table with a cup of tea in front of each of us. Barker shook hands with the officer in charge, Inspector Dunham, one of those fellows in his fifties with white hair but a black mustache and eyebrows that made one wonder if he dyed them. He dipped his mustache into the tea, sipped noisily, and set the mug down again. Sitting down to tea with confreres seemed to be as much a ceremony here as it was in Japan.

"So, Barker, what brings you here today?"

"The body of a girl was found in a sewer in Grafton Street this morning, between ten and fifteen years of age by the size of her. She'd been dead at least two weeks, strangled. I thought it possible there might have been more than one. A strong rainstorm would have washed the body into the Thames."

"She would have washed up at the Isle of Dogs. We get a lot of bodies here—suicides, accidents, stabbings—but when a girl is found strangled, we generally assume it is a crime of passion. Are you suggesting we have one man in London strangling young girls?"

"I don't know yet, but it would be remiss of me not to look."

Dunham screwed up his mouth in thought. "It's true. We have had a few cases. Let me look through my files. Do you want more tea?"

"No, thank you."

The inspector got up from his chair. "I'll be back in a few minutes."

After he left, I looked at my employer. "Would I be correct in assuming that this fellow here hadn't heard a word about Gwendolyn DeVere or the girl found this morning because the Thames Police is in competition with the Metropolitan Police?"

"You're catching on, lad. They'll help us sometimes and up to a point, but never each other. We're not direct competition, after all, and many in our profession are former police officers. But Scotland Yard helping the Railway Police, the City Police, or the lads here at Wapping? Never."

"But if the organizations worked together, they'd solve more crimes," I pointed out.

"True, but a great deal will have to change before that happens. Feuds run as deep here as in Palermo."

Five minutes later, Dunham returned empty-handed.

"We've been scuppered," he said flatly. "Apparently, while I was out on the river this morning, an inspector from Scotland Yard called and the sergeant in charge—who by the end of today will be scraping barnacles from the launch as a constable—allowed him to leave with five files."

"Five files," Barker repeated.

"Yes—and to answer your first question, we have found some bodies in the past month or two. It is an ongoing investigation. Scotland Yard has no right to commandeer those files. The Thames Police is the oldest existing police department in the world."

"What was the name of the inspector who came calling today?"

"It was Swanson."

"He is a canny fellow. We must all be on our toes if we hope to best him." The Guv gave me a glance, and I knew what he was thinking. Inspector Swanson had not mentioned his visit here to us.

"I'm going to complain to A Division," Dunham grumbled. "The minute one's back is turned they crawl in like rats and plunder a man's cases."

"How was the case going?" my employer asked.

"Not well until you showed up. We knew all the victims were probably coming from one location, but it's hard to track down where it is once they've been in the river an hour or two."

"Were they all girls?"

"Yes, and as I recall, they were all between ten and fifteen years of age. Every one of them was in their underclothes and all had been outraged."

"Outraged?" I asked.

"Whoever he is, he has a taste for virgin flesh, I reckon, not that he's alone in London as far as that's concerned, but that ain't the worst of it. Feller collects grisly trophies, a finger here, a toe there. An ear, a nose. Nasty business."

Barker's brow had disappeared beneath the twin moons of his black spectacles. "But there is no profit to be made from killing young girls," he said. "I don't understand."

"What is there to understand?" Dunham said harshly. "He pulled them off the streets, undressed them to their drawers and camisoles, had his way with them, and throttled them. Then he snipped off a bob as a trophy."

"Can such depravity exist?" My employer brooded. "Never mind. I know that it can. So, what we are facing is not a white slave ring as we had at first anticipated. We are dealing with some kind of archfiend, a multiple murderer preying upon young girls."

"And in Bethnal Green, too, that spits them out as regular as candles. He could go on forever if he ain't stopped."

"A new girl has gone missing," Barker finally informed him. "We have been retained to find her. She comes from a middle-class family. Her mother may be a socialist, or at least, her friends appear to be."

Dunham got up and put the teapot on the hob again. I wondered how many pots they went through in a day.

"This is a fine kettle of fish," he commented. "It's not the sort of subject that is put in the papers, but there's nothing the socialists like better than a nice scandal to bring about reform. And here we are in the middle of one."

"Aye," Barker said.

"They think we can just snap our fingers and the criminals come running in to be arrested."

"So, were none of the girls identified?"

"Oh, I found two of the five. I figure the other three might be street orphans. One was a local girl, Fanny Rice, come from a big family. Very quiet they was, seemed glad she'd been identified. The other was a foreigner, Zinnah Goldstein. Her parents really broke down when they identified the body. Her father tried to rend his coat, he was so grieved."

"Were both of these girls snatched off the street?"

"In broad daylight. No clue as to who took them. One minute, they're seen rounding the corner, and the next, they're floaters, as waterlogged as a mackerel."

"Have you noticed any pattern?"

"Both of those girls disappeared on a Friday and were found on Sunday or Monday."

"It must have been a terrible few days for the parents," I commented.

"Is there anything more you remember, since Inspector Swanson has been so good as to take your files?"

"Not much. All of them seemed to be from good families, though they were not without a brush with the law. Fanny ran away once, and Zinnah took an apple from a cart, but it could have been a confusion with her faulty English."

"When you get those files back from Scotland Yard, I would like the last known addresses of their parents. You know it is possible that the parents of the other girls went to the authorities."

"It's possible," Dunham admitted, stroking his mustache. "The feud runs deep. I suppose I must communicate with the Yard over this. I don't want you gentlemen to think we never work for them, but I cannot guarantee their cooperation. I hope Swanson listens to reason. I mean, he has only the one victim, but we have five, and we were first. We have precedence. The case should be ours."

"Come, Thomas," Barker said, easing out of his chair. "Let us go back to the Charity Organization Society and ask some questions."

"The Charity Organization Society?" the inspector repeated.

"What of it?" Barker asked.

"I believe both the Rices and the Goldsteins went through that organization when they first came here. They said so."

"You did not mention it earlier."

"Slipped my mind. I mean, it didn't seem relevant. Is there a connection?"

"The missing girl's mother works there."

Dunham said nothing but nodded solemnly.

"Thank you, Inspector. Come, lad. We've got our work cut out for us."

There was still a pall over the offices of the Charity Organization Society, where the women had assembled even though it was a Saturday, in hope of getting some word about Gwendolyn DeVere. When we entered, the girl's mother came forward through the double line of desks. Hypatia DeVere was no longer bedraggled, but her face was very pale and there were dark circles under her eyes. She must have spent the night in torment.

"Have you found anything?" she asked anxiously.

"No, ma'am," Barker said solemnly. "We circled the district until midnight and showed a photograph from the Carricks to dozens of people. I suspect we shall receive some form of communiqué from her abductors soon, and, of course, Scotland Yard shall begin their search in earnest today as well."

"They have already been here," Miss Hill said, coming up beside the major's wife. "An Inspector Swanson came in not a quarter hour ago."

"Did he make any comment?" my employer asked.

"He was not pleased that we had hired a private agent," Mrs. DeVere said, "but he seemed to know you. Why do you think we might hear from my daughter's abductors?"

"If they originally had hopes of using her for the white slave trade, the quality of her clothing would have told them that she would be worth more for ransom."

"Do you think so?" the poor woman asked, actually clutching Barker's arm. "You think she might be ransomed? I have money of my own. I would give anything to have her back."

"I make no promises, madam," Barker said cautiously. "I merely state that white slavers are motivated by greed and would be intelligent enough to know that more money could be made by selling her back to you."

"And if it isn't a white slave ring?" Miss Hill asked.

"Then we must change our tactics," Barker responded, evading the question. "We will know by the end of the day, I expect. Might I ask some questions? Mrs. DeVere, what do you remember about yesterday morning before the disappearance?"

"It was a typical day with Gwendolyn. I only bring her occasionally. I wanted to teach her the importance of doing charitable work and to appreciate how well off we are."

"What are your duties here?" Barker asked.

"I am the bookkeeper. I have a good head for figures, and a great deal of money passes through the C.O.S."

"We are not a charity, ourselves, although we provide immediate needs, such as blankets and coal," Miss Hill explained. "Our primary duty is to see that donations from private individuals are evenly distributed among charitable organizations. It would be tragic if one group, such as the Salvation Army, receives an abundance of funds while another, like the Poplar Orphanage, receives nothing and must close its doors. We also see that the deserving poor are conveyed to the best institutions to meet their needs."

"I see," Barker responded, turning to Mrs. DeVere. "So what did the wee girl do here while you were busy keeping the books?"

I noticed Miss Hill's lips broaden a little. Barker is a born Scot, but twenty years in the East and five in London had worn the edges off his accent. I hadn't heard the phrase "wee girl" anywhere save the novels of Walter Scott.

"Gwendolyn is a good girl and she amuses herself," her mother explained. "She is becoming quite a young lady. Sometimes she helps Miss Levy and the other girls. She has slipped off before, but always came back within a half hour. She always, always came back."

"Is there any place she might have gone, anyone she knew in the area?"

"No, sir. No one in particular that I know of."

"Did she have a desk at which she sat?" Barker asked.

"Yes, sir. That one," Mrs. DeVere answered, indicating one at the far back of the room. As a group we all moved toward it. It was a smaller desk, not quite in keeping with the others. It looked derelict, and I felt sorry for the girl not merely for what had happened to her now but for being taken here in order to be shown her civic duty. She must have been bored to tears, I thought.

Barker began opening the drawers of the desk, but all he discovered was some paper, a pencil, and a book of fairy stories. The Guv held up the top sheet of paper to the light and scrutinized it, but there were no marks leftover from the sheet that had been on top of it.

"Nothing," he said. There was a back door not far from the desk. Barker crossed to it and gave the handle a turn. It would not open.

"It is always locked," Miss Hill stated. "We had thieves one morning a few years ago who stole some blankets. We've kept it locked ever since."

"Is there any other way of egress?"

"No, sir."

"Were the windows open yesterday morning?"

"Yes, but the ground slopes down from the front," Miss Hill explained. "It is eight feet to the ground here and ten from the windows in my office."

Barker flipped the latch on the window and lifted it. There was a bare alley beside it, but Miss Hill's assessment of the height was correct. A flight of steps led up to the locked back door.

"If she slipped over the sill and hung by the ledge, she might have been able to drop without hurting herself," I said.

"We would have seen her," Miss Levy pointed out.

"Was it busy yesterday morning?" Barker asked.

"Very busy," Miss Hill admitted. "But never so busy as to not see a twelve-year-old girl climbing out the window."

"Is there a water closet in the building?"

"There is. We have had it installed." She led us to the small room and we looked in. There was a window here as well, but it was high on the wall, too high for a child to reach.

"So, it would appear that the only way Miss DeVere could have left was through the front door. Did anyone see her near it?"

"I sit at the first desk," Miss Levy explained. "And I made certain Gwendolyn did not get by. She's gone out before, you see."

"You make it sound as if she escaped, Mr. Barker," Hypatia DeVere objected.

"It seems far more likely that she walked out of here than that a group of white slavers entered and somehow spirited her away under your very noses."

"One minute she was there and the next she was not," Miss Levy said.

"It sounds like a stage magician's trick," I said.

Mrs. Carrick entered then and looked at the group of us. "Has anything happened?" she asked.

"We're trying to discover how Gwendolyn got out," Miss Levy explained.

"Do you know of anyplace she might have gone?" Barker pursued. "Anyone she might have known, perhaps someone her own age?"

"None with whom she cared to associate," Miss Levy said, then realized she had criticized a daughter in front of her mother. "I mean, she preferred to read or talk with us rather than to play with the children who came in here."

Mrs. DeVere's hackles were up immediately and I thought an altercation was about to occur between the overwrought mother and the caustic volunteer, but Barker brought them back to the matter at hand.

He turned to Miss Hill. "Where is the doctor today?"

"Dr. Fitzhugh volunteers from ten until two, normally. He has recently qualified and hopes to open a surgery of his own in London, so he is very busy."

"What would he have to gain by volunteering here?"

"You would have to ask him that question, but as we coordinate among a number of organizations, he would have the opportunity to meet some of London's civic leaders. I feel, however, that the doctor has a genuine heart for the poor."

"Tell me, Miss Hill, are you a socialist? I hope I do not offend you with the word."

"Not at all, Mr. Barker, but there are socialists and then there are socialists. I am a Christian socialist. I believe it is our duty when the churches have been unable to help and some people have fallen through the cracks to step in and save them. It is the only alternative to the workhouse."

"How real do you think the slave trade is in the area?"

"That is the question we have been asking ourselves since yesterday, Mr. Barker. One hears so many rumors, but it isn't always best to give credence to everything that is said. I could name half a dozen fallen women that claim their degradation began through the deviltry of the white slavers, but I believe them all to be embellishing the sordid truth of their own wanton behavior. However, I must admit that children and young women in the area have vanished without a trace. Some, I thought were the victims of their stepfather's wrath or lusts, others desperate or resourceful enough to run away, but now and again I've seen children vanish from good families. And they all have one thing in common, sir. They never return."

"Have you ever spoken to an avowed white slaver, Miss Hill?"

"No, I must admit I have not."

"Nor I, madam. It may be that reports of their activities have been exaggerated, but I believe it is best to play it safe. I have sent a telegram to a gentleman I know in Sussex. He is having the ports watched. Meanwhile, Thomas and I shall be searching the area again, asking questions. We have held up your work. Good afternoon, ladies."

Outside, we headed down Green Street again. I ruminated upon the fact that my feet were still sore from yesterday's walk.

"I still find it hard to believe that there are men, possibly even in this street, whose living is made from snatching young girls."

"Believe it, lad."

"I thought this was a Christian country," I said bitterly.

Barker shook his head. "Then you are misinformed. We live on a mean, sinful planet, Thomas, and it shall only get worse if the Lord should tarry."

Jenkins, our clerk, had awoken during our absence. He had finished his cigarette, the *Police Gazette,* and tea and was dusting the bookshelves. He had also placed a note on the salver on the corner of my employer's desk.

Barker looked at it soberly as it lay in the silver tray. It was a grubby-looking envelope, with the office address written in pencil.

"When did it arrive?" he asked.

"Just after three o'clock, sir."

He lifted it from the salver, weighed it in his hand, then took up his Italian dagger from his desk and slit the envelope open along the flap. He shook the contents onto the desk rather than put his fingers inside the envelope. It was a grayish piece of foolscap. He picked it up, opened it carefully, and began to read.

"Is it a ransom note?" I asked.

He held up a finger and read through the letter again. Then he tossed it down dismissively into the salver and went to his smoking cabinet for a pipe and tobacco. I pounced on the letter. As it turned out, it wasn't a letter at all. It was a poem.

Old Push was seen down in Bethnal Green,
A-smoking on his ivory pipe.
But what he found, 'neath the mouldering ground,
Had grown most decidedly ripe.
Go home, Old Cy, to your garden wall high,
Don't be such a nosy Parker,
Or you'll rue the day that you came my way,
Yours truly,
Mr. Miacca.

"He's watching us," was my first comment. "He saw you with your pipe and he knows about your garden."

"Yes," Barker said, getting another of his pipes going, this one carved in the likeness of the late General Gordon. "We are starting at a disadvantage in that our quarry knows our identity but we do not know his. He's been watching us. Quite possibly, he's been following us about all day."

I got a creeping feeling in the small of my back that such a loathsome person should know our business and who we were. Barker did not seem as concerned, more curious, but then he is over six foot, weighs fifteen stone, and has faced things I'll never see.

"Miacca," he said. "It sounds Jewish or possibly Italian."

"I believe it is English, sir," I told him. "I think it's a fairy tale character." Suddenly it all fell into place. "Good Lord," I muttered.

"What?" Barker insisted. "What is it, lad?"

"I remember. Mr. Miacca was a cannibal, sir. He ate children."

6

"CAN YOU INFER ANYTHING FROM THE NOTE?"
Barker asked.

"The envelope is grubby and of rather poor quality, like the notepaper itself, but the writing is legible enough and it follows the general form of a poem. It reminds me somewhat of Edward Lear."

"Lear? I am not familiar with him."

"He writes nonsense rhymes, limericks and such, mostly for children."

Barker sank back into his swiveling chair and blew smoke toward the ceiling. There was a pause while he made up his mind. "I want you to go to the British Museum," he said. "Track down this Miacca legend for me and Lear as well."

"Yes, sir."

"I'll pay a visit to Scotland Yard and see if I can talk Swanson into letting me look at those files in his possession."

I seized my bowler and stick and stepped out the door into Craig's Court just as Big Ben boomed four times. Research was my favorite part of the investigative process, the hunting of pertinent facts culled from thousands of others in libraries or public record offices. As I raised my stick to hail a cab, however, I thought about how the killer had possibly been watching us today as we walked about Bethnal Green. It made me stop and survey the street and the dozens of anonymous windows that faced me. It is unnerving to know that someone might be scrutinizing you and meaning you harm.

The study area of the Reading Room in the British Museum is formed roughly in the shape of a wheel. The hub is a warren of desks and cabinets for the use of members of staff, and shooting off from it are spokes made up of adjoining desks and chairs for patrons, all in blue-green leather, one of which I had come to think of as my own, P16. I had been coming here since I was sponsored for membership by the patron of my youth, Lord Glendenning, before the unfounded charge of theft leveled upon me by my university nemesis, Palmister Clay. After my personal disgrace and imprisonment, his lordship had seen fit to sever all ties with me but had neglected to withdraw his sponsorship. That written recommendation had been an anchor to me since then. It was here, for example, that I had first come across Barker's advertisement in the Situations Vacant column of *The Times*. I still came here on half days to read and think. Now I had come here to track down the tale of the vile Mr. Miacca.

I made my way to the section on folklore and soon found what I was looking for in a book containing legends and stories of London called *Tales of the Old Town*, published in 1849. I took it back to my desk and flipped through the contents until I found the tale of Mr. Miacca, and turned to the appropriate pages. My memory had been correct. Miacca had been a nasty fellow, but reading the story over, I saw that he was more. There was something of the supernatural in him. After copying the passage into my notebook, I closed the book and set it down on the desk.

Next came the Edward Lear. I didn't suppose Barker considered Mr. Lear a serious suspect, but the author of the little poem in our office was certainly aping his style. I couldn't find his books in the poetry section and had to ask one of the librarians if the British Museum stocked his works. It did, as it turned out, but they had been relegated to the children's section, which I considered shabby treatment. True, children could read and understand his poems and limericks, but they had been intended for adults. I wondered what Barker, a serious if self-taught scholar, would make of "The Owl and the Pussycat," or "The Courtship of the Yonghy-Bonghy-Bò." I chose a copy of his book and sat down again, indulging myself in a poem or two. Mr. Lear is a silly fellow, and, as far as I am concerned, there are not enough like him in the world. After a few pages, I found myself chuckling. Much of his work is repetitious, but occasionally he skewers the foibles of man with his sharp wit. I wasn't about to copy all of Lear's nonsense into my notebook, so I contented myself with a few poems.

I looked over the top of the book to check the time on the wall clock over the door, and out of the corner of my eye caught a sudden movement. Looking about, all seemed as it should be, but I had the unsettling feeling that I was being watched. Was it Mr. Miacca, right there in the Reading Room with me, or was I letting my nerves get the best of me? I dipped back behind the book to collect myself. Why had I not thought to bring the pistol from my desk drawer? I steadied my nerves and attuned my senses before taking action. Barker wasn't there to help me. I had only my training to fall back on.

I looked up suddenly and having done so, my ear caught a sound, the flapping of a newspaper. I looked about casually. Beside me there was a heavyset fellow intent on some work of translation. The rest of the people along my row were all reading with their heads down, as was the row of patrons behind us. I looked at the knot of employees. One held a book in front of his face, but I was certain I'd heard the rustle of newsprint. I continued glancing about the room until eventually I saw it, a newspaper facing me directly, in one of the rows on the other side.

I focused on the hands, which were small. I was being watched by a woman. It had been a while since a woman had stared at me in a library. I was not so naive as to think it was my grace or appearance that had attracted her notice. It must have something to do with the case, I reasoned. The newspaper began to settle slowly. I caught a glimpse of blondish curls before turning back quickly to my studies.

What shall I do now? I asked myself. I couldn't exactly walk over and say, "Pardon, but I couldn't help notice you were watching me just now." On the other hand, any interest I had in fairy tales had evaporated with the attentions of a young lady at hand. I stood, stretched decorously, shooting my cuffs, avoiding the natural desire to glance in the woman's direction. I then turned and made my way to the exit.

Of course, I had no idea whether she might follow. More probably, she would turn her attentions to some other young gentlemen studying at one of the tables. Once outside, I resisted the attentions of a cabman there and turned right, headed along Gower Street, and walked to Regent's Park.

It was warm and sunny, a rare and glorious afternoon. I walked along the path between grassy expanses in the dappled shade of oaks that must have grown there since the park was first designed. I dared not look behind. It was rather like fishing; I didn't want to spook my prey. In all probability, there was no prey to spook, and I was making a fool of myself. I was about to give it up, but as I passed the brass plaque that announced I had reached the Zoological Gardens, I saw in that highly polished metal surface that I was still being shadowed, and by a female in a bowler hat and a trim-fitting black outfit. I rather doubted this was the infamous Mr. Miacca. The glorious day suddenly got that much brighter.

Now that the fish, if I might be so crass as to equate the young lady in question with a fish, had risen to the bait, how was I to set the hook? She could still break off the line were I to change course in midstream. Not really having an idea of what to do, I walked past the lions and seals; finally reaching the wolf cages, which somehow seemed appropriate, I sat down at a bench and, with as much *savoir faire* as I could muster, I raised my hat.

"Good afternoon, miss," I said as she approached. I recognized her as the friend of Miss Levy.

She stopped and actually gaped at me. "Was I that obvious?" she asked.

"No," I replied, "but I am an experienced enquiry agent and it is difficult to pull the wool over my eyes."

She sat down beside me. "My word," she said, "you are good."

"I am Thomas Llewelyn."

"Beatrice Potter."

She was attractive, with light-colored hair swept away from frank blue eyes and delicate features. Her clothes were of the best quality and in the height of fashion. She came from money, obviously. Not landed money, perhaps, but money all the same. When we were children, I wouldn't have been allowed to speak to her, being a mere miner's son, and now she was following me.

"Aren't you going to ask me why I followed you from the museum, or do you know that as well?"

"I assume that you happened to see me in the Reading Room. You didn't follow me there. Are you Jewish?"

"Jewish?" She frowned. "Why do you ask that?"

"Miss Levy, your friend, is Jewish. And you were reading the *Jewish Chronicle* in the museum."

"So I was. I fancy that one of my grandparents was Jewish, but so far I have found little proof. Certainly the other three quarters of me are English enough, and my family is doing its best to deny the other. I find Jews fascinating and have been studying their history and politics. And you?"

"I'm as Welsh as rarebit, but most of my closest friends are from the Jewish quarter and my employer has worked for the Board of Deputies. So, if you happened to recognize me in the Reading Room, why did you follow me?"

"I'll tell you if you'll answer one question first. Why were you reading Lear?"

"It is pertinent to the case. Beyond that I can reveal nothing. Now you tell me why you followed me."

"You wouldn't believe me if I told you."

"Oh, I like that even better," I said. "So come, come. Tell me. I can believe anything, provided it is fanciful enough."

"I am an investigator."

I couldn't help but smile. "Pull the other one. Are you private, or are you in fact working for Scotland Yard?"

"Neither. I am a social investigator."

"I see," I said, though to be frank, I didn't. "I don't suppose that pays very well."

"Nothing at all, actually, but it's very important. That's why I am working in the East End. I wish to know why the greatest empire in history cannot feed, clothe, or shelter many of its people. I wonder why the mistakes and attitudes of one generation are doomed to be repeated in the next and why the arrival of a people with a rich and ancient culture such as the Jews inspires fear and loathing among an otherwise sensible people. And right now I'm wondering what caused a university man to take up what is obviously a dangerous profession."

"What makes you think I was at university?" I asked.

"I may be a woman, but I do have a functioning brain, Mr. Llewelyn. The Reading Room is for scholars. You have a membership. I will even speculate that in spite of your education, you are of humble beginnings. So, was it Oxford or Cambridge?"

"It was Oxford. And you are right about my beginnings. How have I given myself away?"

"If anything, your accent is too perfect. You speak better English than most of the young men in my set."

"Ah," I said. There was an awkward pause, during which I thought about the phrase, "my set." I was right about her class origins. But she was speaking. "I beg your pardon?"

"You haven't answered my question. What caused a university man to take up such a profession?"

"Eight months in Oxford Prison severely limited my choice of occupations, Miss Potter."

"My word," she replied. "That was blunt."

"My apologies," I said. "I misspoke."

"No, no, I admire it, Mr. Llewelyn. You use information like a weapon. That is good. You are in the business of giving and receiving information, as am I. There are people out there attempting to stifle knowledge and mask truth. Sometimes it is private individuals, sometimes it is the government itself."

"Miss Potter, are you one of those crusaders who want to redistribute the wealth and give the vote to women?"

"Do you consider either of those bad things, sir?"

"To tell you the truth, I have no idea. I've never investigated the question before."

"Then you are more intelligent than most of the male population. At least you haven't made up your mind without having researched the issues. There is hope for you, yet."

"Well, good, then," I said, trying not to laugh. "At least there is hope."

"So that man with whom you came into the charity was your employer?"

"Yes. His name is Cyrus Barker."

"He seemed a brusque sort."

He was indeed a brusque sort, but I didn't want Miss Potter to get the wrong impression. "He's a gentleman and a fine employer. And of course, a first-rate enquiry agent."

"I've heard you detectives are very loyal to one another," she noted.

"Sometimes in an inquiry, your employer is the only person you can trust. He's saved my life on more than one occasion. Do you volunteer at the C.O.S.?"

"I did for a while, but now I work at a tenement called the Katherine Building. I interview prospective tenants, collect rents, and see that the building is well maintained. As an investigator, I keep a file on each tenant, their history, occupation, family, and beliefs. When they are gone—and, of course, being poor, they rarely stay long—their social history will be of greater use as a record of conditions during this time."

"So it is a salaried position, then. I am surprised that you work."

She laughed, displaying a set of perfect teeth. No one in need of money had teeth like that.

"I don't need to, of course. My father owns a railway. I'm sure he could buy the Katherine Building twice over."

"It seems an unusual pastime for a young woman, running a slum tenement. Most young ladies would simply marry."

"Some find the institution of marriage to be a form of tyranny not unlike slavery. Most of us at the Charity Organization Society feel that way. We do not need a man to become whole individuals. We are scholars and freethinkers, Mr. Llewelyn. We refuse to be put on a pedestal but instead hope to help bring about social change."

"Mrs. DeVere and Mrs. Carrick are both married," I pointed out.

"True. It is a hard choice. We lose a lot of sisters to marriage. I've turned down several offers myself. It is a difficult decision to remain celibate."

I tried hard not to blush, but I'd never heard a young woman speak so frankly.

"So are there many young women like you in the East End just now?"

"Oh, yes, dozens. Social work is a respectable use of time for young, unmarried women these days. But enough about me. Do you like being a detective?"

"Mr. Barker prefers the term 'enquiry agent.'"

"What is the difference?"

"We take the moral high ground, so to speak. A detective is willing to break the law in order to solve whatever case he is working on. He may break into a house to obtain information."

"So you've never broken a law to obtain information?" Miss Potter asked.

"Well, we've bent it a little once or twice."

"And are you not a former criminal?"

"I was, in a way, but it was complicated."

"Your distinctions have quite gone out the window, then, sir."

"Allow me to return the compliment, Miss Potter. You are good."

"You haven't answered my question, Mr. Llewelyn," she pursued. "Do you like being a detective?"

"No, no. You cannot put me off that easily, Miss Potter. You followed me here for a purpose. What was it, may I ask?"

"I thought I might help you," she said, looking down at a handkerchief she was kneading in her hands. "I could volunteer at the C.O.S. again. Miss Hill would be glad to take me back. Perhaps I might overhear something said by one of the patrons that would lead you to Gwendolyn and her abductors."

I wanted to tell her that we were no longer looking for a white slave ring but instead a madman. However, it was not my secret to reveal.

"What do you think?" she pressed.

"It doesn't matter what I think," I retorted. "It is what my employer thinks that is important. I don't know what he shall say. He keeps a bachelor's home and offices, I should warn you. Why do you wish to help, anyway?"

"Aren't white slave rings a social problem, sir?"

"They are," I admitted.

"You do wish Gwendolyn to be saved and these criminals caught?"

"Of course."

"Then I suppose it is female detectives you don't like."

She argued well, I gave her that, but then, most women do.

"You're building a straw man," I reasoned. "I have neither criticized female detectives, denied wanting Miss De-Vere to be found, nor claimed that white slavery was not a social problem. I merely wondered about your personal motives."

"You're protective of your employer."

"I'm not sure he needs protection, but he doesn't need to be interrupted in his work."

"Very well," she said. "I do have personal reasons. I want to be able to say, if only for my own sake, that I have worked for a professional investigator. It makes me feel I too am a professional and not a rich girl playing games. Tell your Mr. Barker I expect to be paid."

"Do not consider yourself hired just yet, but I shall speak to him tonight. Will you be at the Katherine Building tomorrow?"

"Of course not," she replied. "It's Sunday."

"Then I shall send word of my employer's decision," I said, rising from the bench. "I bid you good afternoon, Miss Potter." I raised my hat to her and left the park. The Guv would be waiting for me, and also, I thought it best to be the one to end the conversation. It was the only control I had.

As I hurried out of the park, my mind gathered impressions. Beatrice Potter was a beautiful and intelligent young woman and seemed genuinely committed to bringing about reform in the East End. I did not think, however, that the girl was being truthful about her motives for wishing to join us in the hunt for Gwendolyn DeVere.

7

"HERE THEY ARE, SIR," I SAID, LAYING THE
newly typed pages on my employer's desk. Barker took the
sheets in his hand and began to read. The tale went as follows:

   "THE TALE OF MR. MIACCA
     "There lived in Old London Town a man, though
some say he was a giant or an ogre, and his name was
Miacca. Mr. Miacca loved good children and would leave
a farthing upon their windowsills, even those who lived
high in attic garrets, but bad children he threw into a
sack and took home for his supper. Mothers used to
warn their children, 'Be good, and do not go out of the
street, or Mr. Miacca shall surely take you.'
     "Now there was a boy named Tommy Grimes who
lived in the Old Town, and like most boys and girls he
was often good, but sometimes he had the devil in him.
His mother warned him about his behavior and about
leaving his street, but one day he turned the corner and

Mr. Miacca took him. He threw the boy in his sack and carried him home for dinner.

"Mr. Miacca pulled Tommy out of the sack and set him on his chopping block. He pinched Tommy's arm.

"'You are too tough for my Sunday joint,' he said, 'but boy meat is good for a stew with herbs. But look, dear me, I have forgotten the herbs! Sally!'

"Mrs. Miacca came in from another room. 'Yes, my dear?'

"'Here is a boy for supper, and bitter he shall taste without some fresh herbs. Watch him while I am gone, and if he moves, hack off a limb with my cleaver.'

"Mrs. Miacca agreed, and Mr. Miacca went off, leaving her alone with Tommy.

"'Does Mr. Miacca often have children for supper?' the boy asked.

"'Now and again,' she replied. 'But only bad ones such as yourself.'

"'And is there no pudding to go with me?' he asked. 'I think I should make a poor meal without pudding.'

"'Ah, I do so love pudding,' Mrs. Miacca admitted, 'but my husband is always giving our farthings away to good children. We can ill afford it.'

"'Why, my mother has made a pudding this very morning,' Tommy Grimes told her. 'And it is sitting this very moment on the windowsill to cool but a street away. I'm sure she will not mind if I take it. Shall I run and get it?'

"'Yes, do,' came the reply. 'But be quick about it. It shall take hours to boil you tender enough for a stew.'

"Tommy Grimes hopped down from the chopping

block and ran out the door. He kept running until he arrived at his own house, safe and sound. That night in his bed, he admitted he had got off cheaply and swore never to be bad again.

"Now, promises are all well and good, but one cannot be good forever. One day Tommy took a step around the corner, and the next thing he knew, he was upside down in Mr. Miacca's sack again.

"'That was a shabby trick you played upon the missus and me,' Mr. Miacca complained as he walked. 'I shall be sure to watch you myself this time.'

"Once they were in Mr. Miacca's house, he thrust the boy under the chopping table.

"'Get under there and don't move while I cut the herbs for the pot. If you stick out so much as one limb, I shall chop it off with my cleaver.'

"Tommy knew he was in desperate straits, but he was a clever boy. There was a pile of kindling by the chopping block, and he pulled one log under him and began whittling it with his pocket knife. He whittled all the time Mr. Miacca was chopping the herbs and adding spices to the stew.

"'It's almost ready, boy. Stick out your leg so I can toss it into the pot.'

"Tommy pulled off a shoe and sock and quickly put them over the end of the log. He poked it out from under the table and yelled when it was cut in twain with the cleaver. While Mr. Miacca was busy simmering the limb, Tommy slipped out unobserved and ran home as fast as his legs could carry him.

"Now, children will be bad from time to time and

Tommy Grimes was no exception, but from hence he was only a menace to his own street. He never dared go into Mr. Miacca's neighborhood until he was a man full grown, and able to care for himself."

Barker put down my notes and leaned back in his chair in thought.

"What do you make of it, sir?" I dared ask.

"I'm not certain," he said. "I have no frame of reference. I have never read a fairy story before."

"Never? Not even when you were a child?"

"No. I was raised in a strict Calvinist home and all we read were the Bible and our clan histories. Reading tales of ogres and such would have been considered desperately wicked. What do you gather from it?"

"It is a variation on the classic giant story," I said. "A child is caught by a slow-witted giant and through an act of cleverness escapes. It is also a morality tale. Be good and do not wander off or else the bogeyman shall get you. The difference is that the tale takes place in the center of London instead of a castle or at the top of a beanstalk."

"The tale is rather gruesome," Barker said. "Boy meat and hacking off limbs."

"Yes, but that's the thrill of it. When a child first hears it, it is harrowing. After that, it is humorous—the slow-witted man and his wife tricked twice by a child."

"Do you think there might have been a Mr. Miacca around whom the legend grew?"

"It is possible. Parents would be sure to point out someone they wished their children to avoid, particularly if he was a foreigner. As you said earlier, the name sounds Jewish or Mediterranean. There's no telling how old the legend is. It could be centuries old."

"You've made a very good analysis, Thomas. I knew I was not mistaken in hiring a scholar. Is there anything else?"

"Well, sir, there is one other legend about cannibalism in Old London."

Barker nodded. "Sweeney Todd."

"Exactly. He's in the book as well, but he's under legends rather than fairy tales. I thought I'd call it to your attention."

"And so you have." He picked up the verses I'd copied from Lear, and began turning the pages. I watched his brows slowly sink behind his round spectacles.

"Poems," he grunted. "Limericks. I have heard many a limerick in my time, mostly from sailors. They were generally ribald. These are not, but I do not understand the humor. What is humorous about a man who has birds nesting in his beard? It does not look like Miacca's note."

"His longer poems do, sir. Look past the limericks."

He flipped impatiently through the pages. Finally, he tossed it onto his blotter with more vehemence than he normally gave the printed word and made his pronouncement. "Rubbish. The similarities are superficial. Anyone with a grasp of English could have written the poem. As for this fellow, I cannot understand Lear's appeal, save to the smallest of tots. Do you have anything else?"

"Well, sir, there is one thing. I was followed from the British Museum."

Barker leaned back in his seat and pressed his fingertips together. He looked rather like a schoolmaster when he did that. "Continue."

I told him about Miss Potter and our conversation. I left out any attempts at flirtation on my part, but I knew he was smart enough to imagine it back in again. Here it comes, I thought, the lecture: *This agency does not exist to provide you with female companionship, etc.*

"She offered to keep an eye on the Charity Organization Society," he stated.

"Yes, sir."

"We may take her up on the offer."

That was all. No lecture.

"Socialists," he growled.

"You do not approve of socialism? If it makes any difference, I believe the term Miss Hill used was 'Christian socialist.'"

"Christian socialist," Barker muttered. "That is even worse."

"What is the difference, pray, in the good works you do in the Tabernacle and the work of the Christian socialist?"

"It starts with their entire worldview, lad. They believe that man is basically good, and that, given the proper nudge by such crusading women, they can turn the earth into a utopia and usher in the millennium."

"And you believe—"

"That man, from the time he is born is at heart selfish and any attempt at utopia shall fail miserably. Heaven shall not be attained on earth."

"But they are helping, sir, are they not? Isn't Brother Mc-Clain over in Mile End Road helping?"

"He is, but he is no socialist. His beliefs are above reproach."

I wanted to say that that meant they were in line with his. McClain was Barker's sparring partner and friend. A former heavyweight champion, he now ran a mission in the East End that was known to have some success with alcohol and opium addicts.

"But they do no harm, at least. The people are fed and cared for."

"I'll grant you that, lad. Miss Hill has the command of a field marshal." My employer took a meerschaum from his smoking cabinet and lit a vesta. "But back to Miacca. He's a depraved monster."

"You think he is a monster, then."

"He is an aberration. He has abdicated all rights to be considered human. He should be hunted down like a mad dog and shot. I have feared something like this would happen. Society continues to grow more and more depraved."

There was a cold supper awaiting us when we arrived home. Mac had set out potted beef and slices of ham on the table, with a thick wedge of cheddar and a loaf of bread. He had brought up one of his small casks of home-made stout from the cellar. It was all perfectly acceptable food, but it was public house fare. After a hard day, I expected one of Etienne's feasts, quails stuffed with *pâté de foie gras* or salmon in aspic.

"What's going on here?" I asked Mac, pointing at the table.

Jacob Maccabee had been making a show of it, acting as if this were simply another night. He wilted under my questioning.

"Mr. Dummolard has quit."

"Quit!"

"Yes, sir. If I recall it correctly, he said henceforth he

shall feed the rats of the city, who have a finer appreciation of cuisine than you two . . . er, gentlemen. He left something for you there."

Mac pointed to my plate. There was a spongy looking mass there, yellow speckled with black.

"An omelet?" I asked, looking at it dubiously.

"Yes, sir. It is the very one he made for you this morning, the one you left behind. Mr. Dummolard took it very hard, I'm afraid. He brought in the truffle specially. In fact, he made a great show of apologizing to it that it gave its life for such an undeserving wastrel. That's close to what he said. My French isn't good, and he was shouting most of it."

I was appalled, of course, but my employer merely sat down and began to help himself to the potted meat. Barker's ward had come into the garden while Dummolard was preparing the omelet that morning, but I daren't bring it up to him now. I wasn't about to get involved in an argument between my employer and his cook. "Oh, do take this away, Mac. It's disgusting."

"Etienne was long overdue for a blowup," Barker said. "In fact, it was your fondness for his cooking that has kept him mollified all this time. He shall return eventually and act as if nothing happened."

"I could go to his restaurant to apologize," I offered.

"It would only make matters worse. He must explode every now and then. You merely gave him an excuse."

Mac cleared his throat discreetly. "Mr. Dummolard was also put out by the cavalier manner in which you consumed the rashers and eggs he made this morning, sir."

"Confound it," Barker exclaimed. "I'm not going to be

dictated to by my cook. I didn't as captain of the *Osprey* and I don't intend to now. Sit down and eat, Thomas. There'll be no fancy Parisian cooking for you tonight."

We ate in silence with only the clinking of cutlery on china for company. In the middle of the meal, Barker evinced a hope that Harm was "getting on" up in Yorkshire. I took it for a rhetorical question and did not answer. Then a question occurred to me and I broke the silence again.

"Shall you tell the DeVeres about Mr. Miacca?"

Barker finished worrying a piece of ham and spoke. "There's no point. I have no real proof of a connection between Miss DeVere and Miacca, only a suspicion. There are still white slavers in England and one may have her for all I know."

He took up his tankard of stout and drained it. Then he pushed himself up out of his chair.

"I had been preparing for a case of child slavery. Now I must prepare to hunt for an archfiend. Mac, I shall need a pot of tea in my room. Thomas, I leave you to your own devices."

He was almost out of the room when he stopped and turned to me. "Perhaps Etienne's absence can be used to our advantage," he said.

Whatever that meant, I didn't like the sound of it.

8

CYRUS BARKER IS LOATH TO MISS SUNDAY morning service at the Baptist Tabernacle, but there was a young girl still missing in Bethnal Green and some things take priority. We had no sooner alighted from the cab in Green Street than we were accosted. The first thing I knew, someone had seized my arm and begun shaking it violently. Automatically, I went into one of the defensive postures Barker taught me, but it was only one of the mudlarks we had spoken to earlier, the woman known as Mum Alice. She was shouting something at us I couldn't make out.

"Slow down, Alice," Barker counseled. "Take a deep breath and speak slowly."

"Ah found 'em," she pronounced slowly. Despite her name, she was not mum. A harelip coupled with a thick Cockney accent and an excitable manner made her difficult to understand, unless one took the time to listen. "Found 'er cwothes."

"You found Miss DeVere's clothes? Where are they?"

"Pe'icoat Wane. Bu' 'e go' Annie!"

"Who's got Annie?"

"Swanson! I wan away 'fore 'e could ge' me."

The next I knew we were climbing back into the hansom, Barker, myself, and Alice, all bound for Petticoat Lane. She was bouncing on her seat in excitement. It may have been her first cab ride. As for me, I found the conditions, squeezed between Barker's hard shoulder and Alice's soft one, like an immense, unwashed pillow, less than ideal.

Once one passes beyond Aldgate pump, Petticoat Lane is the first street one finds on the right. I paid the cabbie. On Sunday it is sheer madness, but the rest of the week the street vendors are gone and only the permanent shops remain. Barker did not object when Alice took his arm and led him down the street. We penetrated farther into the lane than we'd ever gone before. After several hundred yards, the street breaks up into narrow alleyways, with smaller and meaner looking shops. Alice pulled the Guv down one of the alleys. The shallow open booths there were split horizontally, so that while one vendor sat with his legs crossed an inch above the pavement, displaying secondhand collars, his upstairs neighbor sat a few inches above his head, offering ties, handkerchiefs, and suspenders. Inspector Swanson was standing and talking with Dirty Annie, as solid looking as a lamppost.

"Donald," Barker said casually, as if he just happened to be doing a bit of shopping in the area and stumbled across him.

"Cyrus," Swanson responded, affecting the same casual tone.

"It's 'ere, yer worship!" Mum Alice burst out.

Barker followed her to a booth, and she pointed a warty finger at a square of folded clothing arranged among several others. It was blue and white, with an open collar, and a neckerchief with an anchor design embroidered upon it. A sailor suit. My employer crouched down and lifted one end of the fabric, scrutinizing the label sewn in the collar. He nodded once. It was Rowes of Bond Street. The proprietor of the shop, if indeed one could call the small square of paved space a shop, was sitting so close the Guv might have reached out and shaken him, but he ignored him totally for the moment.

"How'd you find this booth?" he asked Swanson over his shoulder.

"I do this for a living, you know," Swanson replied. "You're not the only one who has informants."

"Has he told you from whence the togs came?" Barker continued, this time referring to the proprietor directly. He finally turned the black quartz lens of his spectacles upon him. The vendor was a jowly fellow with a pendulous, unshaven neck, and a bowler too small for his hoary head.

"He's nae said a word," the inspector replied.

"What have you threatened him with?" Barker asked.

"The usual—a hard questioning down at A Division."

"Take a walk, Donald."

"No, Cyrus. There'll be no tossin' suspects about while I'm in the area."

Barker nodded, still squatting there, deep in thought. Then he reached out, plucked the man's greasy tie from inside his moth-eaten waistcoat and slowly pulled the man toward him. He spoke to him in one ear, so low we could not catch a word. Then slowly, he loosed the tie and the man settled down back on the pavement.

"Ask your question again."

"Your name, sir. State your full name and address," the inspector demanded.

"Joseph Perkins, three eleven Flower and Dean Street," the slovenly man muttered.

"Who sold you these clothes?"

"Didn't give their names and I didn't ask 'em."

"Isn't it customary to ask for names and addresses when purchasing clothing?"

"It may be down near Aldgate High Street, in the prime sites. We ain't so p'ticular back here where the sunlight don't get through."

"Were you aware a girl was missing wearing just such clothing?" Swanson demanded.

The man shrugged his shoulders. "Girls go missing every day."

"There is not an epidemic of missing girls in the East End of London," Swanson stated, as if he were giving evidence in court.

"Suit yourself, then," Perkins said with a shrug. "Don't know nothing, didn't see nothing."

"You saw something, all right," Barker growled. "Describe who sold you this sailor suit."

"Were just a girl and her mum. She looked the right size for the clothes, though the frock she had on weren't nothing to speak of. Family resemblance; had to be mother and daughter. Girl looked about twelve, her mum . . . It's hard to tell in Whitechapel."

"She was from Whitechapel?"

"Didn't say that. I assumed. They was pretty draggle-tailed. Came in late yesterday and mum seemed nervous. Didn't speak English much. She wore a 'kerchief round her head. I didn't know about the sailor suit then or I'd a turned her down, but it is a beauty. Gave her a bob for it."

"Do you remember a name?" Barker growled. He was still balanced on the balls of his feet, as solid as if he were cemented there.

The man was quiet a moment. He closed his eyes. "Yer. She called her by an odd name, the mum did. What was it? Orma? Una? No, it was Ona, I think. The girl had stepped over to look at that booth there selling ribbons, and her mum cracked the whip hard. 'Ona, come, child.'"

"That's all you can recall?" Barker demanded, looking as menacing as only he can.

"That's the lot, Push. Honest."

Barker stood then, slowly straightening his knees.

"You're taking the clothes I shelled out for and not leaving a penny, aren't you?" Perkins demanded of the inspector.

"Any time you want to visit them, you can see them in A Division," Swanson replied.

"Like I'm gonna go to the Yard voluntarily," the vendor grumbled.

"How long was your time?" Barker asked.

"Five years hard in Princetown for 'sault. Thought he was a bloke what owed me money. How was I to know he were a solicitor?"

By now the two women were dancing about behind us. Barker instructed me to give them each sixpence to send them on their way. They shot off like horses at Ascot. Finally, he had me pass a shilling to Mr. Perkins.

"You're a gentleman, sir!" Perkins said. "Thank ye."

"What you are," Swanson corrected as he bent down to pick up the clothing, "is a soft touch."

"'Rob not the poor because he is poor,'" Barker quoted.

"I'll see you two gentlemen again," Swanson continued. "The commissioner will want to see these." He disappeared down the lane, or almost. Being a head taller than most, we watched his bowler hat bob through the knots of shoppers.

"We must work a little harder to stay ahead of Donald Swanson," the Guv said.

"He has informants."

"Aye. Canny ones. Let us hurry."

"Why bother?" I asked. "It seems certain now that Gwendolyn DeVere is dead."

"Why do you say that?"

"Her clothes were right there. You're not going to find two outfits by Rowes of Bond Street for sale in the East End, and I think it unlikely she is alive somewhere unclothed."

"Perhaps, but we have a name at least. Ona. I believe it is Lithuanian."

"Jewish?" We were in the heart of the Jewish quarter. In fact, we were surrounded by hoardings in Yiddish.

The minute we were away from the watchful eye of Inspector Donald Swanson, I pulled out my notebook and began flipping pages.

"Ona, Ona, Ona," I repeated until I finally saw the name. "Miss Hill said she was the only girl Miss DeVere would speak to in the Green."

"I believe we should speak to Miss Bellovich and her mother."

"Perhaps. Let us return to the Charity Organization Society."

"But, sir, it is Sunday. Surely they will be closed."

"They have a smaller group of women working on Sunday, headed by Miss Levy. As she is Jewish, it is not her Sabbath and she can tend to the unfortunates who need aid when the society would otherwise be closed."

We caught a cab back toward Bethnal Green. Once inside the C.O.S., Barker walked up to the attractive but tart Miss Levy and asked to speak to her privately.

Amy Levy looked hard at him, trying to come up with a reason to refuse, but finally stepped outside with us.

"What can I do for you, Mr. Barker?"

"Miss Levy, I would like to say a given name to you and perhaps you can supply a surname in return. Are you agreeable?"

She nodded hesitantly.

"The name is Ona."

"Yes," came the immediate response. "Ona Bell. Actually, it is Ona Bellovich. She was one of our charity cases here, along with her mother, Svetlana, when they first arrived in England six months ago. Ona was friendly with Gwendolyn, though I cannot say it was much reciprocated. She is a sweet girl. She acts as interpreter for her mother, who speaks mostly Yiddish. But how have you come across her name? Surely the Belloviches have not done anything criminal."

"Perish the thought, Miss Levy. As enquiry agents, we must track down all leads in an investigation. Her name came up this morning. Perhaps she spoke to Gwendolyn the day of her disappearance. Is it possible that the charity might have their present address?"

Miss Levy held back. "You merely wish to question her, do you not?"

"Of course. Does Mrs. Bellovich have a husband or male relative I might speak to first?"

"No, the two are alone in England. Her husband paid their passage but has been unsuccessful so far in gathering enough to follow."

"I see. And the address?"

She demurred another moment, but finally came to a decision in Barker's favor. "Wait here. I shall look up her file and bring it to you."

She disappeared into the building while we stood on the pavement and watched traffic on Green Street and Globe Road. It was a warm day, warm enough to be uncomfortable in my cutaway. As usual, the building was lined with applicants using the walls for support, as if they had been glued there as ornamentation.

Miss Levy soon returned and pressed a note into Barker's hand. There was a bloom in her olive cheeks. If I had known how many attractive girls the charities employed, I might have become a socialist long ago.

"Thank you," Barker said gruffly.

"You will be gentle, won't you?" Amy Levy asked.

"I am a professional, Miss Levy. Leave it to me." We raised our hats and left her standing there looking pensive.

"They live in Cheshire Street," Barker said, thrusting the note in his pocket. "Now, here is what I want you to do. When we get inside, stand in front of the door and hold your stick in front of you. I want you to do your best to look as imposing as possible."

"That does not sound gentle to me," I said.

"I made no such promise to Miss Levy, if you will recall, lad. This woman and child may be the only people who can lead us to Gwendolyn DeVere, but I fear they shall not give information to us voluntarily. They are Lithuanian, and as such have been subjected to raids by Cossacks and secret police their entire lives. They will not trust us, no matter what inducements we may give."

"How shall we get the information, then?" I asked.

"By giving them what they expect. We must frighten them into giving us the information."

Cyrus Barker smote the rickety door of a squalid tenement in Cheshire Street. His cane, like my own, was malacca with a brass head. Malacca cane is very flexible, and with the weighted head it provides a hard thump, whether on a wooden door or a human skull.

The door was jumping on its hinges, in danger of falling in, but still nobody answered our summons. It wasn't hard to picture Barker as some sort of secret police officer or Russian Cossack. All he needed was a fur hat. Granted, England didn't have secret police, but I'm sure fear of authority had been instilled in them since birth.

Finally, a shrill, quavering voice came from inside and the door opened to reveal a wide-eyed woman of about five and thirty, in a smocked dress with a kerchief tied around her head. Barker pushed his way in, speaking what I assumed was Yiddish. I followed Barker's instructions, closing the door and standing in front of it, my cane held horizontally and a fierce expression on my face. I don't think that I was going to frighten anyone, but I didn't need to. Barker was doing an excellent job of that all by himself.

It was a squalid room full of broken furnishings, and it reminded me of my past. The dining table was heaped with the makings for paper flowers, a depressing little industry in which my late wife's family had been employed. One had to make hundreds in a day, and then sell those hundreds to people who had little use for them, in order to make even the most negligible of profits.

Barker spoke gravely with Mrs. Bellovich for several moments. The poor woman was so terrified, she was trembling. She kept shaking her head as if to confirm that her daughter was not there.

"Ona Bellovich!" the Guv called out in English. "You had better come out at once. I would hate to take this good woman down to police headquarters."

Svetlana Bellovich stared apprehensively at my employer, though it was obvious she didn't understand what he had just said. What a life she must have lived already that the presence of officers of the law, real or spurious, was enough to turn her into a quivering mess. What terrors and deprivations she must have gone through before arriving on our comparatively safe shores.

"Miss Bellovich!" my employer went on in a loud voice. "No one holds you responsible for Miss DeVere's disappearance, but if you do not show yourself, we may be forced to search the house."

Someone began knocking at the door behind me, and I heard men's voices calling out in a foreign tongue. The handle jiggled, but I dug in my heels and refused to allow anyone to enter.

"Very well," Barker said, heaving a sigh. "Mr. Llewelyn, take Mrs. Bellovich to jail. I'll start searching the rooms."

"*Nyen!*" a voice cried from somewhere in the house. A

girl of about twelve years old came running out, into the arms of her mother. The two spoke to each other quietly for a moment, while outside the beating on the door continued.

"Miss Bellovich, I have no wish to cause harm to you or your mother, but you must come forward and speak to the police. I work for Gwendolyn's parents and am trying to find her. You have information that may help us. Do you understand?"

"Yes, sir," she said meekly. The girl looked like a younger version of her mother and wore a similar print dress and kerchief.

"Do you speak English?"

"Yes, sir."

"Good. Why don't you tell the gentlemen outside that you are safe and that we are only going to talk to you? Lad, open the door."

When I did, three men fell in, almost at my feet. They rose quickly. One seized my wrist and I was about to clout him with my stick, while the other two went for Barker, when Madame Bellovich raised her hands and spoke. Whatever she said convinced them to leave with nothing but mutterings and frowns in my direction.

Barker and the mother and daughter sat down at the wobbly table, and Ona began to speak quietly. My employer put questions to the girl, while her mother left and returned minutes later with cracked mugs full of strong, evil-tasting tea. Our assault upon their house began to take on a more domestic aspect. Barker shook his finger in Ona's face like an uncle admonishing his niece. By the end of it, the Guv had both the girl and her mother nodding and smiling, though there were still tears in Ona's eyes and strain on her mother's face.

Barker pushed himself out of his chair, which squeaked in protest. He shook hands with both women, and when he gestured toward me, I raised my bowler in response. When we opened the door, all three men were waiting outside, but we merely made our way past them, like rent collectors on the first day of the month. It confounded them enough to let us pass freely down the stairs and into the street un-molested.

"So let me get this straight," I said, after we were settled into the vehicle trundling down Commercial Street. "Miss DeVere borrowed a dress and kerchief from Ona Bellovich and slipped out of the C.O.S. without being seen. A sailor suit would have been noticed by dozens of people in those streets, as would a cloak in this warm weather. But why did Ona help her?"

"She complied because Gwendolyn insisted upon it. Apparently, this was to be her grand exit. She planned to run away with Ona and stay hidden for the rest of the day, all night, if necessary, until her mother agreed to quit the volunteer work. Ona says Gwendolyn thought her mother's duties to be degrading. She had planned everything rather well, but of course, she had not planned on Mr. Miacca."

"You think he has her?" I asked. "He has definitely not stated as much. It might still be white slavers. With her peasant clothes they might have taken her for a poor girl."

"The slave trade would have tried to get her out of the

country by now, and, as I said, I have an associate guarding the ports, with a competent crew. Scotland Yard is watching Newhaven and Dover, as well. I don't believe anyone could have successfully smuggled her out from under our collective noses. More likely, Miacca has her here, and you know what he does to bad children."

9

"Lo, push!"

The street arab I'd caught the day before came running toward us with a note in his hand. He was out of breath and after delivering it into my employer's hand, he leaned against a building, gasping for breath. It was my experience that these boys were out of doors much of the time and accustomed to walking the city. He must have trotted all over the East End looking for us.

Barker unfolded the note, and I saw his shoulders sag. There was only one event that could have caused such a reaction.

"She's dead, isn't she?" I asked, putting a few bob into the street boy's hand and sending him on his way.

Barker nodded and looked away.

"Floating in the river like the others?" I asked. "Where?"

"She was found among the construction pilings at Tower Bridge. They are bringing the Thames police steam launch to collect the body. We are to meet them in Wapping."

"I'm sorry, sir."

The Guv scratched his ear. "Our chances were even at best, lad. I knew that when I took the case."

No hansom in London could have brought us there fast enough to suit me. I could feel the blood rushing at my temples, and at one point in our journey I wanted to vault over the top, push the driver out of his box, and whip some speed out of our horse. As for Barker, he had retreated into himself. I think he was preparing to be humbled. He had not found Miss DeVere's killer nor had he discovered the body. It is not possible for one man to right every wrong, catch every criminal, or save every victim. I worried that perhaps he felt that success was merely his duty while anything less was failure.

When we arrived, we found that as usual we were late and Inspector Swanson was in possession of the body. The launch had arrived a few minutes before we did, and the little corpse was lying on a flat, two-wheeled barrow, which stood nearly upright. She was huddled down on the bare wood, due to gravity, her sodden clothes and hair dripping on the stone dock. She was dressed in white undergarments: camisole, and pantaloons. Her face, despite the rouge and kohl, was gravely still, and she almost looked as if she were sleeping; almost, I say, for the lids were half open, the bottom of her irises visible and blue. *Hamlet's Ophelia,* I thought. She reminded me of Ophelia drowned in some painting I had seen, though it was obvious she had died another way.

"Strangled," Barker muttered, looking at the purple marks like sooty fingerprints on her slender throat. Then he reached down and raised the delicate wrist of her right arm. The tip of her index finger had been lopped off bloodlessly.

I walked to the edge of the dock and looked down, trying not to be so angry that I started rampaging through the streets.

Swanson and Dunham were arguing. Scotland Yard was taking this case seriously, but I recalled when it was just Barker and I and Major DeVere who were searching Bethnal Green for this missing girl before it became a question of jurisdiction and a feather in someone's cap, with a possible commendation or promotion.

"Have the parents been told?" the Guv asked.

"Not yet," Swanson said.

"May I be the one to tell them?"

"So you can take the credit?"

"Credit for what?" Barker asked, with a bitter edge to his voice. "What have I accomplished? She's dead, isn't she?"

It wasn't fair, I thought. Barker hadn't been called in until after Miss DeVere had been taken. In fact, it had been hours later, after her father in his shining helmet had ridden the length and breadth of Bethnal Green. Cyrus Barker did not undertake a case he felt he had no chance of solving, but when he did, he took sole responsibility even, I thought, over matters he could not control.

Swanson shook his head. "I'm sorry, Barker. You are not officially involved in this investigation. The duty falls to me."

"I need to consult with my client. We're both going to the same destination," Barker reasoned, "and I am already paying for a cab, but it is your decision. Of course, I could leave now on my own and devil take the hindmost."

"I shall take my own vehicle," Swanson offered. "And if you follow and let us do our job, I shall allow you to enter the residence with me unofficially."

"It is the most I can expect under the circumstances," my employer answered.

"Have you examined the body?"

"'Tis a wee lass, Cyrus, and in public," the inspector replied, looking somewhat uncomfortable. "I thought it best left to the coroner."

"Cover her up," Dunham ordered. "Sergeant Bellows, I am leaving you in charge. When the coroner arrives, take down anything he says and then release the body to him."

"Yes, sir," the sergeant said, with a tug on his helmet.

"Come, gentlemen," Swanson said. "We must give the DeVeres the sad news."

"Do you think," I asked as we rattled along in the cab behind Swanson and Dunham's vehicle, "that Major DeVere shall retain our services so we can find Miacca?"

"One never knows in such circumstances," Barker replied. "First of all, I am not certain that DeVere will be motivated more by a desire to get this over with or by a need to punish his daughter's killer. Also, he's got a wife to take into consideration. I doubt he can make any sort of thoughtful decision on the subject just now. We must prepare to be dismissed and we must prepare to continue."

"I do not envy the inspector his duty," I said. "This will not be pleasant."

"It isn't an easy thing, but Donald has done it dozens of times before. It's part and parcel of being a C.I.D. man."

"Forgive me, sir, but are we any closer to finding Mr. Miacca? Do you think we might have caught him if we'd had more time?"

"I'll admit, Thomas, that this case has been difficult. He is a clever adversary and has left us with precious few clues.

But even he shall eventually make a mistake and thereby expose himself, or we shall find that one clue which will break this case open. Miacca isn't going to stop killing girls. A pot can only simmer so long before it blows off the lid."

We eventually pulled up in front of a private residence in Fulham. The DeVere family lived in a terraced house in Dawes Lane and the servants saw that everything was clean and polished and painted. It seemed a cruelty to come in and ruin this domestic order.

Donald Swanson said that he would inform the DeVeres that their daughter was dead, and I suppose in a way, he did. When we were halfway out of our vehicles, the door to one of the residences opened and Hypatia DeVere stepped out, arms out at her sides. Her eyes were as large as saucers, and there was an unspoken question on her lips. Without ado, Swanson answered it by removing his bowler and looking down. Dunham, Barker, and I did likewise. The woman went down just then, the way I've seen a deer go down when it is shot through the heart by a hunter. Her servants caught her, but they could not stop the wail of grief that escaped her. It reverberated down the street. I cannot imagine a more mournful sound than that of a woman who has just been told that her child is no more.

I thought it was over, but I was wrong. She was only getting her breath. The next cry was even louder. Leaving the prostrate woman to her housekeeper, the butler stepped out the door and took charge, which meant that he herded us in quickly before we attracted any more attention. DeVere came downstairs then, a picture of abject misery, and after trying unsuccessfully to soothe his wife, he had the butler send for their physician. The four of us stood about in the entranceway while the major helped his wife up the stairs.

I'd noted how clean the street was, and now I was impressed by the front hall. Fulham, its streets and its houses had the order of a German village. All was fashionable and well tended. Each house was similar to its neighbors, save one thing. It seemed nothing so common as dirt had any place here and yet, one of those houses had a little girl who'd been murdered. I could not see things going on as they were after this.

An ashen-faced and sober Trevor DeVere came down the stairs a short while later.

Swanson cleared his throat. "Sir, we shall need you to come and identify the body."

The man I had seen fall apart when I first met him now summoned control of himself.

"Very well, Inspector," he replied. "Where is she now?"

"In the morgue in Stepney, sir."

"Cannot she be transferred?"

"There must be a postmortem and inquest."

"Postmortem? By the heavens, you shall not take a blade to my child," the major growled, his features turning red.

"It is the law, sir."

"Then change the law. I won't have some idiot elected official hacking away at my child's body so he can have his bloody two quid."

DeVere was well informed. The coroner's position was indeed elected, and for each postmortem he performed he received a payment of two pounds. The Stepney coroner, Dr. Vandeleur, was no drinker, which we knew from working with him on earlier cases. He was a competent coroner and medical man, which I'd heard was not always the case.

"When can you come and identify the body, sir?"

"I'll be there in an hour. I must see that my wife is sedated."

"Afterward," Barker added, "perhaps we might confer about what you wish us to do."

DeVere nodded absently. He rose, nodded again, and left the room. Decorum had been set at naught in deference to the death of a child. We rose and saw ourselves out.

In the street, the Guv thanked Swanson for allowing him to be there, and we left on foot. That morning, Mac had pressed our umbrellas and macintoshes upon us, and I was glad he had, for it began raining. I could not get the image of Gwendolyn DeVere's face out of my head, with its calm features and half-closed lids. For some reason, she made me think of my late wife, Jenny. I had failed her, as we, Barker and I, had failed Miss DeVere. Men make these promises too cavalierly, I thought, to shelter and protect someone from any harm whatsoever. It is pure swank on our part. Man is not omniscient; he cannot watch everyone twenty-four hours a day; and no man is invincible, not even Cyrus Barker. One can no more escape Fate than one can the rain that now fell upon our umbrellas.

We walked in silence. There was little chance of finding a vehicle in this weather. Barker looked as grim as I had ever seen him. We went a half mile to Waltham Green station and boarded a train.

Eventually we reached Whitehall and the blessed dryness of our antechamber. We shook off our raincoats and hung them, greeted Jenkins in monosyllables, and went into our offices. The Guv sat down in his big leather swivel chair and rested his head in the corner of its wing, ignoring the stack of entreaties from people wishing to hire one of the most illustrious private enquiry agents in London. Instead, he sat forlornly, drawing abstract runes with his finger on the edge of his desk. He did not even take solace with his pipe. Perhaps he thought he did not deserve it.

I am suggestible, and being locked up with a brooding employer did not help my confidence. *Barker was going to lose this case,* I thought. *DeVere was going to come soon and dismiss us.* Word would get out of our defeat, and there would be fewer letters requesting our services. The advertisement he placed in *The Times* would suddenly take on a pleading tone. Barker would begin to consider returning to his old life aboard ship. Perhaps he would sign on as captain aboard a vessel bound for Asia, and where would that leave me? There were two very silent and self-absorbed men in Craig's Court that day.

DeVere came in from the pouring rain sometime later, looking as if his face were clay and some sculptor had just carved fresh lines around his mouth and eyes. He fell into our visitor's chair and the breath slowly drained out of him.

"It was she?" Barker asked.

Trevor DeVere nodded.

"You have my condolences, sir, on the loss of your daughter. She is in a better place, but I do not suppose that is of much comfort to you right now. You have several options in front of you. You may discharge me and see to the needs of your wife. In time, perhaps, the two of you will find acceptance in this, if not peace.

"Your second choice is to retain my services and allow me to search for your daughter's killer. It may take time, but I still believe I can do it. It is possible, however, that finding her murderer will give you cold comfort. It shall not bring her back and will allow the memory of her death to linger in your home for months, even years to come."

"I came here to sack you, Barker," DeVere finally said, "though it was against the wishes of my wife. She said that if Gwendolyn could be found, you would be the man to do it. I have no confidence in anyone or anything at the moment, and my wife is too distraught to give me any more advice, but I believe I shall continue to retain your services. That is, if you have the stomach for it."

"That is well," Barker said. "I have made a contract with you that I would find the man who took your daughter and I intended to fulfill that contract whether I was working for you or not. In a way, I suppose, I feel I am working for the parents of the other murdered girls who could never afford my services."

"I do not care for whom you are working, as long as you find the man who murdered my little girl."

"We are of one accord, then, Major DeVere. You should go now and tend your wife. Mr. Llewelyn and I shall pick up the scent once more. We will track him down, you may rest assured."

Barker watched him go from the bow window.

"I cannot imagine the crushing strain he must be under," he said.

"What do we do now?" I asked.

"Let us have lunch at the Northumberland around the corner, and perhaps better fortified, we can see where we erred. We must find our way back onto Miacca's trail."

"So, it's back to Bethnal Green, sir," I said.

"Indeed," Barker answered. "Let us go back and discover if we can see things in a different light."

10

AFTER LUNCH, THE RAIN HAD NOT LET UP, AND cabs being hard to find, we took an omnibus to the City where we then joined the Great Eastern Line to Bethnal Green. We employed our umbrellas until we reached the environs of the Charity Organization Society, but then Barker has always stated that rain is an enquiry agent's friend. It deters crime and empties the streets. Who knows how many crimes are postponed in London due to inclement weather?

I was disinclined to go into the charity, but it turned out that was not what brought Barker here. He was looking at an empty warehouse across the street with boarded-up windows and an estate agent's sign upon the door.

"It looks suitable enough for our purposes, at least from the outside," he said. "We can look out over the rooftops for suspicious activity."

"Why do you think we will get any fresh information here, sir? Wouldn't Miacca have left the area?"

"My instinct tells me he's still here somewhere. I suspect he feeds on the misery he engenders."

"Is this what you meant by a fresh perspective?"

"It is. Don't think this shall be like Claridge's, however. We shall live under Spartan conditions. We shall hide ourselves and watch in shifts, and when the moment is right, pounce upon our prey."

Barker was talking as the rain beat upon our umbrellas, and I heard a cab approaching in just enough time to step back before getting splashed. It was then that I saw him, nestled in the cab out of the wet, comfortable and arrogant as ever, a face out of my past. The Guv had said something would turn up if we came back to Bethnal Green, and he was correct, as usual.

That face drew me down the street effortlessly, as if I'd been chained to the axle of the cab. It pulled me past my employer with a mumbled apology and down to Cambridge Road. I splashed through the gutter, soaking my trousers and shoes, heedless of which direction the rain was blowing. I followed the cab until it stopped at the foot of the street and then jumped into an entranceway while its occupant paid the cabman.

"Well, who is it?" Barker demanded. He was standing on the pavement next to me, holding his umbrella furled, ready for anything. He didn't look angry that I'd bolted, merely curious, as if the case had taken a turn he had not anticipated, which perhaps it had.

"It is Palmister Clay, sir," I said, then poked my head around the corner. Clay was just going in to one of the buildings with a bouquet of flowers in his hand.

"Clay?" Barker said, going through a list of names in his head.

"He's the fellow who put me in prison."

"Ah, the fellow you batted for at university," the Guv stated, docketing him into a specific slot. "And just what do you intend to do?"

"Why, confront him, of course."

"Is that wise?"

"I owe him a beating. That blackguard killed my wife!"

"As I recall, she died of consumption."

"Yes, but he kept me from buying the medicine and beat me up while his two mates held me down. And he had me arrested!"

I was talking to Barker, but in front of my eyes all the memories of that terrible time were flashing by. I remembered the feel of Clay's fist in my stomach and the iron taste of blood. Most of all, I remembered the vision of Jenny, my Jenny, wasting away in a verminous bed, with the dark circles under her eyes and red stains on her handkerchief.

"It is in the past, lad," Barker stated. "We have no reason to confront him in this case."

"But, sir," I said, "this is obviously not his usual neighborhood, and he appears to be taking flowers to someone."

"In Bethnal Green?" Barker asked, tapping his chin with the handle of his umbrella. "He married last year, you know. The announcement was in *The Times*."

"Yes, I saw it, and I do not believe he and his bride have set up housekeeping in Cambridge Road. He's got himself a mistress one year into his marriage. That's just the sort of caddish thing Clay would do. We should speak to him."

"Mmm," Barker grumbled, which in this case meant *Don't press me*.

"Look, we can't know if there's a connection to the case until we ask," I said. "We should question him in the interest of thoroughness."

"Oh, very well, but you must promise me you will not issue him a challenge."

I had wanted to do just that. In fact, I wanted to skip the entire questioning stage and punch him on that pointed chin of his. Over and over again I saw my two knuckles connecting with his jaw and him falling backward.

"Yes, sir," I said. "I promise not to challenge him."

"Very well, let us go."

I controlled myself, walking behind Barker, letting him lead, instead of charging the building like the Light Brigade. It was much better kept than most in the area, a mews which had been divided into flats. My employer ascertained that it wasn't merely one house by glancing through the hall window, and he opened the outer door in that way he has, very silkily for a large man. We were faced with the problem of which flat Clay was in, but the answer came from a single petal in front of one door, as scarlet as sin. I expected Barker to give the door a solid thumping as he had done Mrs. Bellovich's, but instead he chose a discreet knock upon the wood.

The door opened and there he was, the Honorable Palmister Clay, as sneering and officious as ever. I hated his smug good looks and air of superiority. *Let Barker handle this*, I thought. I put my head down, adjusting my bowler.

"Who in hell are you?" he demanded. That was Clay. He hadn't changed a hair since our days at university.

Barker snapped one of his cards out in that way he has and passed it over, still saying nothing.

"I don't need a private enquiry agent." He tried to close the door in our faces, but the Guv moved his boot forward, insinuating it against the frame.

"I am not soliciting custom, Mr. Clay."

"Who is it, Palmsy?" a feminine voice said behind my old enemy. *Palmsy?*

A girl's head peered around his shoulder. Not a woman's, a girl's. No more than thirteen, I should say, but in a frothy dressing gown, her hair up, and very adult-looking pearls in her ears. She was a child trying to act like a woman. This was the paramour his wife did not know about? My eye flicked down her arm. There was no ring on her finger. I wondered what Mrs. Clay looked like. She must be close to twice this young chit's age.

"Nobody," Clay told her flatly. "Get some decent clothes on, Zena."

The girl disappeared again. Clay usually got what he wanted but not this time, I hoped. Please, please not this time.

"Get out of the hall," he said irritably, ushering us in. So far he had not recognized me. "So, I presume you are in the employ of my wife. I've got plenty of money, you know. I think perhaps we can come to some sort of arrangement."

"I don't care about your money or your marital indiscretions, Mr. Clay. I am investigating the disappearances of several young girls in the area, girls not much younger than your lady friend."

"How would I know anything about that?" he demanded.

"You are keeping a young woman here, not two streets from where at least one girl has disappeared. Scotland Yard would be very interested in this piece of information."

"Oh, so that's your game, is it? Blackmail? I might have known. How much do you intend to rook me for?"

"I have no interest in blackmail," my employer said, unperturbed, "but I would like to know how you set up your personal arrangements here. Who introduced the two of you?"

"That's none of your damned business, Barker."

"How does one get set up in one of these little places, I wonder?" the Guv mused aloud. "Is it discussed at the gentlemen's clubs or are the sons of lords approached by the disreputable lot who run these establishments? This really bears investigation."

Clay blanched. "Look," he said, licking his lips, "perhaps I was a bit hasty. I met Zena in Whitechapel. I fancied her and offered to put her up here."

"I see. And her surname is . . . ?"

"Harris, and that's all the information you'll get out of me. She is of legal age. I shall speak to my solicitor. I will not be harassed in this manner by a common detective."

"I have not been harassing you, Mr. Clay. You would definitely know if I were harassing you. You know nothing of the missing girls? They were violated and strangled."

"Look, I don't know anything about any bloody girls. You're wasting my valuable time. Now take your man and go!" He opened the door and waved us to leave.

"Hello, Palmsy," I said, raising my head so that we were face-to-face.

Clay let out a curse. "Tommy Llewelyn. I might have known. I wondered what rock you'd crawled under. So, you've got your revenge, have you? Hired a private 'tec to catch me with a girl, and me a married man."

"As a matter of fact, I work for Mr. Barker."

"I assumed you'd be dead by now. Thought you might have drunk yourself into an early grave."

"I was wondering the same about you," I said tartly.

"Actually, I'm glad you're alive," he countered. He slapped me smartly across the face. "I challenge you to a fight. We never properly finished our little match."

I was ready to begin the match right there and then, but Barker thrust a wall-like shoulder between us.

"I accept," I snapped. "Name the time and place, and I'll be there. This time, you won't have two friends holding my arms."

"Let us say nine o'clock, next Thursday evening. The German Gymnasium. Queensberry rules."

"I'll be looking forward to it!"

"We shall see. Well, gentlemen, unless you intend to march me down to the closest constabulary—which I assure you my father, Lord Hesketh, will have something to say about—I suggest you get off my property."

We left the building and began to walk north to Green Street.

"I believe you promised me not to enter into a fight," Barker finally growled.

"No, sir. I promised not to challenge him. He challenged me. I merely accepted."

"Tell me, lad, how many times have you had a pair of boxing gloves on your hands in your life?"

I thought about that a moment. "Well, just once, actually."

"And how old were you?"

"Eleven."

"And what happened?"

"I was thrashed, as I recall."

"Whereas, Mr. Clay attends the German Gymnasium regularly, from the sound of it."

"But—" I began, but my employer interrupted.

"He is six inches taller than you, has a longer arm length, and outweighs you by almost two stone."

"But my training, sir. I've been training with you for months."

"Your training will be useless in the ring. You'll be fighting under Queensberry rules, with your hands encased in gloves. Yours will feel like pillows, whereas his shall feel more like lead weights when they strike you."

It finally began to sink in then. It was I who was going to be publicly humiliated. Palmister Clay really was going to get what he wanted. "Blast," I said.

"And you'll get no sympathy from me, lad. I warned you. You got yourself into this mess, and you'll just have to fight your way out. Or take your drubbing like a man."

11

"WHERE ARE WE GOING, SIR?" I ASKED. WE were now heading south on his instructions. North, I could see, or west, but not south, unless we were going back to the docks.

"Reverend McClain's."

I was under no misapprehension that the Guv was in need of spiritual advice. It was true that the Reverend Andrew McClain was a firebrand in the pulpit of his Mile End Mission, but more people knew him as Handy Andy, former heavyweight bare-knuckle champion of London in the days before Queensberry rules. He could still deliver a walloping right cross and was Barker's sparring partner. I wondered if he intended for Andy to give me lessons, but the Guv was down to single-word sentences, which was not a good sign. I had used up all his goodwill for the day with my rash actions.

The Mile End Mission is entered by a latched gate covered in peeling brown paint. Inside, there is a pump in the center of a courtyard adjacent to the old church, which caused me to assume this had once been a stable yard. We stopped and washed our hands at the pump, which was as close to a ritual for my employer as I'd ever seen.

The place seemed deserted when we entered. We searched all through the building, until a clanking sound finally drew us down to the cellar. There the reverend sat on the floor in his shirtsleeves, covered in rust, removing a length of pipe. He rubbed a drop of sweat from his nose with the back of his hand, transferring the rust to his face, and glanced at us without interest.

"Plumbing?" Barker asked.

"Boiler," came the reply. "Pipes are full of scale. Come to lend a hand?"

"I don't know the first thing about cleaning boiler pipes," Barker said.

"Nor I, but it hasn't stopped me."

"You'll only break it further. Call someone in. I shall pay for it. I have something else for you to do, something more in your line."

"Saving souls?"

"Busting heads."

"Ah," Andy said with a grin, "the laying on of hands."

"Something like that. Thomas here has gotten himself in a spot of trouble, thanks to that Celtic temper of his. He's been challenged to a boxing match."

"Bare knuckle?"

"No, Qu— that is, the new rules."

McClain got as sour a look as I'd ever seen on his pious face. Since he had been a champion under the old rules, the marquis was not to be mentioned here. "How long does he have to train?"

"Four days."

"Four days!" the missionary repeated, shaking his head. "You want me to train him in half a week? What shall I do after that, walk across the Thames? Or shall I part it, perhaps?"

"Such sarcasm is unbecoming in a man of the cloth. I merely need you to train him."

"I quit that, you know. I don't box professionally and I don't train. I've been asked several times."

"Your retirement has been well documented, Andrew, but Thomas needs the training. I understand the odds are against him and that he cannot be properly trained in a week, but there are . . . mitigating circumstances."

"Buy me a new boiler, and we'll call it square," McClain stated.

"I'll get someone in. He'll clean it and replace what needs to be replaced."

"You don't trust my recommendation?"

"You would recommend this entire pile be razed and built again at my expense."

"Nonsense, unless of course, you are offering." He paused. "Four days. The very idea. Learn piano in four days. Learn Latin, maybe, but not boxing. That takes a lifetime. So, where's it going to be, this match of the century?"

"The German Gymnasium, next Thursday."

"Well, at least there's some reason for hope. Those prigs at the German won't know the difference. He'll have to move in, of course."

"No. I need him. We're in the middle of an investigation. You can have him now and again, around his work. He'll have to be satisfied with that, and so will you."

"You're a hard man, Cyrus Barker."

Barker didn't respond beyond a slight smile.

"Very well," McClain continued, "but I won't stand in his corner. I cannot be seen participating in this momentary aberration known as modern boxing, and I won't back an improperly trained man. You'll have to coach him yourself."

"Done."

"I'm not through yet. One can bring a horse to the track, but he still might not run. You've been as silent as the grave this entire time, Tommy boy. Are you up to this? You'll probably get walloped anyway, but if you're willing to learn something, I'm willing to teach you."

"I'm willing," I replied.

McClain pushed himself up off the floor and smacked his rust-covered hands together.

"Very well," he said. "Give me a chance to get cleaned up a bit, and I shall meet you at the ring upstairs."

A mission with a boxing ring under it would have sounded absurd in the West End, but things are not so hard and fast in Mile End Road, and occasionally one found two unrelated ventures knocked together into one. The reverend didn't make any money from the ring, of course, save from Barker himself, who used it regularly.

I ruminated on the fact that I had displeased my employer with my actions. The training and the fight itself, whatever the outcome, was peripheral to the investigation. It was a waste of time and effort that should have been spent finding Gwendolyn DeVere's killer. I had tried to convince myself that Clay was a part of it all.

"I'm sorry, sir," I said to him when we walked into the ring. "I didn't mean for my personal life to intrude into the case. There is no proof that Clay is involved in Miss De-

Vere's disappearance. Much as I would like to think he is Mr. Miacca, I doubt even he is capable of such heinous deeds."

"I would be inclined to agree with you, lad," Barker said. "I doubt Mr. Clay has even the aplomb to keep his mistress secret from his wife for very long. However, his presence in the district strikes me as a coincidence, and you know I do not believe in coincidence. Follow the line of incidents back far enough, and I'm certain one shall find where the two converge."

"You actually think there is a connection?" I asked.

"Oh, yes, else I'd have stopped you from making a fool of yourself."

"Thank you," I said a trifle bitterly.

"Describe the building for me, lad, the one where Mr. Clay keeps his mistress," Barker said, changing the subject.

"It was a mews converted over to flats, rather well kept up. It had two small evergreens in pots flanking the door, as I recall."

"Aye. Now tell me, who can afford such nice, well-maintained flats in Bethnal Green."

I thought about that. The answer became obvious. "No one."

"Precisely."

"So, you're saying the other flats . . ."

"Are possibly kept by other married men for their paramours. Who knows but that Cambridge Road might be honeycombed with them."

"I thought Bethnal Green had a reputation for being poor but respectable," I said.

"During the day, perhaps."

Brother Andrew came into the room. He was stripped

to the waist and a sight to behold. Though past forty, his chest was heavily muscled and his biceps the size of melons. His neck was connected to each shoulder by a mass of hard muscle; and his stomach, which is usually the first to go as a man grows older, was chiseled. McClain was a little under six foot and weighed about as much as Barker. I could see why the Guv might have chosen him as a sparring partner.

"Don't just stand there gawking, Tommy," the reverend said. "Take your shirt off."

As I removed my jacket and tie, Barker tied the brown leather gloves around McClain's wrists. The look of distaste was writ large across the ex-pugilist's features.

"I hate these things," he complained. "Gone are the days when you could twist your wrists at the last minute and cut open a man's brow with your knuckles. I can hardly feel anything in these mitts. Takes all the enjoyment out of it."

"My singlet, too?" I asked.

"Singlet," McClain muttered, shaking his head.

"Aye, lad, the singlet, too," Barker said. I took it off and walked over to my employer to be laced into the gloves.

I had to admit I didn't like them myself. They didn't feel as if they were designed for humans, too tight in some places, too loose in others. I stood while the Guv tied the laces tightly, then reluctantly I climbed into the ring.

"All right, Tommy," McClain said. "Let's see what you are made of."

I'd done a number of illogical things at my employer's behest but none as obvious as stepping into the ring with a heavyweight champion, gloves or no. I extended my left arm and made a fist, while pulling my right back to guard my chin.

"Pull your left back a bit, boy," the reverend counseled. "You're not in here to have your photograph taken. You need the distance to gain some power behind the blow, being a lightweight."

The next I knew, McClain's glove swiped across my right cheek. It felt hot, then cold; and I wondered if I would start bleeding, but the feeling faded quickly.

"Raise your guard."

I did and took a blow to the stomach. That was enough, I thought. I pictured the organ smashed into my kidneys and all of that wrapped around my spine.

"Ow!" I finally got out.

"'Ow,' is it? There's no 'ow' anymore, Tommy. You're not in the village green. You're part of the Fancy, now, and the code says you take your punishment in silence."

McClain threw a hook to my ear, and miraculously, I was able to brush it away; but then I left myself open for an uppercut to the chin, which knocked my head back. I heard the vertebrae in my neck pop, followed by a slight ringing in my ear, but after I shook my head, I was fine.

"He's got a good jaw, Cyrus. That's a blessing I did not expect."

Just then I took my first tentative jab, which, since he was looking over at Barker, he didn't see until it caught him square upon the nose. He looked over at me and broke into a big grin.

"You pup!" he cried. "Jab at me, will ye?"

The next I knew I was in the midst of a flurry of blows, backing me across the ring. He caught me square in the chest, and that hurt, then he smacked me in the ear, which made me forget about my chest, and then he put another in my stomach that made me forget my ear, and finally he connected with a blow to my chin that knocked me boots over bowler, if I'd been wearing one. The old canvas seemed awfully comforting for the moment. My ear was buzzing and half my teeth felt loose, and this with the gloves to make the sport more civilized. There wasn't enough money in the Royal Mint to make me get into the ring with the reverend bare knuckled.

He bent over, gloves upon knees and looked down at me. "Are you going to stay there and stargaze all day?" he asked. "Get up. Your employer has hired me to see that you don't end up flat on the canvas this way."

"Yes, sir," I said, and pushed my way up to my feet again.

"Your position's all wrong, like I said. Hold your right hand here and your left one there. You see? You can block a hook punch or a jab like this, and bring it down like an axe, brushing away a straight right to the ribs. There's a good deal of wrist work in boxing, though you won't hear it mentioned."

Barker trained me spontaneously several times a week, and never on a regular schedule. He'd stop me in the hall or garden or up in his garret, and only when it involved heavy groundwork would we go to the mat in his cellar. He's a good teacher, if a bit irregular, but sometimes I felt the worst of students. I understand what he wants me to do, but translating that message to my limbs had laughable results. I had hoped to impress McClain or at least not disgrace myself.

"Now, step forward with your left foot, Tommy. No, your other left foot."

"Sorry."

"Do you need me to paint an 'R' and an 'L' on your shoes?"

"No, sir. I've got the hang of it, I think."

"We shall see. Now bring the other foot up behind it. Step again. Again. Again."

"Where is Mr. Barker, Reverend?" I asked suddenly when I realized he was missing.

"Quit breaking your concentration." He put his hands on his hips. "If I know him, he'll take a half hour punching on the heavy bag."

By the time we were done, I was exhausted and dispirited. If I did not train as hard as I possibly could, I was going to lose this match with Palmister Clay.

Afterward, the reverend brewed tea for us in his office.

"You're very quiet today, Cyrus," Andrew McClain said, handing him a steaming cup.

"They found a missing girl this morning. She was in the Thames, outraged and strangled. I could do nothing but stand there and watch the Thames Police and Scotland Yard quarrel over the body. It was galling."

"What do you intend to do?" McClain asked.

"Set up temporary residence in Bethnal Green and thank God I have another chance to catch this fellow."

"You can move in here, if you wish."

"Thank you, Andrew, but I would prefer to remain anonymous and right under our man's nose, if possible. Or rather, over his head."

"Seems to me you're keeping me out of this," McClain said suddenly. "You're not usually reticent about a case."

"I didn't want to burden you with it any more than we have now. You've got enough to deal with as it is."

"No, that won't work," the reverend said. "I'm already in it. I live and work here, right up against the Green. I hear what happens there everyday. The mission is part of the warp and woof of the area."

"Ever hear the name Miacca?" Barker asked.

McClain frowned and shook his head.

"He's an archfiend. He's raped and killed a half dozen girls in the past few months and left their bodies in the sewers or floating in the Thames."

"So why leave me out of it?"

"Because the lad and I are up to our necks in socialists of every description. Young and old, male and female, Christian and otherwise. I knew you were a friend of Bram Booth."

"Knew his dad, the general, too," he said. "Tried to turn me into an officer when his Salvation Army first began. But I was still battling the bottle then, and could not trust myself. Missing girls, eh? I've heard of them. Had to prop up Danny Rice before he went in to identify his daughter. This madman had cut off her nose. Cruel thing, leaving a pretty girl like that dead for her father to find and then hacking off her nose. Makes me feel downright un-Christian. So, you're going after him, are you?"

"I'm after him now," Barker said. "I've been after him."

"Good. Find him. Get your teeth into him. Or the next time we're in the ring together, I'll stop going easy on you."

The two men gave each other a grim smile.

12

"**D**O YOU STILL HAVE THE ADDRESS OF THE estate agent, Thomas?" Barker asked on the walk back to Bethnal Green.

"Yes, sir," I said, pulling out my notebook and flipping pages. "His name is Ezra Levitt. It's on Commercial Street."

"Excellent. He is Jewish. His offices will be open today. I want to see that property as soon as possible. If it all works out, we shall move in tomorrow."

We found Mr. Levitt's office and discussed our need for a short-term rental of the property. The estate agent countered that such a thing was irregular but finally agreed it was best to have some revenue coming in. A possible fee was discussed for a months' use, the Guv counteroffered, and a price was agreed upon, pending approval. Then the agent took us to the site.

There was not much to recommend it. It was an empty warehouse, dusty from disuse, with three floors and a ladder going up to a roof hatch. The grimy windows offered an excellent view of traffic heading east and west along Green Street, and by moving to the window on the far east side, one could see all the way down Globe Road. We were so close to the charity that had I opened a window and shouted, I would have attracted attention from everyone inside the building. Barker pronounced it satisfactory, and we marched back to the agent's office to sign the lease.

Someone said to me once that enquiry work was just the sort of work for men who could not handle routine, implying that we lacked stamina for the eight-to-six workaday world, as if we never fully grew up somehow. Sitting in an office all day, filling out endless reams of paper while gradually emptying inkpots, was obviously his idea of being a man. In my defense, I told him that my position required taking dictation, keeping records, and filling out forms as he did, and that the only difference between our positions was that he didn't have to stop writing every now and then to duck a bullet or receive a fist in the face. I don't know whether I convinced him or not. In any case, sitting in the estate agent's office, filling out forms, signing, countersigning, initialing, stamping, and sealing made me glad for once that I had such an unusual occupation. A week shut up in that office and I'd have been moved right into the lunatic asylum.

After shaking hands with the fellow twice over, we finally quitted the establishment. It was just after six. We stopped at the Prospect of Whitby and had our dinner. A hot leg of lamb with plenty of mashed potatoes was just the thing to drive the dust of the warehouse and the more figurative dust of the estate agent's office from our lungs. The meal, however, was still tempered by the terrible sight we had seen on the dock at Wapping Old Stairs that morning and now that our business was concluded, we naturally fell to talking about it again.

"I expect the funeral shall be in two days," Barker said, pushing back his plate and taking a sip of his tea.

"I hope the DeVeres have close friends and relatives to help them through this," I said. "I cannot see either of them in any condition to attend their daughter's funeral."

"You know that I have limited experience with children, save perhaps with Fu Ying, who was thirteen when she came to live with me," my employer began.

"When she came to live with Harm, you mean," I interjected. The Dowager Empress of China had given this slave girl to the dog to care for him unto death. Harm, in turn, had been a gift for some service the Guv had done the Chinese royal family; but what it was, he would not tell me.

"I was going to say it is amazing how a child upon its birth quickly becomes the focus of its parents' lives, and not merely the mother's. Now their focus is lost. Twelve years of intense caring shall be buried in the ground the day after tomorrow. All their dreams for their daughter—to see her grown, married, having children of her own—are all gone now."

"Perhaps they can have another child."

"Perhaps," Barker repeated. "I hope so, for their sake. There are so many alternatives, none of them good."

"Sir, if I may say it, your plan needs a little working out."

Those were the words I had wanted to say to Barker about our move, but they weren't issuing from my own mouth. Rather, they were coming from the mouth of Barker's factotum, Jacob Maccabee, as he set down a fresh pot of tea in front of him. The Guv frowned behind his spectacles. I couldn't recall the last time Mac had issued an objection. Perhaps he never had.

"A little working out?" the Guv asked.

"You intend to continue the investigation, do you not, interviewing suspects and the like?"

"Certainly."

"Then you shall need fresh changes of clothes. How shall you get food?"

"I had assumed we would go to public houses or tearooms."

"Very good, sir," Mac went on. "But, then, you shall still need meals in the morning and tea in the evening. You gentlemen shall need looking after."

"Hmm," Barker said noncommittally.

"Then there is the problem of the two of you trying to keep a twenty-four-hour watch. First of all, you will both be investigating the area, so there is no one watching what is going on during the day. Also, it's difficult to work during the day and then split a shift at night."

"I see what you are getting at," our employer stated.

I did, as well. Mac wanted to come with us. He was concerned for our welfare, or at least for Barker's, but it was more than that. Mac had very nearly had my position before I arrived, and I believe he coveted the chance to be a part of the investigation. At least it would get him out of the house.

"Well, sir, three is generally better than two in such situations."

Barker took a sip of his tea and began patting his clothes for his postprandial pipe. "You understand the requirements?"

"Yes, sir."

"No pampering, no coddling, strictly Spartan, as they say. And no exceptions. Have you got it?"

"Yes, sir."

"Of course, you may live according to your own dietary restrictions. In fact, if it is easier, you may serve us all kosher now and then. The Bucharest is nearby."

"Mr. Ho's tearoom is not far, either. If you give me the key now, I can take a lantern and sweep and mop the floors this evening and get everything in readiness."

"No," Barker said. "No light. No light at all, in fact. We work in darkness. That goes for you, too, lad. I know you like to read in the evenings, but I do not want to alert Miacca to our presence."

"Yes, sir," I said. This entire exercise was beginning to sound like a punishment.

"How many changes of sheets shall you require, sir?" Mac asked.

"None, Mac. No sheets at all."

I had to stifle a laugh because I knew Mac's idea of roughing it was a small tent set up in the country with a portable dining table and camp chairs, and a large picnic hamper containing everything from *foie gras* to Coleman's mustard.

"And no pillows," Barker added.

"I do not believe I could sleep without a pillow, sir," our butler replied.

"I don't believe I could, either," I put in. "If it is austerity you want, I believe I could do without a pillowcase, but I wouldn't want to wake each morning with a crick in my neck."

"You won't have to worry about that, Thomas," Barker said. "I'm giving you the night shift."

"Thank you, sir," I replied, putting as much irony into the phrase as I dared.

"I suppose that I may bring a small camp stove, sir?"

The Guv gave Mac a sour look. "For what purpose?"

"For your tea."

Barker's face fell. Mac simply wasn't getting into the spirit of the adventure. On the other hand, our employer couldn't do without his pots of green tea. It was what that brain of his ran upon, like coal to a steam engine. "Very well. A small stove. But it must be out from sunset to sunrise. As for Mr. Llewelyn, he shall have to suffice upon tea or forage for his coffee. We cannot coddle a man's whims when we are hunting a killer."

I bit my lip. He was making sure he had his precious gunpowder green tea, shipped in specially to a merchant in Mincing Lane, but my coffee drinking was somehow too capricious for him and therefore expendable. How did he expect me to wake up in the morning? Oh, I'd forgotten. I had the night shift. Eight hours on nothing but green tea, and cold at that. The mind rebels.

"Drat that Etienne," I said.

Mac cleared his throat. He is good at it. It had meaning and inflection.

"Very well, I admit it. This is all my fault. I didn't eat his omelet because I was distracted by a girl."

"May we bring a book or two, anyway?" I asked. "There should be some light."

"That isn't generally the custom," Barker said. "The standard form of entertainment among the Sicilians is a deck of cards. If Mac takes the day shift, I the evening, and you the night, you shall have very little time to read."

I did some mathematical figuring in my head, not my best subject. "So if we are working all day while Mac watches, and you take the evening shift while I sleep, then the two of you bed down while I take the night watch, essentially, we will be working a sixteen-hour shift each day."

"That is correct," Barker said, emphasizing it with a nod. "The work is its own incentive. Track down our killer quickly and we can return to relative luxury."

That evening I chose two novels to take with me, Hardy's *A Pair of Blue Eyes* and George MacDonald's *Donal Grant*. Reading is my chief form of entertainment, and I'd had a bookshelf put in my room to hold my small collection. Barker reads history and philosophy instead of modern fiction. I suppose he thinks the reading of novels something of an indulgence and that my time would be better spent on shooting practice or studying the manuals for self-improvement he often left on my desk. One cannot let these employers always have their way, however, or one should have no time to oneself at all.

My awakening the next morning can only be described as brutal. It was four in the morning when Mac pushed back the curtains. There wasn't even a morning sun to greet me. Barker was already up and about. For all I knew he hadn't gone to sleep at all.

We had chosen the warehouse for its good location and view of the Charity Organization Society on Green Street. When we arrived with the rising sun and I looked at the large warehouse, with its scarred old floor and bare brick walls, I sensed a depressing atmosphere and premonitions of doom, but perhaps I was simply in a sour mood.

"Satisfactory," the Guv pronounced, looking at the empty room with a mattress in its center. Mac had brought his minimum, two trunks and a large hamper. He'd convinced our employer that a supply of food from Fortnum & Mason was better than his going out and foraging every night and possibly being spotted by Miacca or someone who might potentially be spying for him. In the hamper there were sausages, cheeses, tinned kippers, olives, Carr's biscuits, and Barker's inevitable tea. Mac had also brought a small contraption, a stove that allowed one to boil water. Many of the packages were emblazoned with the royal warrant, purveyors to Her Majesty the Queen and all that. It was about as austere as a hunt club breakfast, but I wasn't about to protest. At the bottom of the hamper, our butler had secreted a sack full of coffee.

"I'll have to use the same pot for both," Mac told me *sotto voce.* "Then I'll have to boil water in the pot afterward to get the coffee odor out. You know how sensitive the Guv is about his tea."

It was true. Barker is a mass of contradictions, and no more so than when food is involved. Though he kept a chef, it was more for Dummolard's benefit than his own. The Guv had saved his life on several occasions when they were aboard the *Osprey,* and Etienne felt he was repaying a debt. The fact that Barker could have lumped all his courses into one pile in the middle of his plate and shoveled it down by the spoonful, so careless was he about food, infuriated Etienne. My employer's tea was another matter. He was a stickler for it. The tea had to be the proper color and strength, it had to be at the proper temperature, and it had to be served in the handleless cups he had brought from China that matched his teapot with the bamboo handle. It all went to prove my theory that the austerity was to be observed only on my side.

"While we are here," Barker said, "it would be an excellent time to do some physical culture, gentlemen. Perhaps we can get a skipping rope and some Indian clubs in. Thomas is in training for a match, after all."

It was overcast that morning, and the clouds marched slowly across the leaden sky like chained prisoners. It began to rain, giving me a more practical problem. Barker's austerity had extended to our not bringing umbrellas.

"Are you coming?" he asked after we were settled in. We had work to accomplish, and an archfiend to track down.

"Yes, sir." I turned up the collar of my coat, knowing it would be wet shoes and shoulders for the rest of the day for us, anyway. Mac would be watching as best he could from our window. It would not do to call attention to himself during hours of clear visibility. At night, we could not be seen. I seriously doubted that he could see anything out that window save pelting rain, but I knew Jacob Maccabee would not desert his post for the next eight hours.

We exited the building through the back door, down an alleyway one had to walk sideways to get through, and came out on Globe Road. The moving part of the day was over. It was time to get back to business.

"Swanson!" Barker cried, catching sight of the inspector coming out of the C.O.S. building just after nine o'clock. The man had the common sense to open an umbrella.

"Hallo, Cyrus. Any leads as yet?"

"Nary a one," the Guv admitted. "We're dining on scraps so far. Tell me, have your men been exploring the sewers?"

"They have until today. I'm sure they are rejoicing that this rain is washing them out and they don't have to go down today. I do not think they had any reason to complain. I saw that they were provided with waders."

"Are Dunham's lads watching the river?"

"Aye," Swanson acknowledged. A grim smile came to his lips. "It is river police business, but I just happened to have a few lads standing about with little to do."

"It would be a shame for the good citizens of London to pay for idle constables simply because of a little rain."

I would have felt sorry for them were I not out in the wet weather myself on the same errand as they. At least these two men led by example. So far, the rain had not penetrated my macintosh or my leather boots, but it was only a matter of time. I was careful to keep my head down, for one quick look upward would send a brimful of water down the back of my neck.

"I would have thought," I put in, "that Scotland Yard would have put more patrols in the area. In the streets, I mean, not the sewers."

"Politics," Swanson said, putting as much loathing into the word as possible. "If they put more constables into an area, that would be admitting there is a problem; and if word gets out about this Miacca fellow stealing and killing children, it would set off a panic in every house in the East End. That's thousands of women, and don't think the ones in Wimbledon or Kensington shall feel safe just because the blighter has so far confined himself to Bethnal Green. Every West End mother shall want a bobby on her doorstep, and if they don't get it, the MP will put whatever pressure he has upon the commissioner."

"Then it is in the Yard's interest not to let this get out," Barker said.

Swanson smoothed his mustache. "It may be too late for that. Stead is sniffing about, and you know how he is. This is just the sort of thing for him to smear across the front page of his rag and set off a panic London would never forget."

"So what brought you to the C.O.S.?" Barker asked.

"I was letting them know the sad news. Oh, haven't you gentlemen heard? Mrs. DeVere killed herself last night. Woke up from her laudanum dreams just long enough to swallow the rest of a new bottle."

"Oh, no!" I cried.

"Aye, and your client has gone mad with grief. His servants say after he found her, he threw on his coat and ran out the door. He hasn't been heard from since. I sent word 'round to your house this morning. Apparently, you were out."

13

I WONDERED IF SWANSON WAS TRYING TO BAIT Barker or merely to shock him. My employer put his head down and shook it. As for me, I felt some guilt over Hypatia DeVere, as if I myself had treated her badly. Had she appeared calm and graceful as Miss Hill the first time I met her, I would have accused her in my mind of being cold, and yet I had thought uncharitably of her for being puffy eyed. She was doing what she should have been doing, which was agonizing over the welfare of her daughter.

So there it was, I thought. Gwendolyn DeVere was dead. Hypatia DeVere was dead. Our client had run off in grief. At least six other girls had also been killed and all because of a monster who called himself a name out of a fairy tale.

My employer turned to me after Swanson left. "Come, lad, let us see about the postmortem."

"Do you think it will be finished?" I asked as I followed Barker down Globe Road.

"Dr. Vandeleur runs a tight ship," he said. "If it is not finished, it shall be soon."

There was a big difference in my mind between finished and almost finished. Finished meant I could look at it all on paper, with drawings. Almost finished was "Look here, while I lift up the liver, at the discoloration of the stomach." I'd had the misfortune to have been there several times and viewed close to a dozen bodies at least, but they all had been adult males.

I knew the girl was dead and all sentient thought had left her body. I would even agree with Barker that at one point her soul had departed, as well. But I could not help but think that Gwendolyn DeVere would have objected to lying naked on a slab while men sliced her up like a Billingsgate haddock. I had no desire to see the body.

Vandeleur, it turned out, was at a conference in Glasgow and we were passed on to Dr. Trent, his resident, who had done the postmortem himself. He was a stocky young chap with a round head and a Vandyke who looked as if he didn't allow the nature of his work to interfere with his digestion.

"Have you finished your report on the DeVere child, doctor?" Barker asked.

"Finished an hour ago. How are you connected with it?"

"I am Cyrus Barker, a private enquiry agent. I work for Major DeVere. I saw the corpse where it was found."

"Were you aware it was connected to several other cases?" Trent asked.

"Aye, I was. Did you find anything out of the ordinary in the postmortem?"

"It was the most remarkable I've ever seen."

He reached for the clipboard and began looking through the papers while I gave a sigh of relief. *Perhaps papers were all I would be forced to look at.*

"You noted the traces of rouge and the kohl about her eyes?"

"Yes. She was painted like a Parisian tart."

"When I wiped them off her face, I found burns under her nose and around her lips."

"Chloroform," Barker stated. "It burns the skin."

"Indeed. There was no facial burning in the other cases according to our records, but I still believe chloroform was used, though not directly on the skin. It might have been in a folded handkerchief. I assume the killer had either changed his method of capturing his victims or perhaps the girl struggled and came in contact with the chloroform itself. But then, as I continued the postmortem, another theory occurred to me. Perhaps Miss DeVere was sensitive. I believe she had a reaction to the chemical used."

"Why do you think that?" Barker asked.

"Because she had a reaction to something else. It's all here." He began rustling through the papers. "No, I think it would be best if you saw it on the corpse itself."

Oh, no, I thought, as we were taken to another room and directed to a still form on a table. The resident lifted back the sheet, exposing the girl's face. It truly was a girl's face now, not a child painted to look like an adult. Her skin was clear and pale, and there was a purpling of the upper lip, a smudge like a thumbprint. Then, like a stage magician doing a trick, Dr. Trent whisked away the sheet.

There was a purpling across her entire torso. It formed lines across her body from the right hip to the throat, down to the left hip, from there across to the right shoulder, back to the left shoulder, and down to the right hip again, lines forming the shape of a star. The first thing I thought when I saw the marks was that she had been used in some sort of witchcraft or unholy ritual.

"Do you know what might have left these lines?" Barker prodded.

"It had washed off in the tide, but I found traces of it. It was common whitewash. I believe she had a reaction to the lime. Her skin was so sensitive it left the marks behind, you see."

"What are these random marks on the stomach?" I asked.

"Those are very interesting. They are burns also, but not like the others. They left a residue. Wax. Candle wax, to be precise. And this thin mark just under the breastbone is a bruise. She was struck by something small there, no more than a few centimeters long. It can't have hurt her much. Death was due to manual strangulation, like the other girls."

"May I?" Barker asked. He reached forward and placed his thumbs on the bruises where her killer's thumbs had been, then slid his fingers around. Whoever the killer was, he had hands smaller than my employer.

"He took a souvenir, like the others," I noted.

"Yes, the index finger on the right hand at the first knuckle. It was a clean cut, shears of some sort, I would say. The wound was not ragged."

The slight pressure of Barker's fingers on the corpse's neck was enough to force a small sigh from the corpse's cold lips. The three of us sprang back, but it proved to be a normal reaction. All the same, Dr. Trent settled the sheet around her, unconsciously tucking it in as if she had been merely asleep. Barker continued to regard her while I copied notes from the file into my notebook.

"Has Inspector Swanson read your report?" Barker asked.

"No, sir, not yet."

"That's a mercy, at least."

"Might we borrow that report?" I asked.

Trent shook his head, and Barker looked at me. "Why do you ask?"

"I thought it might give us something to bargain with."

Signing out at the morgue desk, we walked several streets to the Basin Docks and counted seagulls. I bought a penny loaf from a street vendor, and we spent the next half hour breaking it into bits and tossing it into the water while the gulls cartwheeled and dived after them.

"Ho's?" he asked, clapping the crumbs from his fingers.

We weren't more than a few streets from the tearoom where Barker's Chinese friend conducted business and collected information.

"I could not eat, sir."

"No food. Just tea."

Barker and I walked along the waterfront until we found ourselves in the narrow lane leading to the anonymous door, and then we went down the stairs and under the Thames before finally fetching up in Ho's establishment. As usual, it was filled with a secretive crowd. The smoke from several cigars and the smell of food made me nauseous, but after a cup of tea, I felt a little better.

Ho came out of the kitchen and regarded us from under hooded eyes. Perhaps "regard" is too positive a word. He is large and squat, with brawny naked arms covered in tattoos, and an apron tied around his thick waist. He has a shaved forehead and earlobes full of rings that hang to his shoulder.

I felt like a cockroach he was deciding how to squash. Then he spoke directly to me, which is almost unprecedented.

"You boxer now."

Ho could speak English flawlessly, but the more malevolent he feels the more pidgin English he uses.

"Yes," I said. "I had a challenge given me. But how did you know?"

Ho shrugged, which was the closest I'd get to an explanation. He turned to Barker. "Girl is dead. That makes several, right?"

Barker nodded.

"These girls' blood cries out from the grave. You must find this man."

"I am trying."

"Try harder."

I cannot believe the things Ho says to Barker and gets away with. If I'd said that to him, I'd have found myself on the ground with the heel of his boot between my collar stays. With Ho, the remark merely merited a slight rise of the eyebrows.

"Help me, then."

"What do you need?"

"I believe a group of some sort is practicing satanic rituals in London—young English maidens sacrificed on an altar as a spectacle for others."

"Ritual," Ho repeated. "You mean devil worship. Christian, one God, one devil, *neh?* I must consult archives. Come."

He led us through the kitchen into his office, which is dominated by a desk with the legs sawn off. As we sat on the cushions in front of the desk, he moved behind to a wall with a giant silk tapestry covered in dragons and demure Chinese maidens. He pressed a spot and a small door opened in the center of the tapestry. Then the Chinaman pulled out a ledger and settled himself behind the desk. He opened the book and began scanning pages, moving from top to bottom, for it was written in Chinese.

"Give me more information first," he said.

"The girl was found yesterday, so presumably she was killed on Friday. Friday seems a fitting day for a Satanic ritual. I don't believe these are serious occultists, however. More likely they are rakes amusing themselves with halfclad maids while a great deal of alcohol is consumed."

Ho nodded and began to study the ledger as I shifted on my pillow. I could never get comfortable cross-legged. European limbs are not built for such positions. In the kitchen behind us, the cooks and waiters bawled out orders to one another in Mandarin or Cantonese.

"Two young English come in here two Fridays ago," Ho said, looking down at his ledger. "Both had been drinking. One said, 'His lordship throws quite a party.' Other says, 'Too much flash-bang and rituals for my taste, but the girls were choice.' Then they place order and talk of other things."

"'His lordship,'" Barker murmured, "that doesn't narrow it down much."

"Sorry," Ho said, with a look that said he was not sorry at all. "I will start asking men to please speak in full sentences and identify those of whom they speak."

"Do your waiters listen in on every conversation?" I asked.

"Only ones that seem important," the Chinaman replied, giving me what I call his dyspeptic-Buddha expression.

"What do you do with the information?" I said, ignoring Barker's warning look.

"Whatever I think best. Most of the time, nothing. Sometimes tell, sometimes sell."

"To whom do you sell it?"

"Alla time question man. Who? What? When? Where? Shi Shi Ji, send this boy to a temple. Teach him to listen twice, talk once. Maybe never!"

I'd run through Ho's store of patience, which can fit inside one of his thimble-sized teacups, but I'd reached the point where his appearance—half pirate, half temple demon—no longer frightened me.

"Thank you," Barker said to his friend.

As we were about to leave, the Chinaman said, "The Frenchman quit, I hear."

Barker nodded.

Ho, who had a long-standing feud with Dummolard, gave a satisfied smile.

14

"**L**AD, CUT ALONG AND VISIT MISS POTTER AT THE Katherine Building. Bring her to our chambers. If I am satisfied, I shall engage her services, provided she is still serious about her offer."

"If she's anything, she's serious," I said. "I'm certain she hasn't changed her mind. I'll see if she can come."

I took a smart-looking hansom, hoping to impress Miss Potter, and left Barker to take an omnibus.

The Katherine Building where she worked was in a villainous part of Whitechapel, hard by the docks and the fish market. I let the cab driver curse until the air was blue about soiling his pretty wheels among the fish offal–strewn puddles, but we reached a liberal financial agreement. I went inside and found Miss Potter and explained that Barker wanted to see her. She put up the expected argument; she was busy collecting the rents. In turn, I told her this was her only chance. She conferred with a colleague and soon we were traveling through the City on our way to Whitehall. She was nervous about being interviewed by my employer, and I explained that while going into his office was like approaching a lion in its den, he improved upon closer acquaintance. I wasn't certain she believed me. I'm not sure I did either.

Once back in Craig's Court, I sat her in the visitor's chair and left her to look about the room. She was only the second woman I'd seen in that seat since the year began. Barker was nowhere to be found.

"Jenkins?"

Our clerk was staring at our visitor as if she were an apparition from heaven.

"He hasn't come through here, Mr. L.," he said. "Try outside."

I found Barker in the bare courtyard behind our offices, fingering a small, anonymous wildflower that had grown up through the cracks in the pavement.

"I'm thinking of putting in a small garden here," he said, not looking up.

"Really?" I said. "That would be jolly."

"That way, we can do our physical culture exercises out here during our spare moments."

There's nothing I would like better, I thought, *than to come out to the courtyard in all manner of weather and do Barker's exercises on the paving stones.*

"She's here, sir, waiting in your office."

Barker nodded. Before he went inside, he shot his cuffs and resettled his frock coat, like an actor about to go onstage. He'd eschew such a comparison, but it was apt all the same.

"Good afternoon, Miss Potter," he said, striding into his chamber. He took her delicate hand in his calloused one, the same hand I'd seen put bone locks on several men in the year or more since I'd begun working with him. Beatrice

Potter murmured a greeting. She did her best to look undaunted, but Barker had daunted braver people than she.

"Mr. Llewelyn tells me that you are anxious to aid our efforts to find Gwendolyn DeVere's killer. Most women your age," Barker noted, "are concerned with copying the latest fashions from Paris or compiling a list of the eligible young men of their set."

"I am not most women my age, sir."

"I'm glad to hear it. Do you think you could convince Miss Hill to have you take over Mrs. DeVere's duties?"

"I don't foresee a problem. She was sad to see me go to my present position."

"Excellent. I realize you have other duties, but if you could contrive to attend at least an hour a day, I would be grateful."

"Do you suspect someone within the Charity Organization Society of having something to do with Gwendolyn DeVere's murder?" she asked.

"Miss, I suspect everyone in Bethnal Green and several others who haven't set a foot inside it. It is not time to begin eliminating suspects just yet. I am hunting facts and opinions and I think you might be well placed to deliver both."

"I expect this to be a paid position."

"Certainly. I am not one of your charities."

"What duration shall be my employment?"

"It shall be brief, merely a week or two, until I find the man who murdered Miss DeVere."

"You think you shall find him in so short a time?" she dared ask.

"I can but cast my net, Miss Potter, but it is a stout old net, and I am an experienced fisherman. We are no longer looking for a white slave ring. Mr. Llewelyn and I have received a letter from a madman whom we believe has stolen and murdered half a dozen young girls in Bethnal Green."

"My word," Miss Potter murmured, clutching her throat.

"We learned that Miss DeVere's escape from the charity was aided by Miss Ona Bellovich."

"Might I see the letter?"

Cyrus Barker leaned back in his chair and scratched his chin absently, the way he does when deep in thought. He was not inconvenienced in the least that this girl was waiting for him to make a decision.

"Very well," he finally said, pulling the note from the wide middle drawer of his desk. "I would appreciate your opinion."

Beatrice took the letter and read it over a few times without comment. Finally, she set it back upon the desk, face-down.

"Do you believe in woman's intuition?"

"I have no formed opinion. Perhaps."

She tapped the note with a nail. "This is pure evil."

Barker nodded but said nothing.

"He's very . . . harsh. His taunts must be unbearable to you."

I realized then how sensitive the girl was. She was actually concerned over my employer's feelings.

"I can bear them well enough, miss. Do you recognize the hand?"

"I do not."

"What about the poetry? Is anyone at the charity a writer of poems?"

"Miss Levy is a published poet. Amy's work has appeared in several journals. Of course, it's nothing like this. This is quite crude."

"I shall accept your opinion of it."

"Do you really smoke an ivory pipe?" she asked suddenly.

Barker sat a moment, then got up and moved to his bookshelves. He opened his walnut smoking cabinet, displaying two racks of pipes.

"Meerschaum, actually," he said.

"So I see."

"I am satisfied, Miss Potter. Consider your services engaged."

"Is there anything I should look for in particular?" she asked.

"Mr. Llewelyn, have you got the list of victims with you?"

I flipped through my notebook, glad for once that he hadn't called me "lad" in front of Miss Potter. "Here it is, sir."

"Thank you. I would like to know if the girls on this list came through the C.O.S."

"As you wish, sir."

"I hope your enquiry skills are as satisfactory as your manners. The socialism notwithstanding, you give me some hope for the next generation. That will be all."

He rose, gave a solemn nod, and then exited the way he came. He wasn't going anywhere save the empty courtyard again, I knew. Perhaps it was all for Miss Potter's benefit.

"What an unusual person your employer is," she said under her breath.

"He is that," I commented diplomatically.

"He really thinks he'll find Gwendolyn's killer in so short a time?"

"If he says so, I believe him. He does not make inflated promises."

15

CYRUS BARKER AND I WENT TO THE MILE END Mission after that, where he spent his time pummeling Mc-Clain's hanging bag while the reverend tried to tear off my head with his hook punch. Handy Andy complained the entire time about his gloves, but I doubt I would have been conscious if he hadn't worn them. When we were done, he would not vouchsafe that I had learned anything, only that I was "coming along," whatever that meant. I felt as if something had jarred loose in the back of my head, but I knew by now that complaining wouldn't do any good.

We slipped down the alley and entered the back door of the warehouse, then climbed the steps to the first floor. As expected, Mac was intent on his vigil. He had one hand propped high against the side of the window and the other on his waist. At rest he looked like a Greek statue, save the yarmulke.

"Has anything of note happened while we were gone?" the Guv asked.

"Yes, sir," he said, diving into the pocket of his jacket. "Jenkins was here. I'm afraid you received another anonymous note."

Barker grunted and took the envelope, slitting it open with the stiletto he generally kept in a sheath up his sleeve. I realized my employer had probably been expecting one after Gwendolyn DeVere's body was found. The note read:

Poor Push is full of woe;
Doesn't quite know where to go,
A-searching the Green with his Welsh terrier
(The principle is the more the merrier.)

The wee girl's fodder for the grave.
She should have known how to behave.
Drink your tea and smoke your 'bacca—
You can't catch me!
Mr. Miacca.

"Welsh terrier," I commented. When one is small, one is a target for everyone.

"Have you any constructive comments to make, Mr. Llewelyn?"

"No one would write 'a-searching,' sir. They might say it, but they would not write it. It sounds like an educated man trying to sound uneducated."

"Agreed. And?"

"'You can't catch me.' That's from the old tale of the Gingerbread Man," I pointed out.

"Another fairy tale? We may have to get a copy of that. Continue."

"Well, sir, he must know you rather well. He knows you like tea and tobacco and appears to be going out of his way to inform you that he knows what's going on. Either he is someone with whom we come into close contact, or he is remarkably well informed."

"Let's have a bite," my employer said, "and settle in. Mac, some tea, if you will be so kind."

Like Her Majesty, I have only the highest respect for Fortnum & Mason, but my kippers on flavorless wafers tasted as metallic as the tin in which they came and the tea did not successfully wash away the taste. I lay down, hoping to dream of roasted turkeys with mountains of mashed potatoes smothered in steaming gravy. One cannot order one's dreams, however, and I dreamed something else entirely.

I was looking down upon the old and swaybacked, Dickensian roofs of Bethnal Green, and above them, the giant, wraithlike figure of Mr. Miacca strode about, seeking whom he would devour. For some reason, I pictured him with bleached white skin; sunken eyes; and wild, pale hair. He wore a black claw hammer coat, verminous as the grave, with Regency breeches and hose on long, spindly legs. His feet, clad in moldy buckled shoes, were the size of drays; and he was bending down, snatching up bad children and dropping them into his open jaws, as Saturn did his children. For the good little boys and girls, he left presents on their windowsills, the wrapped boxes tiny in his skeletal hands.

I looked down at myself, and suddenly, I was eight again. Beside me, an equally young Palmister Clay was pointing at me and crying that I'd stolen his sovereign. I looked over my shoulder as Miacca's hand came snaking toward me, its claws growing bigger and bigger until they enveloped me. He lifted me high up over the buildings until I was over his gaping maw. Then he released me and I plummeted.

"Lad?"

"Yes, sir?" I said, rubbing my eyes. It was dark, but by the shafts of light coming in through the window, I could see Mac loading shells into his shotgun. Apparently, clothes weren't the only things he had packed in his trunks. "What is it?"

"I'm not certain," Barker stated. "There are a couple of fellows down in Green Street acting suspiciously."

"What are they doing?" I asked, climbing off the hard mattress in my stocking feet.

"Merely walking, but they have passed by every twenty minutes or so since eight o'clock, and it is almost ten. They are dressed in capes and top hats. There, do you see?"

I looked down just as a caped form turned away into Globe Road. "Shall I throw on my boots?"

"Yes, and get your pistol. I have a feeling something is most definitely happening in the Green tonight."

I pulled on my boots and began to fill the chambers of my Webley. Snapping it shut, I pulled on my coat with the built-in holster that Mac had set out, and followed the two of them, still rubbing the sleep from my eyes.

We caught sight of the top-hatted men walking shoulder to shoulder down Green Street. Barker raised his chin in their direction, and we followed them stealthily. Bethnal Green suddenly seemed deserted, as if every hovel, tenement, and rooming house was as empty as the street we padded down.

The fog was pooling about our ankles, and when the river breeze shot out of an alleyway, it whistled against the sharp edges of the brick. *Nothing good could come of this,* I thought, already missing the relative safety of our near-empty room.

"They're gone," I said. One second they had been ahead of us, and now they were not.

"I believe they went down that alley there, sir," Mac said.

We approached it cautiously. It provided room for only one person to go down at a time. The alley came to a thoroughfare, though there was no sign to say which it was. We picked up our quarry on the other side and plunged into another alleyway, a wider one this time. The Guv quickened his pace, and we hurried along behind. As I've said before, he moves quickly for a big man.

"They've gone into that court there," Barker whispered, and we followed them into the yard. It may have been a knacker's yard or a stable at one time. It seemed abandoned now, a cluster of anonymous building backs. We stepped out of the shadows into the center of the empty court, then heard the sudden shutting of the gate behind us. We had been neatly trapped.

The two men stepped out of the gloom ahead and began removing their cloaks and hats. Underneath, they were mere street vermin, poorly dressed. They were in their early twenties, like me, but all resemblance ended there. One had a long scar bisecting his face, while the other must have looked wicked the day he was born. I wasn't sure what to do, but that didn't stop Mac. He pulled out his shotgun and cocked it before pointing it at the duo.

"Easy, Mac, easy," Barker said. "These lads have only been out for a stroll so far."

There was a flaring off to my left and the shadows were illuminated by a vesta. I saw several menacing faces during the brief flare up, as the one in the middle lit a cigarette. Perhaps it was a trick of the light that the men looked particularly demonic in the sudden glare. I didn't wait for permission but dug my pistol from its pocket holder. I spared a glance past Mac at the Guv. There was movement in his direction, too. Barker raised his brace of American Colts. This could quickly degenerate into gunplay. The leader got a look of resolution on his face and stepped forward along with his companions. Slowly, inexorably, they formed a circle around us which grew smaller and smaller with each step. When would they fire? It was a moment before I realized they wouldn't. The dozen men slowly hemming us in were unarmed.

"Stop or I shall shoot!" Jacob Maccabee called out, but his voice wasn't as commanding as he could have hoped. They ignored him and continued to come forward. Another few seconds and the barrel of my pistol would be flat against one of their chests.

"Sir?" Mac asked tensely.

"Steady," Barker growled. "Fire on my word."

Mac prepared to blow the fellows in front of us to pieces, but some code of honor told me it wasn't right. These chaps were unarmed. Theoretically, we were in command. In another step they would be close enough to lay hands on our weapons, at which point what would happen would be anyone's guess.

"Stop, blast you!" Mac cried. As one, they complied, standing shoulder to shoulder, hemming us in. My mind began formulating a plan. I would swing out my right arm and catch the first fellow in the throat with the butt of my pistol. Then I would pull him into his fellow, jump over both of them, and with any luck, catch a third full in the stomach with the heel of my boot.

"Lad, no," Barker said, divining my thoughts. He slid his pistols back into their holsters inside his coat. "Stand down."

"Yes, sir."

"Mac, break open your piece."

Reluctantly our butler eased the hammer down and breached his weapon. I slid my pistol back into its holster.

We stood there immobile, all fifteen of us. The tension was so high, I had to say something or bust.

"Anyone fancy a waltz?"

There was a low chuckle from the group, but it was interrupted by the creak of the gate as it opened again. We heard the jingle of harness and the clopping of iron-shod hooves on paving stone. A brougham pulled in and stopped. One of the men near us went to it and opened the door. A set of collapsible steps unfolded, and a man stepped down to the ground. He was about fifty years of age, in expensive clothes, and knee-length boots, with a nose a Roman senator would envy and a well-tended set of side-whiskers. He was every inch the aristocrat, as blue-blooded as any name in *Burke's Peerage*.

"Thank you," the man said to his subordinate as he crossed the yard and entered the circle through the gap. He gave Mac and me a cursory glance, then his eyes fastened upon my employer. The Guv crossed his arms and waited upon events. He seemed as unruffled as if he were in Hampstead Heath.

"Barker, I would have a word with you," he said.

"I wish to know with whom I am having concourse," the Guv replied.

"'Concourse,' is it?" the man asked. "You are not the dullard I took you to be."

"State your business," Barker growled. "And tell your hirelings to step back a little. I like to have room about me when I talk. If I am not given it, I shall take it."

The man made a gesture and the circle about us enlarged a little. Mac and I breathed easier.

"Never mind about my business for now. Let us discuss yours. You are after a murderer, I understand."

"That is correct."

"And you are working with the Charity Organization Society. You know Octavia Hill and her monstrous regiment of socialist women. You've been seen speaking with William Stead, and I understand you are a close associate of the Reverend McClain."

"So far, all of your assertions are correct."

"Are you a socialist?"

Barker gave a yawn, patting it down with the back of his hand. "Are you keeping me from my bed merely to discuss politics?"

"You have not answered."

"I do not feel compelled to answer your questions, sir."

"Come, Barker, it's a simple question. Are you a socialist, or aren't you?"

"No, sir, I am not. I am a Conservative, not a Fabian."

"Yet you associate with them."

"I have been hired to find a child's murderer. I will associate with whomever helps me find him."

The man got a tight smile on his face. "You have no clue what this is about, do you?"

"Enlighten me," Barker murmured.

"Stead has vowed to see that the age of consent is raised from thirteen to sixteen. I represent a consortium of men who will not allow that to occur."

"And why would they interest themselves in such an issue, sir?" Barker continued.

"That is not your concern. Perhaps the girl was a sacrifice made by the socialists in order to bring attention to the so-called white slave trade."

"Do you know this for a fact, or do you merely suspect it, sir?"

"A blind man could see it. Are you blind behind those black spectacles?"

"I am not, I assure you," Barker said. "Have you any more to recommend to me?"

"Only that the men I represent are very powerful and will not be pleased if the vote should be entered and passed."

"You give me too much credit, sir. I am but an enquiry agent; I cannot control the processes of the House of Commons. I thank you for the information, however, and shall consider it thoroughly."

The man reached into his pocket, pulled out a small sack of coins, and tossed it into one of the gang member's hands. The men could not help but give a short cry of savage joy. No doubt they would be drunk as lords soon, despite the hour. Closing time is variable when there is money to be made.

The man turned and, without a look back, climbed into

his vehicle and rattled off. The gang followed, looking for the nearest public house. In two minutes, we had the courtyard all to ourselves.

"I believe that gang is the Ratcliff Highway Boys, but I've got to find out who that gentleman is," Barker stated.

"Oh, I know who he is, sir," I told him. "That is Lord Hesketh, Palmister Clay's father. I'm surprised he didn't recognize me. It was his money that put me in prison."

16

~~~

"ANY CHANCE FOR SOME COFFEE?" I ASKED MAC
after we came back.

"You drink too much of that brew," he answered.

"Would you rather I fell asleep at my post?"

He made the coffee, though not without a few sighs.
Then he and Barker lay down back to back. Hearing
Barker's spectacles being set on the floor, I took two steps
toward him and then heard Mac cough. There was no
chance of finally seeing the Guv without his spectacles, not
with his watchdog guarding him.

I drank the coffee and watched Green Street from the
window. Mac had set up a notebook and logged various
people as they came and went, presumably from Barker's
descriptions of them. The Guv had continued to record
people through the evening. For once, I had the easier
work; there wasn't much to write down. The night watchman made his early rounds and the constable walked his
beat, swinging his truncheon more out of boredom than
swagger. The night soil cart came through and the waste
of hundreds of horses were shoveled into it, as if it were a

precious thing. A few inebriates were escorted home, and the homeless, forbidden to loiter or sleep in doorways, were herded along by the police like tired sheep. I grew bored with looking through the grimy window and made my way up the ladder to the roof. It was balmy outside that evening, and I could smell the river on the wind. Pigeons cooed in the corners of the roof, not discomfited in the least by my presence. I sat on the ledge, watched the street, and thought.

What I thought of was Jenny Ashby, or rather, Jenny Llewelyn, though she had that name but a short time in this life. It was as if out of some sort of self-preservation I had shut her up in a wardrobe somewhere and seeing Palmister Clay had opened it again. My Jenny, my own sweet girl. I recalled the way the wind caught the curls by her ears and the sun lit them up and turned them red. I remembered the pattern of freckles across her upturned nose as if she were standing in front of me and the warm, soft blue of her eyes, like cornflowers, like the entire June sky reflected therein. I'd been tricked into marrying her, perhaps, but if she were there just now, I'd have married her all over again. Beatrice Potter was a beauty and a great catch for any man in the whole of England, but I would have traded the entire world for just one more afternoon with Jenny.

I'd never have that afternoon, however. Palmister Clay had robbed me of those final months. It washed over me again, like a bucket of scalding water, the deep anger that I felt for that man.

She was gone from me, buried in an unmarked grave somewhere in Oxford, a pauper's grave. At least, that's what a solicitor had told me. Where did she lie, my wife, my dearly departed? How did one look for an unmarked grave? I had not the least idea how to begin.

All this being alone was making me maudlin. I removed my jacket and did a few stretches on the roof the way Barker had taught me. At least it kept me awake. The hours slowly passed. By the light of the gas lamps, I saw the night watchman and the constables continue their rounds. How did they stand the boredom? I knew I should go mad in such a situation.

Eventually, there was a change in the step of the constables below. They began knocking on doors, waking the residents for their daily work. There was money to be made in this, Barker had told me once, as much as four pence a week per residence. No need for a timepiece when someone else can watch the time for you. The constables and the night watchmen were in competition. I watched them hurry through the streets, knocking steadily on doors, then, before I knew it, Mac was at my elbow, with a fresh cup of coffee. It was six in the morning and I had finished my shift.

Jacob Maccabee and I have an unusual relationship. We'd gotten off on the wrong foot on my arrival in Barker's household. Sometimes we treated each other fairly, and other times we traded barbs. Perhaps I was thankful for the coffee or tired or simply overwrought, but just then I felt I needed one less enemy in the world.

"Mac," I said, "I wanted to tell you you've done a good job of looking after us here. You were also rather handy with that gun of yours, even if you didn't actually use it."

"Thank you, sir."

It was a blatant attempt to flatter him. He knew it and I knew it, but it unbent him a little nevertheless.

"Tell me, how came you to be hired by the Guv?"

Mac gave me a guarded look. "I assumed he had told you."

"The Guv? Not a word. Why would you think that?"

"You work with the man."

"You know how he is. One would sooner get blood from a stone. So, come, tell me how he came to hire you."

Mac put a foot up on the ledge and looked out across the rooftops. I thought he might refuse to tell me, but all of a sudden, he began to speak.

"I was working as a second footman to a good family in Islington. The master was a director for the Great Western Railway. When they hired me they called me Mac in order to conceal my religion. I was eighteen years old."

"Why did you want to be a servant? It isn't a normal occupation for a Jew."

"Yes, I know. I was forbidden to let my beard grow and couldn't wear my yarmulke. I can't explain it well. I like order, and I like being a part of something larger than myself. Being a servant is not a bad living, and one always has room and board. Some butlers retire with more than a clergyman or a colonel. If one likes the work, it is not a bad occupation."

"Forgive the interruption."

"Not at all. As I said, I was a second footman. Quite often, I was sent on errands, to get spices for the cook, perhaps, or to carry a message for the lady of the house. One day, I chanced to speak with a young lady about my own age who lived in the neighborhood. Her name was Alice Padgett. She was the daughter of an admiral who had died at sea, and lived with her uncle under reduced circumstances. She spoke to me occasionally after that, and some of the staff would chaff me about having a lady friend in the neighborhood."

"I was waiting for a woman to come into it," I said.

"Are you going to comment on everything I say?" he said severely. "She never became my lady friend because she was murdered."

"Murdered?" I had expected romance.

"Yes. One terrible morning, the police came to the house and spoke to the master. I was summoned, and the next thing I knew I was being locked in darbies and elbowed into a Black Maria. They told me Alice was dead and I was Scotland Yard's main suspect."

"Because you are a Jew, I suppose. That is monumentally unfair."

"They took me to Scotland Yard and put me in a room and berated me for hours. They accused me of slitting Alice's throat, a lover's quarrel, they said; but of course, we weren't. Lovers, I mean. I liked her very much, but we had only spoken in the street. Anyway, they kept saying it would be better if I confessed. Obviously, they didn't care about finding her real killer. They just wanted a confession, and they weren't scrupulous about how to get it. They beat me badly and said I had resisted arrest. I broke down and cried. I was very frightened. When I still didn't confess, they locked me in a cell and brought me pork sausages. *Pork sausages,* for every meal. It was that or nothing."

"Monstrous."

"The next morning they brought in a newspaper. The newspaper had all but convicted me, and with good reason, too. The knife, the murder weapon, covered in Alice's blood, had been found in my room, wrapped in one of my shirts. The inspector in charge interrogated me again brutally. He said he would beat a confession out of me, if he could not get it any other way. When I didn't speak, he sent me back to my cell to think over my confession. He demanded it by morning. I seriously considered giving him one, just to stop the beatings.

"Later that day, I was taken out again but not to the interrogation room. I went to another room, where a man stood waiting to see me. He said his name was Cyrus Barker, and he was a private enquiry agent who had been retained by the Board of Deputies to look into the matter of my arrest."

"So, the first case the Guv had with the Jewish Board of Deputies was actually your case."

"Yes."

"What did he look like—the Guv, I mean?"

"Much the same. A bit rough around the edges, to be truthful. He had a beard and wore those spectacles, of course. He was at least a stone lighter. He looked alien, like a recent arrival, which in fact he was. Perhaps that is why the Board of Deputies hired him in the first place."

"I'm sorry. I've interrupted again."

"Yes, you have," Mac said, looking vaguely annoyed. "After that, Scotland Yard tried even harder to get me to confess, but I noticed they were less likely to slap me about. A solicitor named Abram Salomon came to speak with me and said if they really had anything to charge me with they'd have done so already. They had the murder weapon, but the evening Alice was murdered, my time was accounted for. I shared a room with the first footman, you see.

While Scotland Yard swarmed over the house looking for trapdoors and sliding panels, I hoped the odd-looking private enquiry agent was out in the streets looking for the real killer of my friend.

"Close to a week went by after that. It's hard to tell in prison. The inspector had gone through all his questions and was merely repeating them, hoping I'd break down. Then one morning, I was released and practically tossed into the street. Barker was there, waiting for me, with my parents, Mr. Salomon, and a reporter from the *Jewish Chronicle*. The Guv had found Alice's murderer, a lodger in the next street, who had developed an interest in her that bordered upon mania. He hated me, having seen her speaking with a Jew, and had contrived to gain entry into the house by flattering the charwoman. She also provided an alibi for him; but under questioning, Barker had broken it, and she confessed.

"I was free but completely unemployable. None of the newspapers who had blackened my name had the slightest interest in printing a retraction, though they covered the subsequent trial. Nobody wanted a footman who had been involved in a murder, and so my career was over. Then one day the Guv appeared at my parents' house in Newgate and said he'd purchased a home in Newington and required a manservant. Was I interested? I took charge and at his request ordered all the furnishings for the house. I also suggested he might find more custom if he shaved his beard and that he try a tailor of mine in Holborn."

"Krause brothers?" I asked, remembering the shop Barker had sent me to my first day.

"Indeed. Mr. Dummolard was in France, attending a cooking school, and Mr. Ho had not yet purchased his establishment, so we had most of our meals in from the Elephant and Castle."

"What about his ward, Bok Fu Ying?"

"Apparently when he and Dummolard and Ho arrived in the Isle of Dogs, Barker bought the first vacant building he found in Three Colt Street and installed them both there. When he moved to Newington, she came with him but found the area not to her liking and returned to Limehouse."

"When did he acquire the office in Whitehall?"

"Shortly after he bought the house. I don't know where he got the money for it or Dummolard for his training or Ho for the tearoom he would shortly purchase. I assumed, like many gentlemen, they had acquired their fortunes in the East."

"I suppose Quong and Jenkins came along next," I said.

Barker suddenly stepped onto the roof, and Mac snapped to attention. I realized that was all of the secrets I was to learn that day.

17

"**L**IFT YOUR GUARD, TOMMY."

Barker had sent me on to McClain's as soon as breakfast was over. The time grew short until the match.

"What, so you can batter my liver again?" I asked the reverend, bobbing and weaving.

"Liver, kidneys—makes no difference, boyo."

I ducked and lashed out but caught Handy Andy only on one of his stony shoulders.

"Don't you have anyone my size?" I asked.

"All the kiddies are still abed."

"You should be in the music hall. Boxing and comedy in one act."

"And anyway," he went on as if he hadn't heard, "your opponent isn't your size, as I understand it."

"Is there any chance—Ow!"

McClain had got one over my flimsy guard and caught me across the brow. "Quit jawing while I'm smiting you."

I hopped 'round the ring, sweating like a horse after a mile run. This was no way to win a match against anybody. Twenty-two, and I was to be cut down in the prime of life. I tried to get by; and suddenly I was against the ropes, Andrew McClain hammering me in the stomach and ribs, with an occasional smack to the jaw and nose. I couldn't take much more of this. In fact, I didn't. My opponent hooked me with a right to the ear, and the next I knew I was down on one knee, shaking my head. McClain lifted me by the shoulders and dropped me down on the wooden stool in the corner.

"It's a good thing your boss isn't here. He's not overjoyed about this challenge you've gotten yourself into and wouldn't have gone as easy on you as I have."

"You call this easy?"

"Aye. Break's over," he said, kicking the stool out from under me. "Time for another round."

"This isn't doing me any good!"

"This will be just a walk in the park compared to what your opponent will give you. I've been asking about a little. Nice jab."

I'd managed to tap him on the jaw. It was the first clean hit I'd made since the sparring had started.

"And?"

"General opinion is that Clay is good. Drinks too much and has an eye for female flesh, but so far it hasn't affected his skills. Strictly amateur, of course. I don't want to scare you, but you'll have to do better than this."

"Teach me how to fight, then. I already know how to get hit."

"Just reminding you. Barker's been teaching you that Chinese wrestling, and it's good, don't get me wrong; but if you are gonna wear these pillows on your mitts, you'd better learn you some good, old-fashioned John Bull boxing."

He caught me square on the nose then, and that was the end of the match. I began to bleed like a faucet. The reverend moved me to the stool and held my head back so the blood could flow down my throat, although how that was an improvement, I couldn't see.

"Let me get out of these mitts and I'll mop your face proper, Tommy boy. You know, your right's not bad, but your left is all over the place. You need to learn control, control and follow through."

McClain performed surgery upon me. That is, he ripped the corner from a towel and screwed it into my nostril. Then he sent me in to bathe in a cold tub and get changed. Once outside, I got rid of it. The bleeding had stopped.

When I got back, Barker was pacing and smoking his pipe. Ribbons of smoke hung in the still air.

"Ah," he said, catching sight of me. "Come, we must leave immediately."

"Where are we going?" I asked.

"One of Soho Vic's lads has located Major DeVere. He's in Camden Town. We've got precious time to collect him and sober him up. The funeral is tomorrow."

Barker hailed another cab and ordered the driver north to Camden. I noted the expense in the back of my notebook. Costs were adding up.

"What happened to your nose?" the Guv asked.

"I got too close to one of the reverend's jabs."

"He's got a good one, doesn't he? Someday when you're in your dotage, you'll be able to say Handy Andy McClain once bloodied your nose, but I doubt anyone will believe you. The man's a legend."

★　　　★　　　★

Camden Town was a pleasant surprise. It had a Dickensian feel about it, with old, swaybacked buildings, narrow streets, and a genteel poverty, like a maiden aunt living on a pension. There was one building with the name Fagin on it and another that said Marley.

Barker hired an open carriage at the station and told the driver where to go. He seemed to know this area, as well. *Just how far did his knowledge of the streets go?* I wondered. Had he memorized Tunbridge Wells or Brighton, too?

We pulled up in front of a pub with an open front door spilling light like lager onto the paving stones. It was unremarkable, as public houses go. It might have been a template for every other pub in London.

The publican was a fat, prosperous-looking man, like most I've met. He had a face like a bulldog's, with jowls and rolls of excess flesh, and a stub of a cigar was permanently affixed to the corner of his mouth.

"Is Major DeVere here?" Barker asked.

"Oh, thank God," the owner exclaimed. "He's been doing his best to drink up my cellar these past two days. I've never seen anyone put down so much wine in my life. Thought he'd quit sometime, but every time we thought he'd passed out, here he come down the stair again, askin' for 'nother bottle. Crikey, that man can throw down the liquor."

"His daughter was found murdered, and his wife killed herself," Barker answered, hoping perhaps to shock him into silence, but it didn't work.

"Thought it hadda be something like that," the man said, wiping a glass with a grimy towel. "It was like he was trying to drown hisself, one bottle at a time."

"Where is he?"

He pointed over our heads with his thumb. "Ain't got but the one room."

Barker led me up the stairs, and when he came to the door, opened it without knocking. In the shambles of the inn room, Trevor DeVere sat in a chair with his feet extended and his arms hanging limp. His eyes were glazed, his mustache disordered, and the front of his open shirt stained with wine. He caught sight of us and raised a half-full goblet in the air.

"To your health, gentlemen," he said, draining it in a gulp.

"We have come to retrieve you, sir," Barker said stonily. I don't believe he was as sympathetic to Mr. DeVere's condition as I.

"I'm where I wish to be," came the reply. "Push off, gentlemen."

"No, sir. I'm afraid you're coming with us. We need to make you presentable for your family's funeral."

DeVere came up out of his chair and started to back away, pointing at Barker with one trembling finger while the others wrapped around the neck of a bottle.

"Oh, blazes! Now you've gone and done it! I was trying to forget all about that, and you've reminded me. A fat lot of good you gents have been to me since I walked into your chambers four days ago. I've got a cat left, you know, a nice, fat tom. You can kill him too, if you wish."

"You may complain at the time of the reckoning, when I present your bill. Until then, I am in charge and I'm saying you must come with me."

DeVere splashed more wine into his goblet and drank it.

Then he was back to the finger pointing. This time, he pointed at me.

"You," he said, looking at me with bleary red eyes. "You look like an educated chappy. How many circles of Hell are there?"

I glanced at my employer nervously. "I believe there were nine, according to Dante."

The major shook his head with his eyes closed and a smile on his face. A laugh escaped his lips. "Eleven, there are eleven."

"What do you mean?"

"There's the one I'm in now. You didn't read about that one in old Dante, did you? And then, there's the really, really deep one where they put all the blasted, thieving, useless private enquiry agents!"

He tried to fill his glass again, but the bottle was finally empty. He looked at it woefully. "I keep pouring this stuff down my throat, hoping for release. The damned publican must be watering it down. I'm sorry. I just want oblivion."

"If it's oblivion you want—" Barker said suddenly, his fist coming up under the major's chin, jarring him with the blow. DeVere dropped into his arms like a sack of potatoes. My employer hoisted the major onto his right shoulder and turned to me. "Go downstairs and settle the bill."

I don't believe we had been in the building more than five minutes, and now Barker was leaving with DeVere on his shoulders. I had expected a protracted argument, but Barker had a more expedient method of getting a drunken, angry man out of a public house.

"Where to now, sir?" the cabman asked, once I'd paid DeVere's bill and we were all ensconced in the carriage.

"Fulham," Barker growled.

"That's clear 'cross town, sir!"

"Then you had better not dawdle. I'll make it worth your time."

"Yes, sir."

"I suppose this has turned out as well as could be expected," the Guv said. "There was a chance he would go back to his barracks and blow his brains out."

The major came to halfway through the journey.

"Where the hell am I?" he asked.

"You are going home to sleep," Barker told him. "Tomorrow morning, you're going to bury your wife and daughter."

DeVere sat and stared as the carriage rolled down the street. I wasn't certain whether he'd taken the words in until he spoke again a minute or two later.

"I'm gonna be flogged for this or court-martialed. Or both."

Neither Barker nor I vouchsafed a remark, but DeVere was suddenly garrulous. "You—you're gonna catch this blackguard and make him pay, aren't you?"

"I have every intention of doing so."

"Gwendolyn . . . my little Gwendolyn. Used to rock her on my knee, you know."

"You owe it to her memory to be at her graveside, sober."

"Have you ever lost a child, Mr. Barker?"

"No."

"Have you ever lost a wife?"

Barker didn't respond. My jaw dropped. DeVere, drunk as he was, didn't notice and continued. "Then don't dictate terms to me. I'm paying for the bloody funeral and I'm going to be there. Now leave off."

We arrived at the DeVere residence. The butler, a capable man who looked like he might have seen military before domestic service, met us and helped his master from the vehicle, issuing orders to the maids for a pot of coffee and a hot bath. We left the arrangements for DeVere's appearance in the man's capable hands. On the way back to Bethnal Green, Barker was back to his normal self, watching traffic and turning over aspects of the case, but I pondered the unanswered question in my heart.

18

I SUPPOSE, SOMEWHERE, THERE IS SUCH A THING as an enjoyable funeral. Someone lived a long life, prospered, was revered and loved and was finally ready to greet his Maker once more. His mourners would say, "He lived his life wisely and we will miss him; but he was old. It was his time to die." He might even have been buried in the same cemetery as the one in which Gwendolyn DeVere and her mother were laid to rest the next morning, but this funeral gave no comfort to anyone, for Gwendolyn had been murdered and her mother had taken her life.

I've been to a lot of funerals for one lifetime. In my line of work, death is like a crow that sits upon one's shoulder or hovers over one's head, but this remained in my mind for years afterward. What I recall is the fine weather that Wednesday and the look of shock on the faces of all the participants. It was a day for picnicking in Hyde Park, for playing badminton or rowing on the river, and yet we were here witnessing two coffins being laid in the earth and wishing *bon voyage* to two souls. The sun gave no health or life; it merely accentuated the deaths of two who would still have been alive if we, Barker and I, had only been a little more diligent, if we had only known the right course of action.

DeVere looked as if he had shriveled. His mind seemed to be floating somewhere in the clouds as the service was read. He was not alone. All of us—the unnamed relatives, the ladies and gentlemen who worked at the Charity Organization Society, the Life Guards who stood in silent sympathy with their comrade, and the husbands and wives who knew the DeVeres—stood about looking slightly deflated and out of focus, like dispirited statues. After the rites, in that bright, unnatural sunshine, everyone hemmed and hawed, said the proper thing to the major, and drifted off, their summer day spoiled by this close brush against the sleeve of the specter of Death. There would be no gathering at the home.

Stephen and Rose Carrick came up to us after the funeral.

"How is the investigation coming?" he asked.

"The girl has been found, as you can see," the Guv said. "Now all that remains is to track down her killer."

"I hear he's killed more than once."

"He has, but he will not kill again," Barker stated.

"How do you know?" Mrs. Carrick spoke up, looking over her shoulder at the newly turned earth. "He is still out there somewhere."

"Because he knows I'm breathing down the back of his neck. He'll try again; he is compelled to. But then I'll have him."

Carrick opened his mouth to say something, then shut it again. "Good," he finally said and moved away. I was at a loss for words myself.

We found DeVere and gave him our condolences. Once through the lych-gate and into the lane, Barker and I settled our crepe-banded hats back upon our heads.

"At least," the Guv said, "they allowed Mrs. DeVere to be buried alongside her daughter. Fifty years ago, it would have been forbidden to bury her in consecrated ground."

"Do you really think she killed herself, sir?" I asked. "She was full of laudanum already. Perhaps she woke up and forgot she'd taken any. Perhaps she just took another dose."

"The whole bottle?"

I shrugged. "I don't know. She was half out of her mind and drugged."

"Perhaps," my employer conceded, if only to make me feel better. "In either case, we shall never know."

"I put the blame on Miacca's shoulders. She'd still be alive if it weren't for him. We've got to find him."

"We shall," Barker stated. "He wants to be found. These letters—'catch me if you can'—are cries for attention. The man wants to be infamous. At some point in his life, perhaps very early, his brain began to warp the way a plant sometimes does. It twisted and grew in upon itself, and now we must pull it up by its roots before it infects others, if it is not too late."

Barker stepped up into his cab while I climbed atop my perch behind. Our mare, Juno, had been tricked out with a black ostrich feather. The Guv beat upon the trap and I opened it.

"Shall we have lunch?"

"I am not hungry," I replied.

"You are oversensitive. It is not good to miss a meal just before a bout. You are in training."

"If I get peckish, I'll eat something out of the hamper," I said.

We rode back to Newington to change out of our mourning clothes and to take Juno back to the stable. The house looked forlorn without us, and the rooms had a musty smell. Mac had covered the furniture in the ground floor rooms with sheets, which depressed me, as if we were the ones who had been buried. I took Juno to the stable and saw her brushed down before I walked back down the New Kent Road and entered through the back gate. In the garden, cicadas whined like small machines in the summer sunshine. They contributed to the headache I was getting.

Cyrus Barker had not said what I expected of him: that the DeVere women were not lying there in the ground but were in heaven. Perhaps like me, he was raging at how unfair it all was. We had to find this monster, or nothing— not the daffodils that grew in spring or the stars moving slowly in space vast distances away—would ever be the same.

An hour later, we were finally in Bethnal Green. Mac had cajoled me into taking a plate of food he'd prepared, but the best I could do was nibble a few olives and a cracker. Barker tucked in, as usual. He is rarely put off his food. Mac had just brought the water for tea to a boil when we heard the squeak of the door downstairs. We all froze and looked at one another. Someone was in the building.

Then we heard another sound, a kind of squealing. I might even say caterwauling. I sat up from my seat on the mattress, and Barker put down his plate. Mac took the kettle off the stove. The sound continued, coming up the stair. *What fresh intrusion was this?* I wondered.

It was a street girl, as it turned out, struggling between Soho Vic and another pug-nosed boy. They held her by the shoulders and ankles, but she was giving them the worst of it, I noticed. Both lads had scratches on their faces, and Vic's shirt was rent at the shoulder.

"Pipe down, girl!" he told her, holding his hand over her mouth. "Can't you see you're in the presence of a gentleman?"

She shook her head loose from his filthy grasp. They dropped her unceremoniously on the floor. She was an urchin of about ten years old, with short dark hair and a dirty face, clad in a ragged dress and pinafore and ill-fitting shoes.

"'E don't look like no gentl'man I ever saw," she mumbled, looking at the Guv.

"Good afternoon, Vic," my employer said, ignoring the girl's comment. "To what do we owe this interruption?"

"This young lady, I believe, is in the employ of a Certain Person, an evil personage, if you take my meanin', and has been follerin' you about."

"Is this true, young lady?" Barker demanded. "Have you been following us?"

The girl clapped her hands over her ears. "I don't know nuffin', I ain't sayin' nuffin'."

"A very wise course, to be sure. Won't you have a seat?"

"Where? You ain't got but the mattress," she said, looking about. "I thought gents lived in big houses wif moats and such."

"Never mind about that. What is your name?"

"That's my business," she said defensively. I thought perhaps she was being cheeky, but now I began to wonder if she was actually frightened—and I didn't mean by Barker.

Vic wasn't going to stand for insolence and slapped the back of the girl's head.

"Hold your tongue, you. Sorry, Push. She ain't one o' mine. I'da taught her manners."

"That's all right, Vic." He turned to the butler. "Mac, perhaps our guest would care for some tea and biscuits."

The girl still looked anxious but reluctantly moved forward when Mac opened the large wicker hamper. The two boys were interested, as well. In minutes, he had set out an impromptu picnic on the floor with the children sitting cross-legged around the basket. Even Vic could not resist the charms of the hamper.

"Esme," the girl murmured around a mouthful of cheese and biscuits. "My name is Esme."

"Is that short for Esmeralda?" Barker asked.

"'At's roit. Esmeralda Foster."

"I see. Where is your family, Esme?"

"Ain't got one. Got a bruvver, but 'e's in the workhouse. I din't wanna go, so I'm on me own."

"Tell me about the man you work for, Esme."

"Cain't."

"Has he threatened you?"

"Worse than life, but that ain't the reason. I never seen 'im. 'E allus talks to me from a dark alley. First time, 'e threw a sack over me head and carried me there. He's wicked evil. Ever since then, I've met 'im in the same alley off Collingwood Street."

"How does he pay you, then?" my employer asked.

"'E don't pay me. I do it so I don't get et. 'E's one o' them cannibals. Said I couldn't get away from 'im no matter where I run and that 'e'd eat me for certain if I weren't a good girl. Showed me 'is jar, he did."

"Jar?" Barker said, looking my way.

"Yes, 'is jar. Full o' pickled fingers and such. Bit like Madame Tussaud's Chamber o' Horrors, I reckon, though I never been there."

"How many . . . items would you say were in the jar?"

"More'n I can count."

"I see. How many days have you been following us?"

"Three," she replied.

"Three days. You are to be congratulated, young lady. I would not have thought I could be followed for three days without noticing it."

She smiled between bites of cheese. "Got real close to yer in the charity, sir. No one notices a small girl like me."

"Apparently not. And you went back every night to report to this man?"

"Yes, sir. Daren't otherwise."

"Did he ever give you his name?"

"Miacca, sir."

"Was his voice deep?" the Guv probed.

"Not like yers. Leastways, it was deep enough to know it were a man."

"What do you suppose will happen to you, now that you've told me everything?"

"I'll be et, sir, et for sure," the girl said, giving a shudder.

"Not if he doesn't know."

"Oh, he'll know, all right. Prob'ly knows already. 'E knows everything that goes on in the Green. 'His garden,' he called it. I'm for it, now. I been bad, you see. As long as I was good, he'd let me live. Gave me a sovereign for being good. It weren't a payment. I earned it by not being bad. I don't thieve or go with men like some other girls. I sell flars."

"Flars?" I asked, horrified at what she'd been through.

"Yeah, you know. Roses and such. I promised my bruvver I'd keep me nose clean."

The door down below squeaked again, and Esme was up at once. Unfortunately, there was nowhere for her to go. She ran around the room and finally folded herself up tightly in a corner with her arms around her head. As the footsteps came up the stairs, I reached for the pistol I kept between the wall and the mattress. I needn't have bothered. It was only Jenkins.

"Is this a party?" he asked, looking at us all. Vic and his friend had made inroads into the hamper, and now had crumbs around their mouths.

"You have another message?" Barker asked.

"Yes, sir," Jenkins said, reaching into his pocket, extracting a dirty envelope.

"I knew it! I knew it! He knows!" Esme Foster cried from across the room. "'E'll eat me for sure. 'Oo's gonner tell Bill in the workhouse that I been et?"

"I shall not allow you to be eaten, Miss Foster. You are under my protection now."

He tore open the envelope with a thick finger and perused the third letter from Miacca. I watched his eyes move as he scanned the lines. Then he dismissed it with a shake of his head and passed it to me.

Poor old Push is full of rage
Reading this indignant page.
Don't he know that in our time
Loving children's not a crime?

I'm going on a killing spree
And as I said, you can't catch me.
Smite your doors with cane malacca
It does no good.
Mr. Miacca.

"A spree," I noted, but Barker held up a hand. We were not to speak in front of the girl. I leaned over and spoke low in his ear.

"This has been cribbed, sir. I know I've read 'this indignant page' somewhere before."

"Then go to the Reading Room again and keep a close eye behind you."

"If he knows Esme has been given into our hands, he might try to follow, sir," I continued.

"It would appear so, lad, but that doesn't change anything."

"What about the children? I mean, what will happen to Esme?"

"I'm taking her to Andrew McClain. He'll be able to find someone who can care for her."

"Mr. L.?" Jenkins said, interrupting us. "I've got a message for you as well."

"What?" I asked, getting a sudden chill. "From Miacca?"

"No, sir. It's from your friend Zangwill. He says he needs to speak to you urgently and will be at the usual place."

19

THE "USUAL PLACE" OF WHICH ISRAEL SPOKE was the Barbados coffeehouse of Cornhill, the City, or to be more precise, Saint Michael's Alley, where much of London's coffee is first stored. Israel and I met there often to talk about life, literature, and women, though not necessarily in that order.

When the cab arrived, I jumped down and ran in the door.

"Black Apollo," I called to the proprietor, who always looks as if I had disarrayed his plans merely by showing up. A black Apollo was a large cup of strong black coffee, the house specialty.

"Thomas!" Israel called from one of the high-backed booths that had been built in the 1680s. He looked the same as always: hatchet-faced, with far too much nose and not enough chin. He was wearing his spectacles because the chances were remote that he would be under female scrutiny there.

"Hello, Israel," I said, sliding into the booth across from him. "I'm in a bit of a hurry today. What's going on?"

"We've got something on tonight, if you're interested. In fact, I really must insist you attend."

"I'm not certain if I can," I said. "We're in the middle of a case."

"I assumed that was over," my friend answered. "Amy said it was."

"Amy?"

"Miss Levy, of course."

"You know her?"

"Thomas, you dunderhead, I've been courting her for six months. I told you about her, remember?"

Had he? I wondered. Then gradually, it came back to me. A girl named Amy Levy. Very smart. A published poet. He was trying to impress her. I'd been in the middle of a case then, as I was now, and had only listened with one ear.

"Sorry, Israel. So what's going on?"

"There's a public lecture tonight at the Egyptian Hall. Vernon Lee is speaking. I'm escorting Amy and your presence is required."

My coffee arrived, and I took a sip before refusing. "I can't. I wish I could. For one thing, I attended a funeral this morning. For another, Barker needs me to work tonight."

Zangwill looked crestfallen. He does it with great pathos. "Are you sure you can't come? She asked after you specially."

"What have I done to recommend myself to Miss Levy?" I asked.

"Not Amy. I mean Miss Potter. She's the one who asked if you would attend."

"Did she, by Jove?" I asked. This was something more like.

"Oh, yes. You wouldn't want to refuse her. It's something of a command."

"Hang it," I said. "I'm not certain I can get off."

"You're acting more like your employer every day. How often do such goddesses step down from Mount Olympus, I ask you?"

"But I still have obligations," I wavered.

"Both girls work at the charity. You could question them about events, then tell Mr. Barker that you interrogated them mercilessly. He needn't know the difference."

"I wouldn't lie to him, but if I did ask enough questions to make it worth my while . . ."

"Worth your while? Have you seen Miss Potter? I think you need these spectacles more than I."

"Look, tell her that I shall do my best to be there. If I'm not, it is due to some aspect of the case that required my presence and I'm most sorry. It's the best I can do."

Israel shook his head and then cradled his chin in one of his large, nervous hands. "Your priorities are all confused, Thomas," he said, "but at this rate, you shall have several decades of bachelorhood to straighten them out. Come tonight. Amy insists. You can't imagine how cross she gets when she does not have her way."

"Oh, yes, I can," I said, sliding out of the booth. "I've met her."

I took a cab to the British Museum and began my search. Finding a particular poem from memory can be a lesson in patience, but every now and then one catches a bit of luck. I found what I was looking for in the second anthology of poems I paged through. With the copied pages in my hand, I ran out the front door and hailed a cab disgorging another patron.

"Blake, sir," I said breathlessly when I arrived. "It is William Blake. It's a poem called 'A Little Girl Lost,' appropriately enough. I knew he was cribbing."

I laid it before Barker and pointed at the lines. "See? It says right there 'Reading this indignant page,' and farther down, it should really read 'Love! sweet Love! was thought a crime.'"

"Our collector of young girls seems remarkably well read," Barker noted.

"It's as if he were a member of the Reading Room itself."

"That's not out of the question. Did you not say that you met Miss Potter in the museum?"

"Yes. We could make a list of suspects and compare it to a list of members of the Reading Room."

"The museum would not give it," Barker replied. "They respect the privacy of their members, some of whom are quite wealthy."

"Indeed. Sir, speaking of Miss Potter, I was invited by her to attend a public lecture tonight. It may be relevant to the case."

"But you must rest," he pointed out. "You have a match tomorrow."

"I could go without sleep for one night, I suppose."

"Let us trade schedules for tonight," the Guv replied. "I was going to follow young Dr. Fitzhugh from the C.O.S. and see how he spends his evenings. I'm afraid we have neglected to watch the doctor amid all the chaos."

Jacob Maccabee gave a discreet cough. It is almost as effective as his shotgun, though obviously less messy.

"Yes, Mac?" Barker asked with an air of impatience.

"Forgive me, sir, for stepping into matters that are not my concern, but perhaps I might be permitted to shadow Dr. Fitzhugh?"

"You?" our employer asked doubtfully.

"Indeed, sir. My schedule won't be changed at all, and I shall get a good night's sleep. I am unknown to the good doctor, whereas he has met you both. I have at least a rudimentary understanding of how to follow someone, having read of it in various books."

Mac has a taste for sensational novels, such as the gothic works of Poe and Le Fanu, as well as the modern romances of Mrs. Braddon. I wasn't certain how accurate the methods of detection were in such works, so I was dubious, possibly even more so than Barker.

"But, Mac, you'd stick out like an old nail in your butler's uniform," I said.

"I've brought a less identifiable suit of clothing with me, in case of emergency," came the reply.

"But your face is easily identifiable, and as for your yarmulke—"

"We are less than a quarter mile from the Jewish quarter. Besides, I have a soft hat I can wear over it. As for my face, he shall never see it. Is it not the way when following someone, to stay far enough behind as to just keep him in sight?"

I looked at the Guv. "Well, it would solve the problem."

Barker was standing by the window. "I say that Mac has no time to change clothing. Dr. Fitzhugh has just left the charity. He is young, Mac, and is carrying his medical bag. He is heading east."

"Yes, sir!" Mac said, and turning around, bolted down the stairs. I'm so used to seeing him glide about sedately and silently that I could not imagine him capable of running.

I looked over Barker's shoulder into Green Street. By the time he reached the street, Maccabbee was carrying his coat over his shoulder. He'd pocketed his skullcap and his tie hung down untied. For Mac, it was quite a transformation.

"I guess that settles the matter," I said.

"Perhaps, but there is still enough time to make one more stop."

"Not McClain's," I objected. "I'll look wonderful talking to Miss Potter with a fat lip and a goose egg on my cheek. I'll train all tomorrow, if you wish."

"Who is speaking?"

"A Mr. Lee."

"Is he a socialist?"

"If Miss Levy and Miss Potter are attending, he's bound to be."

"We've got one more errand to run before you go to the Egyptian and I take the sleeping shift."

I followed my employer. I knew better than to ask where we were going.

20

SOME OF THE CABMEN IN LONDON HAD BEGUN to recognize me as well as my employer. Barker knew the importance of getting about quickly and tipped lavishly or, rather, had me do it for him. When we stepped out onto the curb, they moved toward us like the goldfish in Barker's pond when he fed them.

"Regent Street."

We climbed in, and the cab made its way to the busy traffic of the West End.

The Café Royal is the most prominent building in Regent Street. It is a coffeehouse for artists and French expatriates and also where the Honorable Pollock Forbes could generally be found holding court. Forbes was one of Barker's watchers, but I also knew he was the son of a Scottish lord and considered the upper classes to be his particular domain. I would not exactly call him a detective, but he investigated cases for them and made problems go away. He gave a great show of being a dilettante and an aesthete, but the delicate coughs he gave were not an affectation. Forbes was a consumptive.

Our case was focused in the East End, but had several connections to the aristocracy. I'd had a set-to with Palmister Clay and been threatened by his father, Lord Hesketh. Beatrice Potter's father was a wealthy man, and even Rose Carrick's husband, Stephen, came from a nouveau riche family. It was enough, I supposed, to consult with Forbes, who had an encyclopedic knowledge of every noble in the city.

We pulled up at the Royal and went in. I'd like to think I fit in at the café; it was full of young, artistic fellows like myself. Barker was like a pebble in a fine machine, however. He stuck out like Shakespeare's Caliban or Dickens's Magwitch. He did not belong, but he tried to be subtle. Whenever we entered, he made a show of not looking for Pollock Forbes, knowing the fellow would eventually find him.

We ordered mocha coffees, a house specialty, and a few minutes later Forbes appeared at our elbows. He is a slight fellow, whose hair always looks carefully tousled. He slid into the chair across from Barker and set down a box covered in alligator skin.

"Might I interest you gentlemen in dominoes?" he asked, opening the box. It contained a set of ivory tiles, the pips of inlaid coral.

"I have not come to play games," Barker said pointedly, but after Forbes had got them all facedown on the table and moved them about, he began picking his own.

"That's odd," Forbes went on. "I was about to ask you what game you have been playing."

"I've received some notes. Poems, really, from a man calling himself Mr. Miacca," Barker said, putting down the first tile.

"Mmm," Forbes said, pouncing on it with one of his own.

"You don't sound surprised."

"The Yard has a half dozen of them. You don't suppose Mr. Miacca sent a note to you first, do you? He's been trying to draw attention to himself for some time."

"I'd like to see those notes."

"I'm sorry," I interjected. "I'm a trifle confused. How are you privy to Scotland Yard information?"

Barker looked at Forbes, who pursed his lips in false concentration.

"Let us say," my employer explained, "that many aristocrats belong to a certain benevolent organization and that because the London Metropolitan Police Force has no trade union as such, most constables and inspectors are junior members of that same organization. It is not unusual, then, that information or support is shared by both."

I was about to ask what organization he meant, but it was staring me in the face. Through a set of doors leading toward the back of the café was the entrance to a Masonic temple. Forbes himself had a tie tack with the Masonic symbol upon it. I thought about how Swanson seemed to be doing his best to conceal information in this investigation and how Lord Hesketh represented a group of men trying to stop a bill from being passed. It was as if a veil had been lifted. The Freemasons were involved in this case, somehow.

"I wonder," I said, trying to be as tactful as possible, "if Palmister Clay might be inclined to join such an organization."

"I doubt it very much," Forbes stated, setting down a tile, double sixes. "He's more concerned with setting up house and squandering his fortune these days. His father, on the other hand, might have an appreciation for the ancient traditions."

"There is a certain establishment in Cambridge Road," Barker said. "A well-kept mews converted to flats."

"No man is perfect, of course, and some may indulge themselves in the scant pleasures the East End provides."

"Scotland Yard might turn a blind eye to such weaknesses of the flesh," Barker said, taking up the conversation again, "but a half dozen or more dead girls is another matter entirely." He turned back to Forbes and put down another tile. "Or is it?"

"This brotherhood prefers not to mix itself in politics. Sometimes it is unavoidable, especially when both camps have moved away from the center path. If whoever savaged these poor girls should prove to be a member, whoever he is, the organization would consider it necessary to discipline him severely."

"Publicly or secretly?" Barker dared ask.

Forbes gave him a glance. "You really think a public trial is necessary?"

"I do."

"And if he is mad?"

"Then I'll see him in Colney Hatch, but it had better be for a very long time."

"Jean," Forbes turned and summoned a passing waiter, "bring me an absinthe."

We watched as he prepared his mild narcotic, lighting the green liquid with a match and then dousing it with water. Pollock Forbes drank it down, not like a man addicted to a drug but as one taking medicine to kill pain. He held a napkin to his lips as if ready to start a fit of coughing, but controlled it.

"What do you want with Palmister Clay?" he asked.

"He put me in jail."

"Ah. I'm not surprised his name has come up. He runs with a fast set, from what I've heard, despite his bride's objections. She's a pretty little thing, but rather naive."

"Who are his friends?" my employer asked.

"I don't know. I'm not holding back, I promise you. Is Clay part of the investigation? Does he have some relationship to this Miacca person?"

"We are still collecting information at this time," the Guv said. "Inspector Swanson is not as forthcoming as you have been."

"He feels you have gone over to the socialists. You haven't, have you?"

"I think it is abominable that a thirteen-year-old child can legally become a gentleman's bauble," Barker stated, "but I have not 'gone over' to them, as you say. I go as my conscience bids me, regardless of any organization, and I shall not be dictated to by anyone in the midst of an investigation."

"No one is interfering in your investigation, Cyrus," Pollock Forbes said. "Your move."

"Do not rush me." Barker picked a tile from among the others and set it down.

"Thank you. I am out."

"I have not won a game against you, yet, Pollock, but then you've been playing this for sometime. I've got another name for you."

"What is it?"

"Have you heard of a fellow named Stephen Carrick?"

"Son of the soap magnate?" Forbes asked. "I haven't heard that name in ages."

"What do you know of him?"

"He was kicked out of Oxford six or seven years ago for consorting with a fallen woman and had a row with his father, who cut him off without a cent. He's had to make it on his own ever since. I believe he's had a few rough starts and has moved about a lot. Is he in London?"

"He's got a wife and runs a photographic emporium in Bethnal Green."

"Became a tradesman, has he? I'm sure his father left him no alternative, poor chap."

That poor chap was doing better than I, I thought. By Forbes's standards, he had accomplished nothing, yet from mine, he had a wife and ran his own business.

Forbes gave a thin smile. "Would you care for another game?"

"Thank you, no."

"What is wrong? You don't care for a game where one must play by the rules?"

"Let us say I prefer games more evenly matched at the outset. You are far too clever for me."

"I doubt that, Cyrus," he said, giving a cool smile.

The waiter came and asked if we wanted another mocha, but Barker put his hand over the mouth of his cup.

When he was gone, Forbes resumed the conversation. "You are playing a dangerous game, Cyrus. You could get yourself killed making the wrong sort of enemy."

"Death has no sting for me, Pollock. I am more concerned about you. How is your health?"

"About the same. My most recent physician has warned me about the dangers of absinthe and opium smoking, and then he doses me with a treacle syrup laced with laudanum. He also thinks I should take a long voyage to a warm climate. Tahiti, perhaps, or Mexico."

"And will you?"

"Of course not. You know I cannot leave when there are important issues plaguing the nation. Stay for dinner, won't you?"

Those were the words I had been waiting to hear. We hadn't had a proper lunch. Forbes had invited us once before, but the Guv had turned him down, stating that Mac had dinner waiting. Now we were away from our residence, with nothing but the possibility of cold food from the hamper to look forward to. I missed Etienne's *pigeons sur canapés*. Surely my employer would accept a meal from one of London's foremost French restaurants?

"Some other time, Pollock," Barker said. "It does not sit well with me to sup richly when somewhere Miacca is planning more deviltry. Thomas and I are sleeping rough until this fellow is caught, and only then shall we take our ease. Besides, Thomas is in training."

Forbes read the expression on my face. "In that case, gentlemen, I wish you both good hunting."

We left Forbes gathering up his dominoes and stepped out into the street again.

"So I take it that Forbes is some sort of high rank among the Freemasons," I said. "Isn't he rather young for the position?"

"He is young, but his time is precious. An exception was made in his case. Actually, he is the leader of an order within the Freemasons, which also has a long and secret history. There's an old saying, 'Scratch a Scot and you'll find a Mason.'"

"Do you think the Masons in London know who Miacca is? Is there a chance they are helping him?"

"Like Her Majesty's government, the Masons have occasionally needed to make alliances with unsavory persons or organizations."

"Are they are shielding him, then?"

"Not necessarily, but we shouldn't expect much aid from Scotland Yard in this inquiry lad. In fact, I think we should tread lightly. There is little within the structure of English society that the Masons don't have a hand in, and the pyramid goes all the way to the top."

21

I TRIED SEVEN TIES AND THREE COLLARS BEFORE I hit upon a satisfactory combination for the evening's outing. I was out of touch with the fair sex and wanted to impress Miss Potter, who was a cut or two above me. I tied my tie with too much material on one side and then with too much on the other side, and finally got it right on the third try. I was out the door in twenty minutes, and if Miss Potter could fault the man, she could not fault his appearance.

At the Egyptian Hall, I looked about for some time before I saw her. I assumed she would be seated toward the back, where any sensible person would be at a public lecture, with the opportunity to slip out the door at the soonest possible instant, but, no. She and Miss Levy were seated near the front.

The placard announced that Vernon Lee was going to lecture on the subject of the supernatural and aesthetics. I had never heard of the fellow, but I had to congratulate him on connecting two of the most popular topics of the day. Mr. Wilde, whom I noted was in the audience, had been causing a stir in society with his own artistic discourses; while the spiritualists had been thrilling fashionable London with the claims of past lives and communication with the dead. I would sooner shoot my own foot than attend a public lecture, but this seemed slightly more tolerable than most. Then, of course, there was the company.

"Good evening, Miss Potter, Miss Levy," I said, coming up to them. "Is this seat taken?"

They unfolded like a fan in the stalls there, first Beatrice, who looked beautiful in a blue jacket and straw boater, then Amy Levy, leaning forward and fixing me with a sardonic eye. Then Zangwill beyond, waving a long-fingered hand in my direction.

"Hello, Israel," I said over the noise of the crowd. "What are you up to?"

"I'm keeping these two young ladies safe," he called back. "I heard there was a masher about. I see the rumors were not unfounded."

I sat down in the seat next to Beatrice and could not help but catch the scent of gardenia she wore. I think it is my nose that gets me in trouble most. Nothing turns my head like a fine scent.

"You came," Miss Potter said, looking pleased.

"As you see," I responded with a bow.

"I wasn't certain we could expect you."

"I am delighted to attend. I enjoyed our conversation in the zoological gardens very much."

"I hope you don't think badly of us for coming here on the day of the funeral. Amy is awfully keen to see Vernon Lee, and tonight is the only lecture. I'm afraid you must think us the most forward girls in London."

"In fact, I don't," I told her, "but then I suppose it would be better to be thought forward than backward. At least it is progressive."

Beatrice was going to respond, but suddenly Miss Levy seized her wrist and leaned forward. There was a faint flush in her cheeks.

"She's arrived!" she announced.

I wondered who she meant. Just then, a tall, thin woman mounted the platform. She wore pince-nez and her hair was cut so short that she looked mannish. She was a girl, really, not much older than we. She wore a man's collar and a black cape like a university gown. This was Vernon Lee. *Miss* Vernon Lee.

"So, what is she?" I asked Beatrice. "Socialist? Aesthetic? Medium?"

"All of them at once. She is Vernon."

Miss Lee spoke for a good hour. I recall enjoying myself, but I don't remember the substance of her speech. Perhaps it was more the company I was with. The speaker made Beatrice laugh once or twice, and I liked the sound of her laughter. *It would be easy,* I thought, *to fall under Miss Potter's spell.*

Afterward, Miss Levy was all atwitter, having had a brief moment to speak with the Amazon herself. Israel suggested an ABC tearoom, which was respectable enough for young men and women to converse freely. They agreed to accompany us, though I imagine, if pressed by their families why they were late, they would merely say that the traffic had been heavy.

As we waited for the lobby to clear, I noticed a middle-aged gentleman staring at us. He was of medium height, impeccably dressed, with gray at the temples and a monocle, looking so intently at us I thought for a minute he might be Beatrice's father. Then he noticed my stare, turned, and walked into the crowd. I debated whether to follow him, whoever he was, but didn't know what I would say. Knowing it was the quickest way to be told to mind one's own business or go to blazes, I resisted the impulse. Besides, I had ladies to attend to.

"Will you help me on with my wrap, Thomas?" Miss Potter asked.

"Certainly," I said, and all thought of the man was shelved as I settled the thin material over delicate shoulders.

We found a cab and took it to a nearby tearoom. In a very brief time, dainty saucers holding thimblefuls of coffee were brought out, along with cream and sugar, which I noticed the ladies partook of liberally.

"What did you think of this evening's speaker, Mr. Llewelyn?" Miss Levy asked.

"She was certainly . . ." *What?* I thought. *Abstruse? Bizarre?* "Thought provoking."

"Miss Lee is a visionary," Israel stated. "She sees things as they should be, as they must be. Dare I say, as they shall be?"

I knew Israel well. He was quoting someone, himself perhaps, his own column the following morning, which no doubt he had already written before attending the lecture. Zangwill knows who to flatter and when.

"I must say," Amy Levy put in, "that you are quite a surprise as a detective, Mr. Llewelyn. I thought you all had shoes the size of boats and were carved out of granite, like your Mr. Barker."

"I hadn't noticed his shoes before, Miss Levy, but I can attest to the granite."

"So, do you really think he shall find Gwendolyn's killer?" she pressed.

"If anyone can, Mr. Barker can," I said. "Did you know Miss DeVere well?"

"Oh, yes. I was sometimes left to entertain her while her mother was occupied with her duties."

"That must have been somewhat demeaning, considering that you volunteer often while she only comes occasionally. I'm sure you have duties of your own."

"He is astute," she said to Beatrice Potter. "Yes, Hypatia was given preferential treatment, being the wife of a major."

"So, you two ladies are best placed to answer a question I have, and you must be truthful. What kind of child was Gwendolyn DeVere?"

The women locked eyes with each other for a moment. It was Beatrice who spoke, and she did it cautiously. "Miss DeVere came from a very good home and was inclined to be proud."

"What Beatrice means," Miss Levy explained, "is that she was something of a brat. Don't give me that look, Beatrice. You know it's true. She resented being dragged into the East End. Hypatia hoped to give the girl an understanding of the poor, but between my lips and your ear, she was going the other way. She shrunk before any homeless alien and complained of the smell."

"Interesting," I noted. "Did Mrs. DeVere speak of her husband much?"

"Oh, yes," Miss Levy said. "Every other sentence began with 'My Trevor,' but what she said of him didn't strike me as singularly impressive."

"It doesn't sound as if Mrs. DeVere had the ideal life she wished to present to the world," I said.

"That is hitting the nail on the head," Miss Potter replied. "She was rather high-strung. Her daughter was, too. I didn't envy the major living among such nervous females. Oh, dear! Now they are dead. I am terrible."

"No," Israel said gallantly. "You merely said what everyone is thinking."

"What do you ladies think of Miss Hill? Is she a competent directress?"

"Most certainly," Beatrice said, sitting up in her seat.

"Why, yes, the very idea," Miss Levy added, knitting her fine dark brows together. "She is a dear. That is a typical male response."

I put up both hands in defense. "It was a question, not a statement. I am not casting aspersions upon her character, which I am certain is above reproach."

"She is very competent, and you will not find a keener mind in the East End," Beatrice added.

"I can imagine," Israel put in, "that this girl's disappearance would affect the charity negatively, especially if some connection is made to it."

"So far, Octavia has been able to keep the details out of the newspapers, but Stead came into the office this morning and I think the two of them had words. He was upset because she hadn't told him."

"They know each other, then," I said.

"Oh, of course," Miss Levy replied. "We're all Fabians. It's a socialist organization. We're working to create reform."

"All of you?" I asked, looking across the table at Israel.

He suddenly grew quite interested in what was going on in the kitchen.

"So," I commented, "my best friend is a socialist and has neglected to tell me."

"You know me," Israel said, trying to make a joke of it. "A man of mystery."

I looked at him carefully. Sometimes even one's best friends have things about them they'd rather one didn't find out.

"How long has Dr. Fitzhugh been working at the C.O.S.?" I asked, changing the subject tactfully.

"Five or six months now," Miss Levy answered.

"And what kind of fellow is he?" I prompted. "What opinion have you formed?"

Both girls looked at each other then, and Beatrice shrugged slightly.

"He keeps to himself," Amy Levy said. "He's a rather diffident fellow. He seems to carry an air of tragedy about him. I'd even say shame. He'll hardly talk to us, which is rather strange. Being unwed and a rising young surgeon, one would think he'd be glad to make our acquaintance."

"It's very important for a young doctor to marry," Beatrice added. "It gives him respectability. No woman would visit a physician who wasn't married."

"He is not unattractive," I noted.

"He needs to shave his beard or grow it out more," Miss Levy stated. "And he needs to be more cheerful and far less furtive."

"I see."

"So, Mr. Llewelyn," she continued, resting her forearms on the table and leaning forward, so that the light from the candle was reflected in her black eyes. "You must tell us, are we suspects?"

"Of course," I answered.

Both girls smiled. Perhaps it was a delicious feeling to be suspected as a criminal when one knows one is innocent, though having been in such a circumstance, I can state quite the opposite. I remembered Lord Hesketh's assertion that the socialists might have sacrificed the girl in order to bring attention to the white slave trade. If that were true, what exactly had happened? How had she gotten into Miacca's hands?

"Even me?" Zangwill asked. "I'm a suspect, too?"

"Even you, Israel. Mr. Barker casts a wide net. So what do you think of Rose Carrick?"

"She is a good worker. She and her husband, Stephen, make an odd pair, however. They're like mismatched bookends."

"Stephen comes from a merchant family," Miss Potter said. "I believe they make soap—Carrick's Fine Glycerine Soap or something like that. Rose is a bailiff's daughter. When they met, they fell in love on the spot, to hear her tell it. Stephen's parents didn't approve, of course. They threatened to disinherit him; he stood up to them; and when the smoke cleared, he was left without a penny, never to darken the Carrick door again."

"Tragic," Zangwill said.

"Yes, but I don't believe it at all," Amy Levy said. "We're only getting Rose's side of the story. I wonder what old Mr. and Mrs. Carrick have to say about the events."

"It cannot be easy to keep company with someone of a different class," Beatrice said, and it seemed to me she was trying hard not to look my way.

"Does Stead come often to the C.O.S.?" I asked, casting about for something more to ask.

"Just occasionally," Miss Levy replied. "He and Miss Hill have worked on many campaigns together and are old friends."

"I hear the most disparate things about him. Some call him a saint and others wish to tar and feather him."

"He has that effect on people," Beatrice said. "He'll either win you to his cause, which changes day to day, or make an enemy of you. I think he was born in the wrong century. He would have preferred living as an apostle in the late first century, winning Rome or Corinth to Christ at great danger to himself."

The proprietor of the tearoom kept the ladies' cups replenished. I was almost about to tell him to join the conversation or leave. Unfortunately, I should have been paying more attention to Miss Potter and Miss Levy. I let them slip through my fingers.

"We should go," Miss Levy said to Beatrice. "Your papa will wonder what is keeping you."

"Yes, of course. You are right."

"Unless," Amy Levy said, "you are not done questioning us, Mr. Llewelyn. Would you prefer to escort us to Scotland Yard and clap us in irons, perhaps?"

"It is a thought," I said, rising from my seat. "Perhaps I shall hold it in reserve for another time."

We saw the two young ladies into the street and were able to hail a passing cab.

Beatrice Potter held out a gloved hand to me. "Thank you for coming to the lecture, Mr. Llewelyn. It was good of you to remember."

"Not at all," I answered, helping her into the cab. When she let go of my hand, there was a folded slip of paper in it, which I quickly thrust into my pocket.

Israel and I watched the hansom roll away. I turned and looked at my friend. "So, what did you really think of tonight's lecture? I want your true opinion, not the one for publication."

"My foot fell asleep halfway through that interminable lecture. I have never been envious of my own foot before."

"Ah, but, Israel," I said as we put on our gloves and raised our sticks for another cab, "it is the price one pays for female companionship."

22

THE NEXT MORNING WE WERE OUT EARLY, FOR Barker wanted to investigate the addresses Beatrice Potter had tracked down for us at the Charity Organization Society. She was more than the charming companion of the evening before.

"The first," Barker said, "was a girl named Ruth Scoggins, adopted by Mr. and Mrs. Alfred Dodsworth of Twenty-two Saint Stephen's Road. If we hurry, we might catch him."

For once, luck was with us. Our knock upon the door of number 22 brought a large, uncouth man to the door, a serviette tucked into his shirt and his mouth still full.

"Wotcher want?" he demanded, still chewing his breakfast.

"To speak with you and your wife, Mr. Dodsworth, upon a very serious matter, the murder of your adopted daughter."

The man swallowed, perhaps a trifle too quickly. He coughed several times. "Police?" he finally choked out.

"My name is Cyrus Barker. We are private enquiry agents, hired by another parent who lost a child."

"Stay 'ere," he said. "I'll arsk the missus. She weren't expecting company."

We waited on the doorstep a good five minutes before the door opened and the woman of the house ushered us in. She looked like him, perhaps because married couples, through living together, take on the same shape and mannerisms. Mrs. Dodsworth was round and buxom and unkempt, but I suspected she had a good heart. She drew us into the kitchen that smelled of pie crust and almost belligerently tried to feed us. It took several protests and the acceptance of a cup of tea each before she relented and we were able to get to the matter at hand.

"It is no longer a secret that there is a man in the area that has been taking young girls and killing them," my employer said. "I'm afraid your daughter was one of them. Scotland Yard has withheld the names of some of them from us, and yours was the first we uncovered. Would you be able to speak about it? It's possible that even the most wee bit of information might offer a clue that will help us."

Dodsworth looked at his wife and after she nodded, he did the same.

"It were a bad experience, sirs, I can tell you," the man said. "She was a tough nut, was our Ruthie, and it came as no surprise she came to a bad end. Emmy and me, sir, we was never blessed with little ones, and one day she says, 'Let's go to the Poplar Orphanage and see about adopting a girl.' She gets lonely when I'm at work, you see, and a girl would liven up the place. We went there, expecting to get a child of five or six, but Emmy clapped eye upon ten-year-old Ruthie and that was it. She wouldn't be happy until Ruthie was home in our kitchen. She had the face of an angel, but the devil of a time during her early days. Blackguard of a father beat and half starved her. She walked to London all the way from Bristol, I 'ear, after he died o' drink. Came to the orphanage by way of the Charity Organization Society."

He sipped noisily from his cup. His wife, standing by the sink, had kneaded her apron in a bunch and was sniffing.

"It weren't hard to adopt her. Most don't want the older children 'cept as farm workers. Within a few days we had her in this very kitchen and Emmy promising to make her all manner of dresses. But the child were distant like and distrustful, not that I blame her. She weren't in the house a fortnight 'fore she slipped anchor and took the best Sunday china with her."

"She didn't mean to do it," Mrs. Dodsworth explained. "She weren't happy and needed money to live on."

"Now, don't take on, Emmy, in front o' the nice gentlemen."

"Did you ever see her again?" my employer asked.

"I should say I did, and a sorry sight it was. I was coming home from the 'bacconist with a new twist one day, when I all but run into her in Cambridge Road, all dressed up like a dollymop with a swell on her arm. I laid into her, I can tell you, for breaking my Em's heart. Almost got into it with her fancy man, as well, I were that angry.

"Didn't see her after that, not alive, anyway. Three months later the River Police called me in to identify the body. A sorrier sight I've never seen and ne'er shall again. Her face, well, I'd rather not describe it, with Emmy in the room."

Mrs. Dodsworth was crying now but doing it soundlessly. *This poor couple,* I thought. *They didn't deserve such grief.*

"So, that's it, then. We decided we ain't gonner adopt no more childrens. We let ourselves open and that were the consequence. We was happy before, weren't we, Em? And we'll be happy again, I reckon. Now, if you gentlemen don't mind, I've got to get to work."

"This man Ruth was with," I spoke up. "Was he blond, with a pointed chin?"

"No, young man," Mr. Dodsworth replied. "Dark fella, with a beard, not much above your own age."

"Thank you, sir, for being so forthcoming. We regret any distress we may have caused. Come, Thomas."

The second couple we visited was the Goldsteins. Their story began differently, but ended the same. Zinnah Goldstein was their own daughter, and they had high hopes for her future, until she was fourteen and took up with a young Irishman, despite their objections. She would not listen to her parents, and when he finally threw her over, she no longer cared for her reputation or her religion. The rabbi of Bevis Marks tried to forge a reconciliation, but before that could happen, she disappeared. It was the opinion of the Goldsteins that Zinnah threw herself off London Bridge. Sad as it was, it was more respectable a death than being murdered. Barker did not attempt to change their mind, even after learning the Goldsteins had come to the area through the C.O.S.

Alice Childers of Stepney had a penchant for dipping pockets. Her father, a former sailor, tossed her out to fend for herself. She'd been found in the river missing one ear. She'd once come to the C.O.S. to seek help after her father beat her.

Fanny Rice was thrown out by her parents, when she was found to be with child at aged twelve. The charity helped her through the baby's birth, brief life, and death. Fanny had become a Whitechapel prostitute but eventually went missing. Her parents learned about her from the local constable, who read it on her police record.

Finally, Lizzy Gilbert, the last name on the list, was a good girl, her parents maintained, and would not hear otherwise. We were obliged to ask a neighbor about her. The girl, as it turned out, was given freedom to act as she pleased, and she did. She also had a police record at the tender age of thirteen.

Afterward, we were seated at a table in a public house called the Bread and Treacle, overlooking the Thames. Barker was finishing a plate of fried potatoes and egg. As with most meals, he pushed everything together. I prefer space between my food.

"Impressions?" Barker asked, patting his pockets for his tobacco pouch.

"Mine?" I foundered for a moment. "Well, sir, either accidentally or intentionally, they all are linked to the C.O.S."

"We should continue to consider the connection between it and Mr. Miacca," the Guv replied.

"He seems to hover over it like a malevolent spirit."

"Apt, if a trifle flowery," Barker said around the mouthpiece of his pipe. "Can you picture him putting gifts on the windowsills of good children in the area?"

"Yes, and punishing those like Ruth Scoggins."

"It is not true, however, that all of Miacca's victims were kept women. Gwendolyn DeVere certainly was not. I would think that while they are valuable mistresses they are safe, but once discarded by their patrons, they become candidates for Miacca's attention."

I looked at Barker, knowing some connection had just occurred in his brain.

"Blast!" he bellowed, shocking everyone in the room. He pulled a letter out of his pocket and opened it so quickly it ripped. It was Miacca's last poem.

"What is it?"

"He's toying with us."

"Sir!" the manager said, coming to our table. "I must ask you to modulate your voice or leave."

"Pay the man, lad," my employer said, rising. "We've stayed here too long as it is."

I paid him and followed the Guv outside. "What is it?" I asked. "Show me."

"Look here," he said. "'I'm going on a killing spree.' Do you see how the 'a' is out of place here. It's too close to the word 'on.' Miacca is speaking of Ona Bellovich."

23

―――∽⎰⎱∾―――

"ONA BELLOVICH," I REPEATED IN HORROR.
"But she's a good child. Everyone at the charity says so."

"Not by Miacca's standards, lad. She helped Gwendolyn
DeVere escape and then sold her clothes. That would be
enough to merit punishment in his book. We must go now. I
just pray we are not too late."

We squeezed our way through the narrow alleys until
we came into Green Street. There were few cabs in Bethnal
Green at this hour, but neither was there any decorum to
uphold. Barker turned and began to run. I could do no
more than follow as best I could.

We made our way to the tenement in Cheshire Street
and plunged into it. The corridors were filled with loungers,
most of them smoking or talking. Barker pushed his way
through like a whaling ship breaking through Arctic ice.
The Belloviches' door was open. If I had any doubts the
child was really gone, they fled now.

Svetlana Bellovich was seated at the table with a look of
stark tragedy on her face. Her kerchief was off, her black
hair wild and uncombed. Within a few hours fear and grief

had etched circles under her eyes, and yet there was a grace to her grief that I believe Hypatia DeVere had not possessed. Tears poured down her face, but she sat rigid in her chair with her hands in her lap.

She looked up as Barker came toward her, and I wondered what he would do. He was not a comforting sort and always avoided emotion in others. He bent down and spoke quietly in her ear. After a moment, she rose from her chair and reached for him, clutching his lapels. In a shrill voice, she responded vehemently, and then my employer nodded and gently removed her hands. Then he turned, and the two of us quitted the room. I had misgivings about what had just occurred, but waited until we were in the street again before I voiced them.

"You promised her, didn't you, sir?" I asked. "You promised you would bring her daughter back alive."

"Aye," came the impassive response.

"But you've warned me about making promises I was not sure I could keep."

"I know, lad," he said.

"You cannot guarantee the girl's safety," I pointed out.

"No," he replied, swinging his cane as he walked. "I can only pledge that I will give my life, if necessary, to stop that monster from harming her. I have but one assurance."

"What is that?"

"His pattern. At one point, he keeps his victims drugged. It's likely they undergo some sort of ceremony or ritual. Then I suspect almost immediately afterward, his lusts become uncontrollable and he violates and murders them. Finally, sated, he clips off an extremity as a souvenir and discards the bodies, probably in a different place each time. He might even carry them in a sack. A young woman is generally small and light. Since the bodies have always been found on a Saturday or Sunday, the ceremony is probably held on a Friday, and this is but Thursday."

"Are we going anywhere in particular, sir?" I asked.

"Of course. We're not walking for our health. I am looking for the last place Miacca was seen. The child, Esme, said she met him in Collingwood Street."

We headed south in the direction of the Jew's burial ground. Slowly, we inspected each alley. Most were doorless or featured lodgings that were too well lit or cheerful for Miacca's purposes, that is, until we came to the foot of the street, not far from Mile End Road, and found one that was narrow, dark, and crooked, perfect for the archfiend's purposes. We passed into it and walked until we came to a heavily shadowed doorway with an overhanging eave. Barker stepped forward and seized a few boards that had been fastened across the door, rending them off the frame.

"They were screwed in," he said, lighting a vesta, "and the brass heads are still new."

"No tarnish on them," I noted, shaking my head.

He blew out the match and dug in his waistcoat pocket. He generally kept a skeleton key there.

"Keep an eye out," he ordered, going to work on the lock.

"You're sure this is his lair?" I asked.

"It's either his, or it's deserted, if these boards are any indication."

He worked on the lock for a few minutes before the door opened soundlessly in his hands.

"The hinges have been oiled," my employer pointed out. "People don't generally oil doors in the East End, unless they don't want something to be heard." The Guv pushed the door open with his arm against it, while I leaned over his shoulder. I got a glimpse of a dingy room with faded wallpaper and a few pieces of furniture. Then there was a loud pop, and suddenly my hat was knocked from my head.

"Damn and blast," Barker growled. "You're bleeding."

My knees started to quiver, and the top of my head suddenly went cold. I could feel the blood seeping through my hair.

"Who—" I began, but Barker held up his hand.

"Nobody. It is a device, set to go off when the door was opened. Come here."

Barker pulled a handkerchief from his pocket and laid it atop my head. "Hold it there," he told me. "'Tis but a scratch. It is fortunate you're such a wee lad, but then the bullet wasn't meant for you, but Swanson or me. It would have caught either of us square in the face."

I was only half listening, because I was staring at the engine that had tried to part my hair. It stood in the middle of the room, a vertical mass of planks and rusty gears, which cradled an old hunting rifle, still smoking and filling the room with the scent of gunpowder. There was a long dowel of wood projecting from it, with a tennis ball at the end. When the edge of the door struck the ball, it set off the mechanism that pulled the trigger. Miacca had planned to blow off the head of whoever first walked in here, and it was very nearly my own.

"My hat," I said, bending down with one hand while clamping the Guv's handkerchief to my head. I picked up my ruined bowler. There was a neat hole almost dead center in the front and back. I didn't know if it was training or providence that had told Barker to push the door open while standing at the side of the doorway, but I felt a perfect donkey standing there in the middle like a target. Had I been five foot six instead of five foot four, I'd have been lying half out in the alleyway, on my way to the hereafter.

"Bolted," Barker said, looking about. The room contained a metal bedstead with rumpled sheets, a table and two chairs, the infernal contraption, and a fireplace. There was a layer of fine soot over everything, not much, just enough to say Miacca had not been here in days. Naturally, our eyes were on the mechanism.

"Ingenious," Barker said, moving the dowel back and forth. It had a metal cup at the end of a rod, with a piston-like piece attached to the trigger. They looked like manufactured parts, the kind one could find at an ironmonger's. It was clever, in an evil, malignant sort of way.

"Sir," I said. Something had caught my eye. A meerschaum pipe lay upon the table. Not Barker's traveling pipe, which was now wrapped in the sealskin pouch in his pocket, but the new one from his office smoking cabinet, carved into a likeness of General Gordon. The only other item on the table was a box of vestas. Miacca was telling us he could go wherever he wished and that the instrument that just blew off my hat could as easily have blown off the head of our clerk, Jenkins. Barker snatched the pipe from the desk and thrust it into his pocket.

While Barker inspected the room, I dared lift his handkerchief from the top of my head. There is always something horrifying about looking at one's own blood, scarlet against the white of a handkerchief. The Guv was right, however; I had merely been nicked and the blood had already begun to coagulate. I had cheated death once more.

"Here's where the jar lay," my employer said, pointing toward a spot on the mantel. Then he crossed to the bed and drew back the sheets. "A child has been kept here, by the looks of it. I assume it was Miss DeVere."

"Was she sensible at any time, do you suppose, sir?" I asked. "She was drugged with chloroform or laudanum."

"It cannot be easy to regulate drugs in an unwilling child. I am afraid she must have been awake for part of her time here."

"Poor girl," I said. There are times when words are so feeble as to be meaningless.

Barker lifted the mattress and began to look under it.

"What are you doing, sir?"

"I'm looking for a note. It is not like Miacca to be silent."

He crossed to the door and closed it. As he predicted, there was the message, written in chalk across the back.

The man who ducks my ventilation
Deserves to read this small notation,
Whichever bloodhound he might be.
But I still say you can't catch me.

The girl I trussed up on this bed
Is surely now long gone and dead.
And you, the brave and valiant tracker,

Are far too late.
Mr. Miacca.

Barker fished in his waistcoat pocket and retrieved a small whistle with the word "Metropolitan" engraved across it and handed it to me.

"Lad, step into Collingwood Street and blow this until a constable arrives."

I did and was almost dizzy by the time a constable finally pushed his way through the gathering crowd. Nothing attracts attention like the screech of a policeman's whistle: the street was choked with people asking me questions about my head. The Guv had to bar the door with his arm, or the room would have filled with the curious and the bored, looking for something to excite their interest.

It took about half an hour for Inspector Swanson to arrive. He posted two constables outside to keep the rabble at bay and closed the door behind him.

Donald Swanson was a smart fellow, a "canny" sort, in Barker's terms, and not a talkative man. He silently inspected the contraption in the center of the room, the message left by the killer, and the bed where Miacca's victims once lay. He even noticed the ring of dust on the mantelpiece. Then, he examined the table, without touching the vestas. Finally, he looked at the layer of soot on the table. "What was here?" he asked.

The Guv pulled the pipe from his pocket and showed it to him.

"Gordon," the inspector noted. "I would wash that in spirits if I were you. I wonder if it's possible to poison a pipe." He got down on his knees and very gently opened the box of matches, as if it would explode or contained a deadly spider, but no. It was only vestas.

"Shall we compare notes now?" my employer asked.

Swanson shook his head. "No, but if you wish, when this is all over, I'll buy you a dram at the Red Lion and tell you as much as I dare."

"I couldn't live with the conditions you work under, Donald," Barker said, "not for all the tea in Canton."

"That's all right," Swanson said with a grim smile. "We would not have you."

Barker grinned as well.

"Clear out, now," the inspector said, pointing his thumb over his shoulder toward the door. "I'd ask you how you came to find this wretched lair, but you'd only want to trade it for a glimpse of the cards in my hand. We'll talk later."

"It's just as well," came the reply. "We have an urgent appointment."

We left Swanson in charge of the room and headed back toward Green Street, pushing our way through the crowded alleyway.

"What urgent appointment do we have?" I asked, wondering if he had made it up to make us sound more professional.

"That bullet must have rattled you worse than I thought," Barker said. "Have you forgotten you shall be stepping into the ring with Palmister Clay in an hour?"

24

We ARRIVED IN CHENEY STREET IN SCARCE enough time to begin the match. I was still anxious to conclude my personal matter against Clay, but the combination of Ona Bellovich's disappearance and the bullet that had grazed me was giving me a headache. I wanted to get the fight over with once and for all, even if I took a drubbing.

The German Gymnasium in King's Cross was the cleanest athletic building I had ever seen. Where was that stale odor of male perspiration, wet towels, and old leather one always found in such establishments? Leave it to the Germans to replace it with bleach and carbolic.

Our fight, I would even say our feud, was not publicized; but a number of men had come to see the match anyway, perhaps a result of Clay's bragging. Though this was an establishment for amateurs and betting was forbidden, it was not difficult to spot the bet takers in the audience.

In the dressing room, I found that Barker had provided an outfit for me: a pair of silk drawers in black, a white cotton singlet, and a pair of rubber gymnasium shoes. Only the gloves were old.

"The softer they are, the harder they'll feel against Clay's face when you put them there," Barker explained.

"I—I don't know what to say. Thank you, sir."

Barker shrugged it off. Being thanked always made him uncomfortable. "We can't have you in shabby togs. It makes the agency look second-rate."

I felt more confident once I'd changed. Looking at myself in a full-length mirror, I could say I looked like a boxer, if only a bantamweight. I was clean-limbed, with no fat on my frame; and almost two years of training under Barker had packed a layer of muscle across my arms and chest. I was in the best physical condition I had ever been, and I prayed it would be enough.

Stepping into the ring, I began to warm up, trying to project an air of confidence. I wanted the anonymous men standing about to think I was a serious fighter, because if they were confident, perhaps it might rub off on me. Though it was far too late to say it, particularly after I'd wished so hard for this fight, I was beginning to have my doubts.

Clay came in just then, looking as superior as ever. I noticed he'd put on a stone or two since I'd known him at university, and he showed signs of dissipation. Too many rich meals, late-night drinking bouts, and keeping up with the needs of two women told in his somewhat baggy eyes and slight paunch. I'd like to say we were evenly matched, but his arms were still much longer than mine, and his many supporters in the audience told me that he still boxed here.

This was no prizefight and there was little fanfare once we entered the ring. The referee—a short, pugnacious-looking older man with side-whiskers and a truculent manner—called us together brusquely. He looked familiar, and then I realized why. Our referee was the Marquis of Queensberry himself, creator of the famous rules of boxing. He had to be a crony of Lord Hesketh, I wagered. I looked through the crowd and saw his lordship smoking a cigar at the back, speaking with a haughty fellow with curling hair and a patrician nose. The marquis told us he expected a fair fight, and we agreed and went to our corners. Cyrus Barker was in mine, I was glad to see, with a stool, a towel, and a bottle of water. He stood behind the post in his shirtsleeves, though he still looked dapper in his waistcoat. When I reached him, he turned me and whispered last-minute instructions.

"Remember, lad, let him come to you. Change positions often, left to right. Stay on the balls of your feet, and when you hit, hit cleanly and put your shoulder behind it. Throw off any clinches. Go, and Godspeed."

At the bell, I dashed out of my corner. Clay took advantage of his longer reach early, jabbing first and following up with solid punches. I danced out of the way of most and caught him a jab once or twice. He gave me one full in the stomach; but in the next clinch, I caught him a good one in the ribs. We began to sweat though we were scarcely a minute into the fight.

"I'll see you in the gutter yet," he muttered under his breath.

"Only if you're looking up," I told him.

At that moment, I would have given even odds, but I was being optimistic. He hooked me suddenly, catching me on the side of the chin, and I felt something give in the back of my head. I still battled it out, but I felt wobbly and there was a ringing in my ears.

I switched positions, leading with my right fist, but I couldn't remember all the things Barker had told me. *I couldn't possibly lose,* I told myself as we pummeled each other with a flurry of ineffectual blows. *It wouldn't be fair or just.* But as Barker has told me on numerous occasions, don't expect fairness or justice on this side of the grave; that is what the other side is for.

Clay kept poking me with his long stinging left, but it was slowing. I batted it out of the way several times; but whenever I stepped under it for a volley of my own, there was his right, quicker and more lethal, a coiled serpent waiting to strike.

The bell sounded, and Barker shoved the stool between the ropes. I could hardly believe that only three minutes had sped by. I'd gotten in only one really clean punch, yet I had fared well enough. However, when I moved my head, I felt as if there were gravel in the base of my skull. All the while, Barker was issuing more instructions in my ear.

"Don't telegraph your punches, lad. He can see them coming. Fire them off cleanly. When you get under his guard, hook him or give him the uppercut."

"His right, sir," I said, gasping for air. "It's good."

"Redirect it, then. Take it on the shoulder or the elbow. Then go for his stomach. Keep dancing; you'll soon wear him out. You're in better condition than he. Don't swallow this."

He put the bottle to my mouth. I swirled the water about and spat it over the ropes. Then the bell rang and I charged in again.

Palmister Clay was more confident now on the strength of the one good punch he'd gotten to my chin. I, on the other hand, was determined to shorten the odds, so there was a furious exchange of punches that we each absorbed. It was a typical amateur bout, two young men trying to prove themselves, throwing punches that landed nowhere. That is, until near the end of the round when I stepped under and gave him a smart uppercut that everyone saw. Though Clay was not rocked by it, there was an appreciative sound from the crowd.

Then disaster struck. Clay got in another jab, and when I blocked it, he came in with a right that opened up my left brow. A split brow is the end of many a fight, and I feared this was going to be one of them. Clay was the first to draw blood. Suddenly, the audience, the same men who had been cheering me on not a minute before, became a pack of baying hounds. I was now their prey.

My opponent redoubled his efforts, but I was more inconvenienced by the trickle of blood than harmed. I began an assault of my own to show him how much fight he was still facing when the bell rang again.

There were no instructions this time. A doctor climbed up into my corner and applied a hasty sticking plaster, while Barker pinched the cut to staunch the blood. My heart was pumping too hard to notice or care about the pain. I kept telling myself that this was for Jenny. Barker was mopping my face as the bell rang, and I launched out into the ring again.

Something was different about this round. My arms and legs felt sluggish, as if weights had been attached to them, and I was dizzy. Blast it, it was only a little cut. The one I had from Miacca's bullet was longer. I launched a hook at Clay's odious head, but he parried it easily, and his first jab knocked the new plaster off. What blood was not going down into my eye, I actually saw spraying outward in droplets. The next I knew I was against the ropes, he was assaulting my stomach, and I could do little to prevent him beyond guarding my head with my forearms. I felt my knees buckle and saw the marquis waving Clay away. He was counting me out, but it sounded like he was in the next room. I've been called pigheaded before, and that day was no exception. I pushed myself back onto my legs and lurched toward him again. I planned to get him with a classic combination of jab-jab-punch, when suddenly Clay's glove came over mine and downward, a kind of reverse uppercut that landed on my chin. The next I knew, I was flat on the canvas, my head ringing. Cheers went up, and there was scattered applause. Clay had won. As it turned out, I hadn't even been conscious during the ten count. The marquis held Clay's arm aloft while his father, Lord Hesketh, climbed into the ring, a satisfied smirk on his face. Barker lifted me up by the shoulders and seated me on the stool a final time.

So that was it, I thought. *I'd lost. There would be no punishment for what Palmister Clay had done to Jenny and me, no retribution for the final days we never had together, as she choked out her life in a dilapidated tenement.* The knowledge was as bitter and caustic as a draught from the Lake of Fire itself.

Barker and the physician crowded over me, blocking my vision of Clay's triumph. I felt the tug of the needle and thread as my brow was stitched. The ring was full of gentlemen, standing about discussing the match dispassionately, as if I weren't there. I wanted to crawl off somewhere and die. I wanted to go home and lick my wounds, not to the warehouse, not even to my room in Newington, but to Wales.

"Gentlemen!" Barker's voice bellowed above me. I lifted my head as best I could and looked at him. He had stepped up on the outside of the corner, a foot on either side of the pole, his knees balanced against the ropes. "Gentlemen! A challenge! We demand a rematch!"

I looked at the crowd in front of me. Everyone was looking at the Guv as if he were out of his mind. I had just been outclassed, and handily. To put us together in the ring a second time seemed superfluous. The better man had already proven himself.

"What is your challenge?" Hesketh demanded. "That your boy here shall stand within the next half hour?"

That brought a rough chuckle from the crowd. I must have been a sight. Momentarily, I wanted a mirror, then thought better of it.

"I demand a rematch, sir," Barker growled. "And I shall cover all bets myself."

25

⚜

"**I** SHALL COVER ALL BETS," HE REPEATED, "AT
ten to one odds"

I frowned, or would have if my brow wasn't filled with
waxed cotton thread and covered with fresh plaster. I
couldn't believe my ears. Perhaps I was hallucinating. I was
in no condition to box soon, if ever, and Barker never bet.
He thought it wrong for a gentleman to make wagers of
any kind. And what odds! Did he think I could improve
enough to beat Clay in a month?

The men parted and Clay came closer. He wore a blue-
and-red-striped silk robe over his shoulders and looked as
fresh as if he'd been only skipping rope. His father, I noticed, was smiling at me in a condescending way as he came
forward.

"You think your boy shall be up to it?" Hesketh asked.

"Certainly," Barker said.

"Very well," his lordship said, after his son nodded confi-
dently back at him. "Where and when?"

"Here and now," Barker responded.

"What?" Hesketh said with a laugh. "You're mad. Your lad's done for the night. Probably for the week."

"Do you concede the rematch, then?"

"Of course not!" Hesketh barked. "But two more rounds and your boy could be dead. You have a responsibility to look after him."

"My responsibility, your lordship, is my own affair."

"But Queensberry has left. There is no official from the boxing fraternity to referee the match."

"So much the better," Barker answered. "The gloves are off this time, gentlemen. Anything goes, no holds barred, unless, of course, your boy is not up for such sport."

Hesketh looked about for a second. He was considering whether to decline the rematch. After all, Clay was on top at the moment, and he knew not what dirty tricks Barker might have taught me. But no matter what the conditions, it is bad form to turn down a challenger; and by doing so he would deny the men standing there, many of whom were friends and influential men, an opportunity for what they saw to be easy money.

"Very well," he said at last. "We accept the challenge. But who shall referee?"

"The choice is yours, sir."

Hesketh called up the crony with whom he'd been talking to be referee, and the ring began to clear. Barker climbed down, and I pushed myself up into a standing position. I accepted the fact that, like a gladiator, I was being sent back into the ring no matter how much pain I was in. The Guv climbed between the ropes and, seizing one of my gloves, unlaced it.

"I have trained you now, Thomas Llewelyn, for almost a

year and a half. You were at a disadvantage going into this match with your hands in these mitts, but they are now coming off. You came here to seek revenge today—don't attempt to deny it—and you failed. It may be wrong of me, but I am giving you a second chance. You can trounce this popinjay, if you remember all that I have taught you. Otherwise, I shall be several hundred pounds poorer. If you don't win this match, you might as well pack your bag and go back to Wales, for your name shall be ruined in London for years to come. Nothing you can possibly do could ever repair it."

A bellow welled up out of my gut, all the anger that was still festering in my soul.

"No anger, Thomas, it does no good. Just get the work done. Are you ready?"

"Yes!"

"Remember all I've taught you, lad. Now take this man down."

We were called into the center of the ring again, and, though he had just defeated me, there was an uneasy look in Clay's eyes. Perhaps it was due to what he saw in mine. We went back into our corners and the bell rang. I turned and charged.

Clay, now gloveless, threw a left, hoping to open the cut over my eye again. I caught his wrist and twisted it, bending his entire frame downward. I caught him once or twice with kicks to the right side of his face, then thrust him into the corner and began to pummel him, not with gloves like sacks of sand, but with bare knuckles like grapeshot. I could not let the man land a punch. It was time to put the odious Palmister Clay out of commission.

Seizing his head with both hands I fell back with my

foot against his abdomen, kicking him over me into the center of the ring. Then I rolled over, took his right arm, and thrust my feet into his chest and neck, tugging on the arm for all it was worth. The limb was about to come out of the socket. Clay's only choice would be to tap the mat and accept defeat. Or so I thought.

Clay flailed his body about. He raised one of his legs and then brought it down hard on my chest. Once, twice. I had no choice but to let go. We staggered to our feet and without hesitation attacked at once. Gone were the gentlemanly arts of the British boxing fraternity.

"Form!" Barker growled from the sideline as he'd done a thousand times in our practices. I stepped into a cat stance, most of my weight on my back leg, arms curled in front of me. Clay threw a punch that I caught between my forearms for just long enough to kick him in a place the marquis had definitely excluded from his rules. I heard the men about us groan in sympathy and hoped I made a few men approach the bet takers in the room with changes in their bets.

Stepping gingerly now, Clay swung at my head with his right, the one that had caused such devastation earlier. I got out of the way this time, blocking it with my left, and caught him in the chest with a palm. An open hand is not a weapon in Western culture, but Barker taught me how effective it can be when thrust into a solar plexus. My opponent's face was now scarcely a foot from mine, and there was a look on it I had never seen before: consternation. No doubt it was the same expression he had so recently seen on mine.

My mind went back two years then, to the day he'd caught me picking up a sovereign from his mantelpiece. I hadn't actually taken it yet, but I was considering it. The coins had sat there for weeks, while my wife, Jenny, was fading away from tuberculosis, in desperate want of a doctor's attention that I could not afford. I remember the look of triumph on his face when he caught me. I'd punched him on the chin, more a reaction of nerves than an attack; but his friends had seized me, and Clay administered a beating. Now it was my turn, but the bell rang just then.

I leaned against my corner and glared at my opponent, while Barker issued orders in my ear. I was snorting like a bull and not paying much attention. I'd become an animal. The bell rang again and I burst out of the corner.

Clay got in a few blows, but I was beyond feeling them anymore. As I was not trained completely in boxing, he was not trained in how to fight against gang members or footpads. He clapped me on my injured brow, hoping to open it again, but I countered with a chop to the mastoid that felled him. I stepped away reluctantly, hoping he wouldn't get up. The referee moved forward and began to count him out. Clay was game, however, and up again at the count of three.

Clay jabbed at me again, but his arms were getting tired. I lashed out with a perfect right, an actual boxing move that caught him on the tip of his pointed chin. He stepped back, but I followed and caught him a second right on the temple. Then, as we each took one more step, I swung my left out in a perfect arc, a move I didn't think I had in me. My hand turned mid-motion, knuckles out, and I raked Clay across the nose. I watched him go down. He was out cold before he hit the canvas.

There was silence, then a cheer. It occurred to me for the first time that perhaps some of the men in the room did not care for the bullying ways of Clay *père* or *fils,* that perhaps they found the duo as odious as I. I moved back as his lordship's friend stepped in and reluctantly counted Clay out. Then he raised my sweaty arm just long enough to show I'd won, and turned back to Hesketh's side. Before I knew it, I was surrounded by men shaking my hand and pounding me on the back.

I nodded and grinned away at the men chattering in my face. My stitches had come loose and I was bleeding again, so I was led over to the doctor for more patching. Barker mopped my face with a slight smile under his brush of a mustache, like he'd known I'd win all the while.

"How'd I do, sir?" I finally asked.

"Terribly," he informed me. "Your form was sloppy and your moves erratic. It's a wonder he didn't see every move coming. But, all in all, satisfactory."

This is what counts as high praise with Cyrus Barker and I drank it in like wine. Effusiveness is not one of his qualities. It is a sign of the drubbing I'd taken that I stood still for stitches with no anesthetic. Had the doctor tried it that very morning in the warehouse, I'd have protested to high heaven.

Barker arranged with one of the well-established betting gentlemen to deliver our winnings to our offices the next day. I could no more imagine the Guv walking about with a bag full of gambling swag than I could the Archbishop of Canterbury, but I knew he hadn't done it out of the desire for money. Rather, he'd risked the loss of it for me. He'd given me the opportunity to lay to rest a ghost that had haunted me for over two years.

"Thank you, sir," I said, but the doctor took the remark for himself.

"Not at all. You'll be right as rain in a few days. Take it easy and rotate your head slowly every couple of hours or your neck muscles will seize up. You'll be black and blue and three shades of purple come morning, but I reckon you'll live."

"Come, lad," my employer said.

Barker led me back to the dressing room. My muscles were seizing up by the minute and I needed help getting into my clothes. After that, we stepped out into the blessed cool air of a July evening. The Guv helped me into a hansom and out of it again when we reached Green Street. I vaguely recall shrugging into my nightshirt before settling onto the hard, lumpy mattress and into a deep sleep.

26

I HAVE ACCEPTED THE FACT THAT, AS IT IS MY LOT in life to be Cyrus Barker's assistant, I should often wake up in some degree of pain. If I wasn't injured during a case, such as when I was nearly crucified a year and a half before or blown off a bridge, to give but two examples, then there were the occasional sessions in the basement where he attempted to teach me Chinese wrestling. If I had become a connoisseur of pain, the morning after the fight with Palmister Clay, I was treated to a feast.

I inspected my face with the aid of my shaving mirror. Overnight, my lips had swollen, as had the brow that contained the stitches. It was a whitish lump, surrounded by a ring of purple, with outlying areas in a kind of gaudy yellow. My face was sporting colors I'd never seen before, and I was amazed at how a subtle swelling here and there could make a fellow look almost unrecognizable.

Mac tsk-tsked over my face as if I were a child who had covered himself in paint. My lips seemed to belong to someone else. They did not want to quite open for the roll Mac brought for breakfast, nor did they want to completely close for the coffee that accompanied it. All my teeth felt loose, and I prayed that that would change, as young women are not attracted to toothless men, no matter what their age.

Barker had attended the fight, stayed up all night, and was ready for another day. When he saw me, one brow went up and then one side of his mustache. It is a sad day when an employer considers the sight of his employee battered and stitched to be comical.

"Perhaps it would be best if you took the morning off," he said. "I had nothing definite planned, merely to push until someone pushes back. I shall return for lunch."

He carried himself off. Mac took up his position at the window, notebook in hand, noting arrivals at the C.O.S. and suspicious persons in the area. Since I was there and he was lonely, he announced each person's arrival as if he were a footman at Buckingham Palace.

I alternated between reading Hardy and aching. I felt like a machine that had been assembled incorrectly, with half the muscles in my body pulled too tight and the other half too loose. Therefore, I did the only logical thing: I complained.

"It hurts when I move."

"Then don't move. Shouldn't you be sleeping?" Mac took his duties, in my opinion, far too seriously.

"You know very well I've been sleeping all night and I'm scheduled to sleep again this evening. Do you expect me to sleep 'round the clock?"

"It might help. Nothing is better for healing the body than sleep. Perhaps if you try sleeping, your face will stop swelling so." He directed his attention outside. "I see Dr. Fitzhugh is just getting in."

"He's a funny cove," I commented. "There he is, an unmarried man, working among marriageable girls like Miss Potter and Miss Levy, and he avoids them as if they were lepers. There's something suspicious about it."

"Perhaps not," Mac said. "It is possible he's not inclined to matrimony. My impression of him was that he's merely diffident."

"He's a bit odd."

"Just because he's not like you, with your nose in the air like a pointer after every woman's scent, you act like he's an enigma. He's only an enigma to you."

"All right, I'm sorry," I said. "I didn't mean to cast aspersions upon his good name. And as far as I'm concerned—"

Just then the door on the ground floor creaked open. Mac jumped up and rooted among his copious trunks for his shotgun. Less concerned, and far less able to move, I made certain my Webley was still tucked between the mattress and the wall.

It took a moment or two before our visitor showed himself on the stairs. Soho Vic shambled up casually in his baggy coat. His dark hair, as always, pointed in every direction, and he was rolling the end of a cigar in his mouth.

"'Allo, fatheads. Is the master about?"

"Mr. Barker is occupied at present," Mac replied frostily.

I'm perfectly fine with being referred to as "fathead" from time to time, but being a butler has given Mac exaggerated opinions of decorum. He arched his brows, and his delicate nostrils flared. It was a comfort to know someone despised Vic even more than I.

"And here I am ready to give the case into his hands. I figure with you two gents sittin' on yer backsides and hangin' on his coattails, he might need some actual help."

Mac was going to either give him a good talking to or blow his head off, either of which would have suited me, but I was curious and got a word in first.

"What do you mean, give it into his hands?"

"Don't know as I should tell you now," he replied, looking at his grimy nails as if they'd just been buffed and polished. "I've had me feelin's hurt. I feel less than welcome."

"You'll feel less than alive if you are not forthcoming with the information."

"Don't get riled. I s'pose I do owe you. You won me money last night. Twice."

It took a minute for the import of what he was saying to sink in. I was a bit slow that morning. "So you bet against me in the main bout."

"Yes, and for you in the second. You looked as if you'd finally gotten your mettle up and were ready to fight. I hadn't realized till just now that you'd boxed the entire night with your face."

"That's very humorous. You're a regular Little Tich. So, out with it. What have you got?"

"What I've got is a woman drinking herself into the soak of her life on the strength of havin' sold her daughter this morning to a bloke for five pounds outright."

"Where? When?" I asked.

"This morning, not five streets from this very spot. More important is who."

"That was my next question."

"I'll bet. Well, it was an old procuress named Jarrett who done the actual buying, but she left the mother in no doubt as to the ultimate purchaser."

"Who was it?" Mac and I said at once.

Always one to savor having someone off guard, the young street urchin pulled out a vesta and made a show of lighting the cigar, which looked as if it cost more money than all the clothing he wore put together, shoes included. He let out a mouthful of smoke into the air.

"Just William T. Stead, is all."

Mac was off his stool and I upright on the mattress, all my muscles seizing up again. "Stead!"

"That's a nice little act you two have, sayin' the same thing at the same time. Reckon you could make a killin' at the Alhambra."

"Barker needs to hear this," I said to Mac. "Perhaps I should look for him."

"He said he'd be back at lunch. The only place I can say he isn't is the Charity Organization Society."

"Which pub is she in?" I asked Soho Vic.

"She's been crawlin' since they opened the doors. Already kicked out of the Juniper Lane Gin Shop. She's holdin' court at the Rosy Crown now, and will for a while if they don't chuck her out on her straw hat, as well."

"Thanks." I tossed him a sovereign. It was Barker's standard price for information. Vic caught and pocketed it.

"Got what I came for. Ta-ta, laddies." Soho Vic trundled down the stairs, whistling the lastest music hall song.

"I'm going to kill him one of these days," I contented myself with saying.

"Not if I get there first," Mac replied. "Drat! Someone just went in and I didn't see who it was. That street arab has thrown off my records."

"I should go looking for him—the Guv, I mean. He'll

want to know this. If Stead should prove to be openly buying children in Bethnal Green, then he could quite possibly be Miacca himself. Or could he be doing it to corroborate the white slaver stories."

"That would be scandalous," Mac said. "I mean, doesn't Stead have a reputation as a reformer and a brilliant newspaperman? If this should be true . . . I mean, it's unthinkable."

"I'm not one who ascribes weaknesses to the masses," I answered. "Even great men can have their flaws. In fact, it would take a strong mind to come up with a plan even Scotland Yard and Cyrus Barker are unable to foil. I really should look for him."

"But where? He could be anywhere in the Green or even out of it. You can't just walk the area. If you go straight down Globe Road, he's liable to come in from Green Street looking for you. It's best for you to stay here. Hallo! This is interesting."

"What?" I asked, sitting up.

"Your Miss Potter is giving a gentleman a piece of her mind."

"A gentleman?"

"Yes, I think it was the one who slipped in a few minutes ago. Middle-aged fellow with a monocle."

Despite my protesting limbs, I pulled myself to the window and peered over the sill.

"My word," I said. "She's really laying in to him."

I was spying upon the poor girl, but I could not help it. She was in the midst of a strong argument with the fellow I'd seen at the Egyptian Hall. They were outside the charity building, just out of earshot, and she was shaking a finger at him and speaking animatedly. The gentleman, if I dare call him that, had his arms crossed and responded to her every now and then coolly. He was unflappable. I felt despite all her words and gestures, he was in control of the situation. What was going on? Who was this chap and what was he to her? What on earth were they arguing about?

"I suppose it's her father," Mac stated.

I'd forgotten I wasn't alone.

"No doubt he prefers she give up this socialist nonsense and come home."

"You think it nonsense?" I asked.

With a flounce, Beatrice turned and marched back into the building. This was a side of her I had not seen and did not wish to see again, not if that finger was waving in my face. The gentleman took out his watch and consulted it, then turned, raised his hat to a man passing by, and walked down Globe Road. The man to whom he had raised his hat was Cyrus Barker.

Below, the door squealed and I heard the Guv's steady tread upon the stair. He came up and stood at the top, staring at us.

"What has happened?" he asked.

"Who did you speak to in the street, sir?" I asked. "We just witnessed an argument between him and Miss Potter."

"It was quite heated," Jacob Maccabee put in.

"Was it the gentleman you saw at the Egyptian Hall?" the Guv asked.

"It was."

"That is Joseph Chamberlain, the MP, leader of the radical party."

I turned to Mac. "So much for your father theory."

"He could be a friend of the family," our factotum maintained. "Perhaps her father objects to her being in such a dangerous area and sent a family friend to make his wishes known."

"She spoke awfully heatedly to him," I argued. "That's not the way a girl usually speaks to her father's friends."

"But she's one of those women who sets propriety at naught."

"Is that all, gentlemen?" Barker asked, ending the discussion, which could have gone all day unresolved.

"No, sir," I answered. "Vic's just been here. An agent working for Mr. Stead purchased a child from her mother this morning for the princely sum of five pounds."

"That is news. If you wish to accompany me, you had better get dressed."

In the hansom that took us to Northumberland Street, Barker appeared to be off in his own private world. The actual solving of the case, the tracking down of Miacca, was Barker's doing, though I knew someday I would be required to attempt such solutions myself. Had it really been Stead all along, killing those girls and sending us taunting messages? I was content to let Barker discern the mystery.

In Northumberland Street, the Guv passed one of his agency cards to a clerk of the *Pall Mall Gazette*. After five minutes' delay, we were shown into Stead's office. The editor himself was behind his desk, which was covered in papers, messages, telegrams, rival newspapers, notes, a wrapper containing half a sandwich, and a tankard of stout. Stead did not look like a fugitive ready to leave for the Continent any time soon.

"Where is the child?" Barker demanded. "The one you purchased from her mother for five pounds."

"Ah. You mean Eliza Armstrong. Sweet girl. Yes, she and the woman who purchased her for me are on their way to Dover." He consulted his watch from his waistcoat pocket. "They should arrive in half an hour or so."

I could not believe my ears. Stead was admitting everything to us.

"And what shall become of them, then?" my employer demanded.

"Oh, the child is to be spirited to a secluded house in the French countryside owned by the Salvation Army. They are helping me in this endeavor. Won't you gentlemen have a chair?"

The Guv and I sat down.

"What you have done today will become known—" my employer said.

"Oh, I shall announce it in the *Gazette* soon. I plan a special supplement. I shall call it 'Maiden Tribute of Modern Babylon.' I'll confess everything freely."

"You shall go to jail for it," Barker warned.

"Oh, most certainly. My solicitor says I will be lucky to get less than six months. But that was not my purpose. There are easier ways to get into jail."

"You mean to force the bill raising the age of consent."

"Precisely. They'll be reading 'Maiden Tribute' from Lyme Regis to the Outer Hebrides. If that doesn't pass the bill, then London really has become Babylon, and I shall step down from the helm of this newspaper and retire."

"'Maiden Tribute,'" Barker said, frowning.

"Greek mythology, sir," I supplied. "Children in Crete

were sacrificed to appease the lusts of a monster named the Minotaur."

"You should have left London, Mr. Stead," Barker said.

"That would add fuel to the rumor that I truly was transporting Miss Armstrong for immoral purposes."

"True, but you would be out of harm's way. Is there not some other way?" Barker implored. "This is ruinous to your career."

"My constituents claim they shall support me, should this go to trial. If they do not, I should start my own journal in competition with the *Gazette* when I am a free man again. Have you any other option?"

"None, now that the machinery is in place. I should warn you that there is a group of nobles who are ready to fight against any possible bill—and I do not mean merely in the houses of Parliament. They have procured the services of a local gang. This may be dangerous for you."

"I thank you for your concern, sir, but I have already taken such a possibility into account. I expect siegelike conditions upon these offices when it is announced. To be frank, Mr. Barker, I would appreciate your support. I'm told you are a good man in a scrap."

"Those sound like Andy McClain's words. Is he involved in this?"

"Not directly," Stead answered. "He has been occupied these last few days but said I could count on him if things grew violent."

I felt bad then, having wasted McClain's time on a personal quarrel, when such large events were brewing.

"Alas, I cannot guarantee my participation," Barker said. "I am after a murderer, and that must take precedence. If I can be here, I will, but I wish you to understand that I do not believe in a socialist platform, merely in this one issue."

"Understood," Stead said, rising. The two men shook hands.

"It is another dead end, but I am pleased to take you off my list of suspects. Come, Thomas."

27

WE HAD JUST COME BACK FROM STEAD'S OFFICE. Some of the swelling had gone down in my face, but now muscles that had been silent before began to ache, and I was glad for a few moments rest. Barker was halfway through one of his exercises in the back of the empty room, moving slowly and deliberately. I was content to watch him from the mattress. Mac was boiling hot water for tea while keeping an eye on the activity in the street and announcing arrivals and departures from the charity as it began to close for the day.

"Mrs. Carrick is coming back from delivering an elderly man, probably to the Stranger's Home. Miss Levy is informing the poor applicants that the charity is shutting down for the day and shooing them away."

"What do you think Israel's chances are with her?" I asked as he handed me a fresh cup of the nearly colorless green tea.

"Let us see," Mac said, who as a Jew might offer better insight. "She's from a better family than he, she's devilishly attractive, she's the first Jewish female to attend Cambridge, and she's a published poet. As for Israel, he's from Whitechapel, works as a reporter, and is a known socialist. Were you a matchmaker, what would you think?"

"That he doesn't stand a chance," I said, but I wasn't thinking of Israel and Miss Levy just then. I was thinking more of Miss Potter and myself. Did I really think our relationship might go any further? What had I, an enquiry agent's assistant and a former felon, have to offer a beautiful, ambitious, and intellectual girl of good family—or any girl at all, for that matter? How would she feel if she saw me now, I wondered, with my face mottled and bruised?

Barker finished his final movements and then took a dainty sip from his cup. A man his size could have used a bowl instead, but he used small, handleless cups from the Orient that held almost nothing.

"Dr. Fitzhugh is leaving," Mac returned to his narration. "He's turned left. That's not his usual route. He's heading toward Cambridge Road."

"Come, lad," Barker said, actually tossing his empty cup onto the mattress at my feet. "Any deviation in Fitzhugh's routine is of interest to me."

I pulled myself out of bed, and the two of us took the staircase quickly. We sprinted across the road and when we reached Cambridge Road, Barker waved me across. I walked one side of the pavement, while he took the other. Our quarry was easy to spot because of a new silk top hat he wore that caught the late afternoon sun. The first way to convince the populace that one is a respectable doctor is to dress like one, I suppose. The problem was, I soon discovered, Dr. Fitzhugh was not as respectable as I thought he was.

Barker's method of stalking his prey is to hang back enough to avoid being noticed, and to wait until it goes to ground. In this case, Fitzhugh turned into a brick building around the corner in North Street. Barker crossed the street as I reached the door he had entered.

"Old Sal," Barker said. "I would not have believed it."

"Sal?"

"Sally Forth. Not her real name, of course, her professional name. She's an abbess."

"Some sort of religious organization?"

"You're being marvelously dense this evening, lad. She keeps a brothel."

I knew such an establishment provided a constant source of temptation to men, young, old, and even married. Illicit pleasure could be sampled for just a few shillings, even less from the prostitutes of Whitechapel, but such moments of pleasure had another, higher price. Too many men, even highborn ones, had contracted diseases for which modern medical science had no cure. Young men I had known had slid into dementia and eventual death. Word of such catastrophes were discussed among youths and mentioned in vague terms by clergymen as object lessons. Despite the fact that young women in better establishments received regular examinations to verify that they were disease free, as an acquaintance once warned me, it only had to happen once.

"Shall we wait for him to come out?"

"We don't have time to wait," Barker said, and before I could prepare myself, he was pushing me through the front door.

"Welcome, gentlemen," a robust, blond woman with large teeth cried, swooping down on us. Then she recognized Barker. "Oh, it's you, Push. What in hell are you doing here? Have you come to shut me down? Because if you have, you'd better think the better of it."

"No, Sal. I shall leave that to the Moral Purity League. I have a question or two to put to Dr. Fitzhugh."

"He's in the back. Last door on the right. And do go out the back way. You'll scare off the customers!"

A painted girl clad only in bloomers and a chemise had come up and was attempting to catch my attention. I was doing my best to ignore her, despite her lack of proper clothing. When Barker gave the signal to follow, I took the opportunity to do so.

Barker and I reached the end of the corridor, and he roughly threw open a door. I came in after him and, despite our locale, was surprised at what I saw.

Fitzhugh had been engaged with a young woman wearing an outfit much like that of the girl I had seen in the hall. At our entry, he stumbled back and flushed a deep crimson, but the girl took it as a sort of joke, tying up her clothing and laughing harshly at us before leaving.

"I thought it was something like this," Barker said, leaning against the doorframe.

"Surely you don't think—" Fitzhugh blustered. "I don't avail myself of these women, sir. I work here. These women must be examined and certified to be free of disease. It's the only way I can make enough money to both live and save for my own surgery."

"And the work at the charity?" Barker asked.

The doctor sat down on the edge of a bed. "It is to assuage the sense of guilt I feel over the work I'm forced to do. I despise this, gentlemen. I cannot put it any more plainly. I've been searching for a junior position with an established physician, but there are none to be had. I've got close to a dozen letters out at the moment. I've written to doctors as far away as Edinburgh, but there has been a large crop of new physicians this year."

Fitzhugh turned to a ewer and bowl, poured water, and lathered his arms up to the elbow. It was as if he was trying to scrub his own soul.

"So you examine these women to determine if they have any disease," Barker prompted.

"Yes. If I find anything wrong, I report it to Miss Forth and the police to make certain the girl doesn't work. I've treated some with mercury, though I find it an unsatisfactory treatment in most cases and downright dangerous. The various venereal diseases are fatal, you understand."

"And that is all you do here?" The Guv continued to push him.

Fitzhugh dropped his head and shook out his hands before taking a towel. "I suppose I should make a clean breast of it. I also issue certificates of virginity."

Barker went as cold and immobile as I've ever seen him. "And how exactly does that work?"

"Well, sir, a young girl is brought in—"

"How young?" Barker growled.

"I don't ask. A few have been quite young, indeed, and have been genuine virgins. With most, however, it is merely a ruse. I do not examine them at all. I merely issue the certificate. It should be obvious they are not virgins, but it is what the market demands. I am not proud of what I do, Mr. Barker, but I must eat. The Charity Organization Society cannot afford to keep a physician on staff. I am merely a volunteer."

"You know what I am going to ask you next, do you not, Dr. Fitzhugh?"

"Yes, sir. Miss DeVere was not brought here to be examined. As far as I know, no girl from the charity has. I don't know how Miss Forth engages these young women."

"I see. May I trouble you for your address, doctor?"

The doctor gave me the address of a boardinghouse in Morpeth Street, not far from the C.O.S. I heard girls laughing behind me. I turned and saw a group lined up in the hall. One or two winked at us. Barker frowned and I don't believe it was due to his Puritan roots.

"What's going on?" he demanded.

"What do you mean? I've told you all I know."

"I mean now. Why are all these women here now?"

"It's Friday, sir," Fitzhugh said drily. "It is their biggest night."

"What certificates are you here for, ladies? Disease or virginity?"

"Both, sir," a bold girl answered.

"Is there a special event occurring this evening?" he asked.

"A party at some estate," she said nonchalantly.

"Out of town?"

"There ain't none in town that I know of."

Barker drew himself up to his full height. "None of your lip, girl."

I'm sure she faced rough men often. A girl can quickly grow tough and cynical in her profession. But even she would not take on a man like Cyrus Barker.

"No, sir. I dunno where it is exactly. Along the river somewhere."

"Get Sal."

The last girl in line scampered off to get her. The rest of us stood in a somewhat embarrassed silence.

We heard Sally Forth before we saw her. She came down the hallway of her establishment emitting curses the way a steam engine lets off puffs of steam, in full throttle by the time she reached Barker.

"You better not be interfering with my business, Push."

"If you anger me, Sal, I'll be back with Swanson of the Yard, and we'll shut this place down. No Friday night business and no fancy parties out of town."

Miss Forth's only answer was "All right. What is it you want?"

"The name of your client tonight."

"Not that," Sally said, lowering her voice. "I ain't stayed open for business these ten years by squealing on my gentlemen."

"One name, Sal," Barker maintained. "You press me and you'll find out how hard I can press back. I'm after a multiple murderer. I don't care about your fancy girls."

"This ain't the normal client," Sal admitted. "This is the best money I've made in years. I could retire on it. He's highborn. Best if you leave it, Push. Not just for my sake. It could make more trouble than even you could handle." She turned back toward the young women. "Girls! Out. Hop it."

They seemed relieved to be dismissed and quickly left.

"I wasn't going to be seen discussing this, and *you*," she said, pointing a long-nailed finger at Dr. Fitzhugh, "had better keep your bloody mouth shut."

"Yes, madam."

"I shouldn't do this," she continued, "but I know all about your temper."

"It is wearing thinner by the moment. The name, Sal. Give me the name."

She looked reluctant, but somehow it slipped out of her mouth. "Dashwood."

Barker stood for a moment, then pushed his bowler hat up and ran his hand across his forehead and put his other hand on his hip. It was as if even he had not expected such an answer.

"Thank you, Sal," he finally said. "Doctor, we shall speak again. Come, lad."

Outside, we walked along Cambridge Road, but Barker wasn't paying attention. One of his broad shoulders almost knocked a man over.

"Who is Dashwood, sir?" I asked.

"Does the name have any meaning to you?" he asked.

"It is the name of a family in one of Jane Austen's novels, sir. Beyond that, I'm afraid I do not know."

"Francis Dashwood, the Earl of le Despencer. He was the leader of a group of upperclass rakes a century ago. They were involved in satanic rituals and mad revels amidst London's upper classes. It was the most infamous organization in the history of London."

"My word," I said. "You're speaking of the Hellfire Club."

"Yes, Thomas. It would appear they have returned. It all fits together. Such an organization would be a perfect cloak for Miacca's activities. Most of the victims were found between Saturday and Monday. They were likely sacrificed on Friday night, ritually outraged and murdered by these most vicious of libertines. Like Miss DeVere, their bodies were painted. When the Hellfire Club was done with them, they tossed them away like empty tins."

"That is vile."

"Yes, and, lad, there is the link you were looking for. Richard Dashwood, the latest baron who owns the estate in Buckinghamshire, is a friend of Lord Hesketh's and was the referee for your second match with Palmister Clay."

"My word."

"And do not forget today is Friday. I believe the Hellfire Club is going to sacrifice Ona Bellovich tonight."

28

"SHALL WE GO TO DASHWOOD'S ESTATE NOW, SIR?"

Barker thought a moment. I'm sure he was itching to re-connoiter the area himself, but ultimately he shook his head. "Best not. There's no need to be tipping our hand. Come, I fancy a pint."

We took an omnibus into the City. I knew Barker could not mean what he said about fancying a pint. From the little he had told me about his time in the East I knew he had been a terrible drinker and brawler when the mood was on him, but since then he carefully watched his own intake, never more than a glass of wine or ale per day, and often a week without either. The only stimulant he preferred was his gunpowder green tea, the little pellets of rolled leaves he had imported for him. Fancying a pint was one thing, allowing himself to indulge in one was another. *So, what,* I wondered, *was he really up to?*

At Aldgate Station we got out and stretched our limbs. We both liked the City, from St. Paul's in the west to the Jewish quarter in the east. North was Newgate, where Mac's parents lived and where he was briefly imprisoned, and south was the river and the Tower. The Guv led me deep into the center of the district and for a moment shocked me when he stopped in front of St. Michael's Alley, where the Barbados stood. Then he moved into the next street which was Lombard, and led me into a chophouse called the George and Vulture.

As we stepped inside, I couldn't help think that I knew the name from somewhere. When I saw a gentleman stretched in front of the fire with a handkerchief over his face, sound asleep, I recognized the pub's name.

"Pickwick!" I cried, which only served to attract the attention of everyone in the room.

"I beg your pardon?" Barker asked.

"This is the setting for Dickens' novel *The Pickwick Papers,* sir. Sam Weller stayed here."

"Is that relevant to the case?" my employer asked patiently.

"I don't know. Is it?"

Barker didn't favor my question with a reply but ordered two half and halfs at the bar, and then we squeezed ourselves into a corner; for the place was filled with solicitors, barristers, and bankers just let out for the day.

"So why are we here, sir?" I asked after a sip of the stout and porter.

"This is where the Hellfire Club began, lad, and here is where the George and Vulture nearly ended. It was on this spot in 1749 that the original chophouse burnt down and was rebuilt. Some say it was consumed with brimstone, but I think we can safely separate truth from legend now."

"So tell me more about the Hellfire Club, sir," I said.

Barker dug out his pipe and filled it. With the pint glass

in his left hand and the charged pipe in his right, he began.

"The Hellfire Club was the name of a short-lived group in the 1720s that began in this very building. Then in 1746, another group was formed here with the same name, led by Francis Dashwood, the fifteenth Baron le Despencer. It was a group of fast-living politicians and City men—including the Earl of Sandwich and the artist William Hogarth—a notorious club of debauchery, drunkenness, and satanic ritual. The acolytes were known as monks and nuns and the motto was *'Fay ce que voudras.'*"

"*'Do what thou wilt,'*" I translated.

"Precisely. But the club wasn't merely for licentiousness. The members were also building ties and making alliances, not only in England but also around the world. The American diplomat Benjamin Franklin was one of hundreds of members. Dashwood was brilliant but a confirmed student of witchcraft. It has been said he founded an order called the Dilettenti, based upon rituals borrowed from the Freemasons."

"There are the Masons again."

"Indeed. If one believes they are a benevolent organization, then Dashwood's club was its evil brother, out for plunder and power."

"So what happened to them?"

"There was a time they wielded great power. Dashwood excavated elaborate catacombs within his grounds at West Wycombe and built a temple, but soon factions grew and political rivalries compromised the club. Even evil sometimes falls prey to petty jealousies. By 1765, the Hellfire Club had disbanded."

"Now it is back again."

"Aye. The new Baron le Despencer is apparently compounding the earlier baron's traits of lust, drunkenness, and satanism; and it appears he already has a constituency upon which to rely, including Lord Hesketh and possibly the Marquis of Queensberry. He's gaining influence among the aristocracy, and yet, so far, he has not attracted notoriety like his ancestor."

"Did the original Hellfire Club sacrifice virgins?" I asked.

"They did, but it was both voluntary and symbolic. There was no abducting and butchering of children. In that way, this fellow is worse, and yet I still have questions. The bruise, for instance."

"What bruise?"

"There was a bruise on Gwendolyn DeVere's rib cage. It was in the very place where the fatal blade would have entered to cut out her heart. I believe it was symbolic, a wooden knife, or a false one loaded on a spring. If it was symbolic, then why kill her afterward? If not, why not really sacrifice her, in which case, there was no need to strangle her? It is perplexing."

"What exactly do you plan for us to do tonight?"

"I wish to break up their meeting. Surely they are not all ardent satanists. If I prove that their secret activities are known, then it is possible that those who are merely there for sport shall panic and run away, never to return."

"What if they are all 'ardent satanists'?"

"Then we'll be in for it, I suppose."

"Why not call the Yard?"

"The club has not broken the law conclusively, and the baron wields a great deal of power in Buckinghamshire.

Hmmm." Barker began scratching absently under his chin as another thought occurred to him.

"What is it?"

"I just recalled something else about the original Dashwood. He was a Freemason."

"I see."

"There may be no connection. The Hellfire Club might have nothing to do with the Freemasons and Pollock Forbes. They may be little more than a group of libertines drinking and consorting with fallen women and indulging in a bit of theater. But they could be much more than that, and you and I must ascertain which it is."

"Is there no way to assemble a group of us?" I asked. "Mac would wish to come and Handy Andy's folks are always good for a scrap."

"No," Barker said, giving a sigh. "I shall not endanger them or their good names."

"I suppose," I said, looking at the bustling pub of professional men, "that there is something *apropos* about planning to bring down a satanic society in the very public house where they first began it."

"That's the spirit, lad."

I thought about the fact that everyone here in the pub would be going home soon, to their homes and families, while Barker and I were about to challenge a satanic cult. It gives one pause.

"What made you decide to become a detective?"

The Guv looked at me appraisingly before answering. "I'd done similar work in China from time to time before I owned the *Osprey*—bodyguard work, finding things, small investigations."

"That's not a complete answer, if I may say it. There is the London Metropolitan Police, the Criminal Investigation Department, and even the Special Branch for such work. Why set up as an enquiry agent?"

"Scotland Yard is a branch of the government, whose purpose is to defend society as a whole, to lower the number of crimes, and deter criminals. It's not set up to help private individuals like Major DeVere."

I sat back in my chair and tried not to smile.

"You're looking awfully smug, Thomas. Out with it, then."

"You're a socialist, sir."

"What do you mean, you rascal?"

"The Salvation Army and the Charity Organization Society are set up to meet the needs of individuals who have fallen through the cracks. Wouldn't you say you do the same? You are the last hope of inquiry. That's why DeVere came to you."

There was a rumbling in Barker's chest. He was chuckling.

"Very good, lad. You are using your reason. I could argue with you, but let us cut through all that and say you are right, with one caveat. I am not a socialist, but I do something similar to what they do."

"I still have one question, sir, that I would ask if we are to go charging in blindly tonight after an entire cabal of satanists."

"Ask it."

"Well, sir, from what you have said and what I've gleaned from the sermons we've heard at the Baptist Tabernacle, you believe that society is wearing down and getting worse and worse, moving toward chaos and that it must be so because that is what has been predicted."

"I don't know if I would have worded it quite that way, but I'll accept the analysis. So what is the question?"

"The question is why? Why do you do what you do? The government probably doesn't appreciate your interference, and Scotland Yard is often against you. The Home Office has used you a time or two but thinks you questionable. Why care what happens here? I'm not saying it's not needful, but why us?"

"Did you see the night soil men on your watch, Thomas, shoveling the horse dung from the streets?"

"Yes," I said doubtfully. "I could not miss it."

"Do you know why they do what they do? Because the work must be done. Because there is a little money in it, and most especially because no one else is willing to undertake the work."

He picked up his untouched half and half, took one large draft of it and put it away from him, then wiped the foam from his mustache with a finger. "Have I given you a satisfactory answer?"

"Well, it wasn't the answer I expected, sir," I admitted, "but it was an answer."

29

OUR DESTINATION WAS WEST OF LONDON, AN area I had not visited since coming to town. Many of Barker's cases had taken us to the East End or the City but not to the west. Still, we were traveling by river which is the same from Hampton Court to Woolwich. After dinner we were soon to meet a boatman at a dock in Brentford.

"Per'aps I should go with you," Jenkins suggested, from the security of his booth. He was the Rising Sun's premier patron, in residence from five thirty to nine every night that the pub was open. To deviate from his chosen schedule was unthinkable. Profits would tumble, the crown slip from Victoria's brow, and the earth veer from its axis.

"That will not be necessary, Jenkins," Barker murmured. "Thomas and I shall get along well enough."

"Right," Jenkins said, having made the offer. I think he was relieved to be dismissed, but then, he's no tiger like Mac. He's more for creature comforts like good ale and conversation.

"Do you punt?" Barker asked me as we left Whitehall.

"Punt? Good heavens, no. Punting was never part of my curriculum at Magdalen College. I could not afford the time or the money. I assumed you hired a steam launch or something."

"No, no, merely a punt. It is vital that we don't attract attention to ourselves by arriving with a loud, steaming boiler. Besides, the exercise will do us good."

Every time Barker says something will be good for me, I know I shall live to regret it and that night was no exception. We arrived at the docks around eight o'clock, and Barker spoke to a sailor who led us to our vessel for the evening. I paid the old salt more than double the price he deserved and surveyed our transportation dubiously.

Cyrus Barker was not as rich as Croesus, but I suspected he had a pile of money from his days as a captain in the China Seas. He is a generous man, but he is also a Scot, and these two opposites in one man sometimes cause war within. At times, he could be especially generous, always seeing that my tailor was well paid, but at other times he was appallingly cheap, as with the dusty warehouse and the mattress. He himself is naturally stoical. All this I contemplated as I looked down at the vessel that Barker would punt all the way to the Dashwood estate.

"It's not the newest boat in the fleet," I noted, studying the bare, gray wood of the punt. It had begun its days several decades before on the more prestigious Oxford portion of the Thames, but after it lost its looks, had been sent over to this working end of the waterway. The most I could say in its behalf was that it looked sound, by which I mean it did not have six inches of water in the bottom of it.

"Here, put one of these on," Barker said, handing me an oilskin coat in dark gray. The coats must have been included in the price. The old sailor seemed to take grim delight in our donning these villainous garments, rank with sweat and fish scales.

"And just why am I wearing this?" I dared ask.

"We do not want to attract attention."

"Two gentlemen punting in the dark when anyone else on the river would be camping for the night? Couldn't we have gone by train or something?"

"This was the way the original denizens of the Hellfire Club came, and I have no doubt this is how they shall arrive tonight."

"How do you know Miacca really exists? Couldn't he be an invention of the Hellfire Club to cover their illicit activities?"

"No, lad. My professional experience tells me that those letters are genuine. Only a very warped individual would think like that."

The moon had risen, a pale yellow crescent with the features of a man curious about our endeavors. Clouds moved slowly across the sky, concealing and revealing the moon, like a bull's-eye lantern. Barker stood in the stern, pulling the pole out of the sediment behind and setting it down in front of him. It is not a fast means of transportation, but he got into such a steady rhythm, I was conscious of the passage of land on either side.

I soon saw why he had chosen this mode of transport. Once out of the town proper, we reached a series of locks. In some cases, the lockkeepers were vigilant, and in others, they had to be hailed. Money changed hands in two instances. On others, we punted to the side, and bodily dragged the old boat around the lock.

"Come here, lad," Barker ordered. "I'll teach you how to punt."

He showed me how to stand with my feet braced and to pull and push on the long length of spruce. Like all things new, it was awkward at first, until I got accustomed to it. As long as I was not interrupted by another lock, my pole sunk into sandy silt and all was fine.

The moonlight, when it wasn't playing peekaboo with the clouds, painted everything in argent hues. It was cool and there was a light breeze, but my exertions made me want to take off my oilskin and jacket and roll up my sleeves. The town had given way to open countryside where all sensible people had gone to bed. There wasn't a light to be seen anywhere.

"Lad, pull over to the bank quickly."

The Guv hadn't shown me how to stop, so it was awkward, but I still managed to guide the boat over to the side, though I lost my footing, falling into the stern.

"What is it?"

"Shhh!"

A boat was coming along behind us. We huddled down and tried to look inconspicuous, as though we were anglers fishing by moonlight. I heard the steady putt of a steam launch, and over it, the sound of men singing. I could hear the words distinctly across the water, though the singers tended to slur their words, a song about a maiden aunt whom a family would not acknowledge after she had run off to Paris. The song was bawdy, and the singers, young rakes of university age or older, sang it with fervor. There was nothing out here to interest them, save the very meeting we were going to disrupt. I wondered how many people would actually be there.

The launch passed with a wake that set us bobbing and soon Barker was punting again. A half hour later, we floated under a bridge, and on the other side, my employer ran the boat aground. We dragged it up on shore against the side of the bridge and began walking.

"We are in Buckinghamshire," he said. "The baron's estate is less than a mile away. I thought he might have men at the dock, and we do not wish to be seen."

The two of us crept along a wagon path. I saw the estate in the distance, well lit against the dark night, and my mind imagined something sinister about it. Barker lit a dark lantern of his own and shone the circle of light upon a large scale ordinance map. A breeze came up, and I felt a chill despite the oilskin.

My employer led me into a valley, and we approached a structure standing tall in the night, a church or abbey. It had a circular courtyard and a pair of open gates lit by torches that bathed everything in a shimmering light.

"That is the entrance to the caves," the Guv explained.

"It looks deserted," I said.

"They may be within the labyrinth. It was heavily quarried, according to Dashwood's design, with some sort of temple at the far end, deep within the earth."

"How do you know so much about it, sir?" I asked as we came up to the entrance.

"I thought the subject worthy of study. I have a book upon it in my garret back in Newington."

"I don't hear anything," I whispered. "Should we go in?"

"We have come this far," came the reply.

"Dare I hope you brought a pistol?" I asked.

"It wasn't wise," he answered. "This is private property and we are trespassers."

We headed into the cave. The tunnel was narrow and faced with brick, an endless corridor of gothic arches.

We followed the corridor to the left and had only gone a few yards when I heard a chilling sound, the squeal of gates behind us. They crashed together, setting off echoes throughout the cave.

"Caught like a rat in a trap, Barker!" a rough voice echoed down the corridor. "We have been expecting you. I hope you enjoy your tour of my caves. You will have until the morning to enjoy my hospitality."

We heard the sound of a heavy chain being wrapped around the gates and a lock clicking shut, then the harsh, raucous laughter of some of Dashwood's guests, male and female, drifted to us from the entrance of the cave.

"Sir?" I asked in a low voice.

Barker raised a finger to his lips. I told myself it was too early to panic. Trapped we were, but our lives were not in immediate danger. All the same, any chance to lay hands on Miacca tonight had vanished. If we were jailed here all night, who would stop Ona Bellovich from being murdered? What kind of saviors were we?

Barker turned and led me back down the tunnel to the entrance. The gates were closed and padlocked, and a guard had been set outside to watch us, armed with a hunting rifle.

The Guv ignored the guard, flipping up the large padlock that held us in.

"Drop that!" the guard ordered at once.

"Stop me if you wish. Lad, hold this lantern for me."

I took the lamp as Barker rummaged about in his pockets. Finally, he pulled out a ring of skeleton keys and inserted one into the lock.

"Stop that or I will shoot!" the guard warned, looking a trifle desperate. No one had thought that Barker might have his own keys.

"I doubt the baron has given you permission to shoot me," my employer stated, taking out the key and inserting another. "You are merely to see that I don't escape."

The mechanism clicked as the lock sprung open. The guard raised his rifle, and then the Guv flung out his arm. The distance between them was suddenly full of pennies glittering in the torchlight, the sharpened ones he called his "calling cards." They caught the man in the wrist, the chest, and the cheek. The guard fell back with a cry, not even able to fire off his gun in warning. Meanwhile, Barker removed the lock and pulled apart the chains before pushing open the massive gate. He charged out, bent double, covering the ground between them quickly. I heard a loud impact, and the guard fell at Barker's feet. He wouldn't be getting up any time soon.

"Should I take the rifle?" I asked, glad for something to hold onto.

"No," he replied. "No guns." He seized it and swung it against the wall of the entrance, shattering the stock. "This has slowed us down. Come."

There was a marble, hexagonal building nearby and we headed toward it. As we approached, I saw that it was a large, open mausoleum for the Dashwood ancestors. This, too, was deserted, but after we passed it, we saw a well-lit building a few hundred yards away, and my ear caught the sound of music and raucous laughter. This was where the satyrs were having their party.

"They are having their unholy revels in a church!" Barker growled. He tossed his lantern to the ground and began to run, with me in pursuit.

Two men stood in the entrance of the old church, and when the Guv entered, he thrust their heads hard against the old wood. As they slid to the floor, I jumped over their sprawling limbs.

Inside, it was a scene from Hogarth. Most of the men were clad in garments from the previous century, breeches, long coats, and tricorns, their faces covered by half masks of black silk. As for the women, they too had their faces covered, but precious little else. They looked like Georgian strumpets, with elaborate wigs and tight bodices and pantaloons. Bottles of whiskey and goblets of wine littered the tables; and the pews had been replaced with banqueting tables, long couches, and chairs. In one corner, a small orchestra sat, wearing powdered wigs and blindfolds, churning out a merry air. But that was not the worst of it.

In the center of the room, a man was just laying a young girl down upon a marble altar. She wore a heavy cape, but it was half open, exposing her bare flesh. I recognized Ona Bellovich. The man wore a similar cape down to his feet, but his face was hidden by an elaborate goat mask, with large horns and a pentagram painted on the forehead.

"This is a raid!" Barker bellowed. "Everyone, stay where you are!"

In fact, they did just the opposite. His demand caused pandemonium. Old roués parted from the women with whom they caroused and grabbed for their breeches. Women screamed and the music trailed off. Some of the men ran for the door, while others turned to stop us. I kicked one in his paunch, and he went down easily. Barker lashed out, catching one in the jaw and stomach who, for all we knew, might be a cabinet minister or judge. From a nearby table, he lifted a cat-o'-nine-tails, whose reason for being there I didn't want to consider, and began to flail at the legs of the men and women running by.

"Out!" he cried. "Get out!"

In the tumult, I lost sight of Ona Bellovich.

Barker continued to thrash at the escaping crowd, while I pushed my way forward. The man in the goat mask had disappeared, nor could I see his captive. I saw the crowd for what they were: portly bankers and merchants and politicians consorting with low women from Sal's bawdy house hired for the evening's frivolity. But what of the sacrifice? Was the girl really meant to be killed on the altar, raped, and strangled in front of all these people?

The room rapidly cleared. The orchestra members tried to carry their precious instruments through the fleeing crowd. I was suddenly seized from behind, and I did not hesitate, giving the fellow a sharp blow to the stomach with my elbow, then stamping on his instep with my heel. I wrapped my arm around the fellow's neck and was about to smash my fist into his nose when I recognized him. Swanson of the Criminal Investigation Department had materialized in the midst of this raucous crowd.

"Inspector!" I cried, but what was done could not be undone.

"Assaulting an officer of the law!" Swanson sputtered above the din, thrusting me into the waiting arms of two of his constables. "And, Cyrus Barker, you are under arrest!"

My employer swung around.

"On what charge?" he asked.

Swanson came close, and they stood nose to nose. The inspector ticked off points on his fingers. "Trespassing. Assault. Destruction of property. That's just to start. No doubt you are responsible for the unconscious man back there with the sharpened coins sticking out of him."

A group of men approached, still clad in Georgian costumes, without their wigs and masks. Lord Hesketh stepped forward, followed by a man whom I assumed was Baron le Despencer himself.

"Get these men out of here!" the latter cried. "I demand that they be punished to the fullest extent of the law!"

"Yes, your lordship," Swanson replied. "I was just in the process of arresting them, thank you very much."

"How dare you interrupt my party and chase away my guests," the baron demanded of Barker. "I shall see that you do time for this."

"And I, your lordship, shall see that every villager knows exactly what sort of orgy has been going on in this church."

"There is nothing wrong with a harmless function on my private estate with my friends."

"There is when young women are being outraged and murdered!"

"That is slander, and I am a witness!" Lord Hesketh spoke up.

"Arrest him. Both of them!" the baron ordered. "I want them both in chains!"

Barker raised the cat-o'-nine-tails, and the man ducked and winced. Instead, my employer offered it to the noble.

"Your property, I believe, your lordship."

Whether it belonged to him or not, he took it. Then Barker held out his wrists for Inspector Swanson's darbies.

"You always push," the inspector complained. "You won't let anything alone. You cannot let other men decide what is right."

"Do you mean those men consorting with fallen women here tonight, the MPs disporting themselves, the aldermen and aristocrats observing a satanic ritual that murders innocent maidens? No, I will not let that alone." He held up his chained hands. "Do you know the difference between you and me, Donald? Your wrists have been chained since the very beginning."

"That's it. Get him out of here," Swanson said, thrusting Barker toward one of the constables.

Reluctantly, I held out my own wrists. The cold steel of the Hiatt darbies closed about them. I was going to a jail cell, something I had sworn to myself would never happen again.

The constables marched us past the mausoleum to the dock. It had been quiet when we passed here earlier, but all was chaos now. The steam launch that had brought the party was gone, leaving a dozen or more carousers and their female companions stranded. At least the gentlemen had the manners to lend their old-fashioned coats to the partly clad women. It was chilly on the river, with a fog settling in.

Our plans were set at naught. Who knew where Ona Bellovich had been taken, or if Miacca had been the man in the cape and goat mask. There was no opportunity for us to save her now. As we were loaded onto the police launch, I thought any chance of this case ending well was over.

"Hello, gentlemen," a man said, as we were thrust into a seat. He came forward and gave us a slight smile under his impossibly black mustache. It was Inspector Dunham of the Thames Police.

30

We were on our way back to London in a police launch destined for a jail cell or the interrogation room in Scotland Yard. The darbies around my wrists were cold, and the fog had spread over the surface of the Thames like icing on a cake. We had punted here slowly, but were speeding back, thanks to the powerful boiler on the police steam launch. I was about as wretched as a man could be, knowing I would be in a cell soon. So why, I wondered, did Cyrus Barker seem so cheerful?

"If your constables are going to arrest a fellow," he said over the thrumming of the engine, "they would do well to check his pockets."

So saying, he reached inside his coat as both constables lunged at him. However, he came up with nothing more dangerous than his sealskin tobacco pouch.

Both constables flanked him, arms akimbo, while Inspector Dunham shook his head. "Go ahead, Barker, have your fun."

Barker charged his pipe, lit it, and leaned back, hooking an elbow over the gunwale and crossing his ankles. All he had to do was hoist himself up over the ledge and he'd be in the water with the vesta he had just thrown in, leaving me to suffer the consequences alone.

"Swanson shall be quite the hero when he brings in a desperate pair of enquiry agents who work so near Scotland Yard they can toss a stone through the front window," the Guv said, contributing his pipe smoke to the surrounding haze.

Dunham gave him a quizzical look but gave no answer.

"What would your superiors say if I could deliver the killer of the girls into the hands of the Thames Police? Or would you rather I tell them that you allowed a child murderer to escape when you nearly had him in your clutches?"

"I'd have to be positive you could do so," Dunham said, raising an eyebrow. "Convince me."

"Describe Miacca for the inspector, lad," the Guv said to me. "He's been awaiting Inspector Swanson's command here on the launch."

"He was wearing a long cape and a goat's head mask with horns. Of course, he's probably tossed those off by now. But there's one sure way of knowing him. He's got a young girl with him who is probably drugged."

"You saw them at the party?" Dunham demanded.

I spoke first. "I would hardly call it a party. Miacca was just about to sacrifice her when we broke in!"

"Where are they now?"

"In the launch ahead of us, heading back to London. We've spoiled his entertainment, and now he is taking his victim to salvage what is left of the night for his pleasures."

"You know who Miacca is?"

"Of course," Barker said coolly.

Inspector Dunham looked at him skeptically. "Tell me," he said.

"Oh, I am just a prisoner, Inspector."

"If I take off the bracelets, will you tell me?"

"If you free us to continue the investigation, I'll take you right to him."

"Impossible," Dunham scoffed.

"I shall, of course, report myself over Dashwood's complaints after this is over, but right now I demand a free hand. Both of them, in fact."

"Slip his darbies," the inspector ordered. The constables, Swanson's men, looked at him dubiously. "Are you gentlemen in charge, or am I?" he barked at them. They quickly freed my employer's hands.

"And Llewelyn's," Barker demanded.

"I didn't say anything about your man here."

"He is my right hand," Barker insisted. "I need him."

Dunham heaved a sigh. "Him, too. But here's the lock coming up. If nobody's come through here I'm putting the darbies on you again."

The lockkeeper was standing at the dock in his nightshirt and cap, looking irate.

"Look here," he cried as we came up. "This is too much. I'll not have such shenanigans on my lock, racing at such at hour!"

"Someone just came through?" Dunham asked.

"Not ten minutes ago, and in such a hurry he scraped my gate!" He pointed at a scratch of white paint that ran horizontally across the wood.

"Describe them!"

"White steam launch, sir. Just one man aboard that I could see."

The inspector swiveled his head toward us. Was Barker tricking him? his expression seemed to ask. Or worse, had the man tossed Ona overboard?

"She may have been lying in the bottom of the boat," I dared say.

"Open this blasted gate!" Dunham bellowed.

In a moment we were through, the constables shoveling coal into the boiler for all they were worth. Meanwhile, the inspector pushed the handle on the throttle, gaining more speed. Barker abandoned the casual pose that had driven Dunham so mad, and made his way to the bow. He seemed glad to be in a boat and extended his chin forward in the breeze as the shreds of fog whipped by.

When we reached London, the vessel slowed, causing barges and other boats to clank against the docks like toys in a tub.

"Stop!" Barker cried, but it was too late to shut the valve. Miacca's launch was floating unmanned in the middle of the Thames. Dunham swerved, but we plowed into the back end of it with a rending of wood. The inspector was knocked off his perch, and Barker and I nearly fell overboard. The boat narrowly avoided a dock, and slid up an embankment before smashing into a hut. Both constables were covered in hot coals and began patting out the fire on each other. Barker jumped down onto the shore.

"Come! There's not a moment to lose, if we are to save Ona Bellovich."

We had passed under the Tower Bridge, still in mid-construction. Barker spread those long legs of his and ran for all he was worth, his oilskin flapping behind, while we struggled to keep up. In Royal Mint Street, he flagged down a cab, and he, Dunham, and I clambered aboard, leaving the constables to find another or be left behind.

"Who is it?" Dunham demanded. "Won't you please tell me who we are after?"

Barker only gave him an adamantine look.

"Blast your hide, Barker!" the inspector swore. "Must everything be a secret to you?"

"They cannot be far ahead. Turn onto Cambridge Road, driver!"

It's Palmister Clay, I told myself. *My word, he's Miacca!*

But no, we swept past Clay's little snuggery, and when we came to Green Street, we did not turn left toward the charity, pressing on northward instead. Barker seemed to know exactly where he was going. I just prayed we were not too late.

31

"**H**ALT!" BARKER CRIED WHEN WE REACHED the Old Ford Road and flung open the doors of the cab. He clattered down to the pavement and ran, leaving Dunham and me a tangle of limbs trying simultaneously to exit the vehicle and pay the cabman. We struggled to the ground and followed my employer. There were scant seconds to lose if we were going to save Ona Bellovich from violation, murder, and mutilation. I knew where we were going now and the identity of Miacca.

The Carrick Photographic Emporium was in sight, and Barker had almost reached it. He did not slow as he approached, but several feet away launched himself into the air. Both of his boots struck the door at once, bursting it from its hinges; and when the door fell, he slid across the room upon it until it crashed into the counter. He vaulted it and landed on the other side.

"Stephen Carrick!" Cyrus Barker bellowed. "Bring the girl here now! Gentlemen, the next room!"

The three of us charged into the room where Carrick took his photographs. It was empty, but there was a half-opened door beyond it. I thrust it open in time to see the face of Stephen Carrick regarding us furiously from a small bedstead, his black cape spread across it like the wings of a bat. Underneath him I could see the still form of Ona Bellovich, dazed from whatever drug he had given her. Carrick began to rise, a look of mad triumph on his face.

Dunham and I tackled him, knocking him from the bed. He struggled forcefully, and I was obliged to seize his hair and bang his head once or twice against the brick wall while Barker covered Ona Bellovich's body with the cape.

A sound like a cat hissing came from behind me, and I turned in time to be confronted by Rose Carrick. She held a large rectangular tray in her hand, the kind used for developing photographs, and she threw the contents at me. It would have soaked me completely, had Barker not stepped between us, raising the oilskin he wore as a shield. The coat caught most of the liquid, but some splashed over his head and onto Dunham and me, and began to burn.

"Acid!" Dunham cried. I looked up to see Barker's long oilskin begin to smoke. He tore it off, but I could see that his hand already had angry red blisters on it. He ran it over his scalp and came away with a lock of loose hair.

"Sir!" I cried, reaching for him, but Carrick took the opportunity to dash between us. He glanced back at us and there was a look upon his face of sheer maniacal glee. Another few steps and he would be able to flee into the night with his wife.

I wasn't going to let that happen while I could do something about it. I latched onto his ankle as he passed, and he dragged me with him across the room. The weight of my body slowed him down enough to allow Dunham a good swing of his truncheon, which broke Carrick's nose. He went down, dazed by the blow, while his wife dropped her pan and loped for the safety of the darkroom.

"I've got him this time," Dunham said grimly, clasping his darbies about the killer's wrists. "Get his bloody wife!"

Leaving Miss Bellovich with Barker and Carrick in Dunham's custody, I ran to the door of the darkroom and beat upon it, ordering her to open it. Stepping back, I began to kick near the lock with the heel of my boot as hard as I could.

Suddenly there was a roar within and a sharp scream from Rose Carrick. Barker and I looked at one another incredulously as we realized she had set the room on fire with herself in it. Smoke began to billow from under the door. A darkroom must contain flammable chemicals, I was sure. "Mrs. Carrick," I cried. "Open the door! Can you get to the door?"

But the screaming became even louder and more plaintive as the fire inside grew. I looked about for something with which to batter the door, but there was nothing nearby that would serve, so I put all my weight into one strong kick.

"No, lad!" Barker cried from behind me, as the door sprung open. He pulled me down as a huge ball of flame flew over our heads, igniting the room. My employer's mustache and brows were kindled and our clothing caught fire. We rolled over and over across the floor to quench the flames, while overhead the rafters began to burn.

"Ona," Barker rasped. "Get Ona, lad."

I pushed myself off the floor and ran into the back room. The fire had not reached there yet, but the room was filling with smoke. I made my way to the bedstead and scooped her up in my arms. Her eyes opened slightly, but she was still heavily drugged.

"I'll get you out of here safely," I said, but even as I said the words, I wondered if it was a rash promise. The front room was now an inferno. Dunham and Barker were trying to drag Carrick through the open entranceway with the aid of Swanson's constables who had finally found us. I took as much smoky air into my lungs as I dared hold, then dashed through the burning room to the front entrance. The heat was excruciating and I wondered if my clothes had caught fire again, but then I was suddenly out in the Old Ford Road, alive, comparatively safe, and with Ona Bellovich in my arms. My coat was so charred, it smoldered in the night air. There was a cheer, and people moved forward to pat my clothing. The fire had attracted residents and merchants who had no idea what had just happened inside.

There was another explosion from the building. The first floor windows blew out, showering us all in glass, and a tongue of fire rose out of the burning chimney.

Stephen Carrick sat up then and pushed himself onto his feet despite his shackled hands. He watched as the shop he had built was engulfed in flames along with the wife who had tried to protect him.

"No! No!" he cried, trying to dash back into the burning building, despite the constables who held him on either side. "No! My jar, my trophy jar! I must have it!"

"Shut it, you little ghoul," Dunham said, raking him across the shoulders with his club.

"Sir," I said, kneeling down by Barker. "You're in bad shape. Let me go and get Dr. Fitzhugh."

"Go, then," the Guv said, gritting his teeth in pain. "Miss Bellovich will need medical attention after her ordeal." Leave it to Barker to disregard his own needs in order to meet another's.

For once, I was glad to be in Bethnal Green. I ran through the streets on my way to find the doctor, but though I attracted stares from everyone I passed in my smoldering clothes, no one dared stop me. In Kensington or Chelsea, I would have been arrested for disturbing the public peace, but here I ran all the way to Fitzhugh's boarding-house without interference.

"My god!" Fitzhugh said when he saw me. "Come in and let me treat you at once."

"No time," I choked out. "Barker is in the Old Ford Road in far worse shape than I, and we've got a girl in our custody who has been drugged. Get your bag and come!"

Fitzhugh ran up the stairs to pack his medical bag and was back in two minutes ready to give aid. He led me through alleys and side streets I didn't know about, until we were back in front of the burning structure again.

We found Ona Bellovich being tended by a pair of female Salvation Army workers who had pinned the cape about her body and put a tin cup of cocoa in her hands. A combination of shock from the events and the effects of the drug made her sit forlornly, head cocked to the side, like a doll that had been dropped. I doubted she even knew she held the cocoa. Within minutes, one of the female officers and a constable carefully lifted her into the back of a hansom cab.

Barker's head had been bathed by another Salvation Army officer. Fitzhugh took over for her, applying sticking plaster to the major lesions and painting the rest of my employer's face in iodine. I was glad for once that he always wore dark spectacles, else he might have been blinded. By the time the doctor had finished tending him, the iodine and plaster made him look worse than before he had been treated.

"Bloody hell," a man said behind us. I looked over my shoulder into the eyes of Inspector Swanson. "Why aren't these men locked up, as I ordered?"

"I discarded your suggestion," Dunham said, emphasizing the final word, "and decided to go after the killer of all those girls I found in the river. His name is Stephen Carrick and he's here in my custody."

"In case you didn't notice, Dunham, you ain't on the river now. This is Yard business."

"I came here on the river," the Thames Police inspector maintained. "I found those girls in the first place and I wrote the reports you stole and never returned. I won't have you giving me orders. Why don't you go back to Whitehall where you belong?"

While the inspectors continued their jurisdictional argument, I hefted my employer to his feet, and the two of us shuffled through the alleyways to the warehouse. Once inside, I called for Mac and together, we got the Guv upstairs and onto the mattress. I believe he fell asleep almost instantly.

"Oy, Thomas," Mac said, using my Christian name for the first time that I could recall. "You are a fright."

I looked down at myself. My oilskin was in tatters and there was a large hole burned through my jacket and waistcoat to my shirt beneath. There were blisters on my hand. I went in search of my shaving mirror, and when I found it, wished I hadn't. My nose and forehead were red from the fireball and my face black with soot. My hair had been singed by fire and would have to be cut short to look normal.

I suddenly began to shake as it all caught up with me, but I fought back the attack of nerves. I had made a temporary truce with Mac but didn't want to show any sign of weakness. "I say," I said in my most casual voice, "any chance for a cup of coffee?"

"Of course, but I think first I must attend to your wounds. I've got a medical kit among my things."

"Is there anything you neglected to bring?" I dared ask.

"Shoe polish," he responded, taking my remark literally. "I have had to buff my shoes with a cloth. I shall remember it the next time the Guv decides to move us into temporary quarters."

"I hope that won't be for a very long while."

"I do, as well," Mac said. "To be quite candid, I've hated it here. I do not believe I would have made a good Sicilian."

Mac pulled a box full of gauze and other medical supplies from one of his trunks and set to work. I flinched as he applied iodine to one of my burns.

"So," Mac said as he painted my face. "I assume you got Miacca."

"Bagged him but good," I answered. "He's in police custody, though I'm not certain which police."

"So, tell me who it was and what happened."

I told him everything from the time Barker first put the punting pole into the water until we had staggered into the warehouse still smoldering. It took almost half an hour of explaining. We had had an eventful evening.

"So it was Carrick," Mac said. "How long do you suppose the Guv had known?"

"I have no idea," I said, looking at the slumbering figure on the bed. "The important thing is it's done. Miacca is in custody, Bethnal Green is safe, and we can go back to Newington again. No more stony mattresses."

"No more eight-hour vigils."

"No more meals served at room temperature."

"Fresh sheets, clean laundry, fresh cream on the doorstep every morning."

"And best of all, no infernal exercises."

"Do you gentlemen intend to talk all night?" Barker spoke from the bed. "Be so good as to give me twenty-five of your best."

32

⁓⁓⁓

THE NEXT DAY WE MOVED OUT OF BETHNAL Green. I was very happy to return the key to the estate agents and be shed of it. In Newington, we put our injured employer to bed and called in his personal physician, Dr. Applegate. He had to cut Barker out of his clothing. Some of the fabric that adhered to his burned skin had to be slowly removed with salad oil. The physician trussed him up like an Egyptian mummy. When he offered to treat me as well, I politely refused.

Afterward, Barker had me summon a barber to his bed. I had to keep raising my offered fee for the man's services until he stopped grumbling and we reached a settlement. He came and cut all our hair, Mac's included, clucking over the state of our appearance, as if acid throwing were some new fashion of which he disapproved, but he left having more than made up for the time he'd shut down his shop.

Barker was awake in the center of his old cabinet bed, with the curtains all drawn back. He was not the most handsome of men, but I hoped for his sake he would heal quickly.

"Sir," I said. "Mac and I were wondering when you first suspected Carrick."

"The second I saw him," he replied.

My brows went up.

"Don't think me a genius, yet, lad. I thought the same thing about Dr. Fitzhugh and William Stead. Detection is not about finding someone and fashioning a charge that will stick to him. It's more like a footrace. One knows the winner is among the runners, but only when the others have dropped out and the race is finished will you know who it is. In this case, I began with a couple of assumptions.

"My first was that Miacca was mad. He worked from a compulsion to kill young girls, but his madness was not patently obvious or he would have been arrested by Scotland Yard immediately. They are not simpletons, and they have great resources. Dunham is a good man, but Swanson is a first-rate detective. It was a challenge to work against him in this case.

"My second assumption was that Miacca was educated, for only an educated person would quote Blake or parrot your Mr. Lear. The problem was that so many of our suspects were well educated. Carrick, Miss Levy, Dr. Fitzhugh, William Stead, Mr. Clay, Lord Hesketh, and Dashwood had seen time at university. My assumption has been proven false. I now believe that Rose Carrick worked in collaboration with her husband in writing the taunting notes. She's the one who chose the victims."

"Now wait," I said. "Are you claiming Rose Carrick helped her husband? That implies that she knew what he was and what he did."

"More than that, it implies that she did not care. Her

own husband assaulted and murdered children, and she helped him do so. I believe it was her task to get rid of the bodies when he was done with them. He would not have cared what became of the corpses. She was the organized one, the planner sitting in the British Museum, cribbing poems to use in taunting letters. She was his helpmeet and protector. She would have done anything for him, suffered anything. In fact, she did."

"But why?" I asked. "Who would put up with that?"

"Do you recall how Stephen Carrick ran into trouble at university and ended up losing his inheritance?"

"Yes, he was consorting with a fallen woman."

"That fallen woman, I believe, was Rose Carrick. Her life had reached the point where she was living as a prostitute in Oxford. The senior Carrick found that they had taken up together and demanded he give her up. Carrick refused, not because he was in love with her but because he would not be dictated to by his father. Rose may have interpreted it as such, and no doubt, she persuaded herself she was in love. She molded her life around him and defended him fully. In her mind, she had somehow won the prize, the handsomest, most intelligent, wealthy gentleman she'd ever met. By the time she discovered that he was less than perfect, that in fact, he was a monster, it was too late. She had committed herself and would do so unto death. She loved him fully, while he, in turn, was incapable of love but knew a good thing when he saw it. I believe she even selected candidates for his abductions. It is perhaps the reason she volunteered at the Charity Organization Society in the first place."

"That's like another kind of madness," I said.

Barker raised a bandaged finger. "No, not quite. Not in the eyes of the law. It was why she locked herself in the darkroom and set it ablaze. Had they both been captured, he would like have gone to the asylum, for it is probable that he is mad, but she would have been hanged as an accessory to many murders. It was a long, dangerous journey for the two of them, but she must have known it would eventually come to a bad end. He would never willingly stop adding specimens to his jar."

"What kind of husband—"

"Husband!" Barker scoffed. "I doubt he understood the meaning of the word. A husband tries to shelter and protect his wife. He wants what's best for her and reveres and admires her all of his days. The Carricks' relationship was as twisted and unstable as Stephen's mind."

I recalled Barker's earlier mention of marriage. I still could not quite believe he might have been married, but had he been so, I had no doubt he would have performed his duties with the steadiness he showed in all other ways. *What of me?* I wondered. *Had I been all the husband I could have been?*

"I think," Barker went on, "that Carrick's time at Oxford was worse than we have taken it to be. Consorting with a woman of the streets, even vowing never to give her up, is hardly a rare occurrence among undergraduates, but I believe Carrick committed his first murder there. The Carrick fortune was able to cover up the affair, but Stephen's father saw the serious defects in his son's character and gave him up, cutting him off without a penny. It was good that he did so. Can you imagine what deviltry he'd have gotten into with funds and plenty of leisure time?"

"How did you know it was not the Hellfire Club, sir?"

"I do not believe London so debased just yet that one could assemble a group of men together in one room willing to watch a young girl be murdered. It would be easy, on the other hand, to find a number of men like Palmister Clay, young hedonists willing to meet together, to drink and carouse in the name of an old and infamous group and to watch a young and almost naked girl being 'sacrificed' in a satanic ritual, providing they know it was a magician's trick and that she was in no real danger. They weren't men on Carrick's level and did not know how corrupt he really was. At some point, he must have met Dashwood, using his former connections, and offered to provide not only some chilling entertainment but also the young girl to go with it. They had no idea what he did with the girls afterward and probably did not think to question him about it. I also believe he provided another service for them."

"What is that?"

"When Rose Carrick ferried young girls into new homes or institutions, she told some that if they were not satisfied with their new surroundings, she could help set them up with young gentlemen as mistresses."

"Clay," I stated.

"Aye, Clay, and whoever occupies the other nests along Cambridge Road. I imagine Carrick got paid for brokering the little arrangements. He was in need of money constantly for his photographic emporium."

"Very well," I said. "I understand why you did not suspect the Hellfire Club, but why not Clay in particular?"

Barker gave a faint smile. "Clay was married, kept a mistress, and without doubt was a member with his father of the Hellfire Club. Do you think he still had enough stamina left to outrage a new girl every Friday? He's leading a dissipated life. I doubt personally that he has the prowess."

"Much as I would like to connect the murders to him, I suppose you are correct. I don't believe Clay was involved . . . much."

"I am glad to hear it. Is honor still not satisfied? You drubbed him well."

"I don't know. I don't know that I can ever forgive him."

"If revenge is what you seek, you need do nothing. I'm certain his wife suspects his dalliance. His way of life shall surely catch up with him in the fullness of time."

"Of course you are right. But tell me, why did you not suspect Dr. Fitzhugh?"

"I did, for a time, but let us say you were a young physician in need of money as well as a malevolent killer of children. What would you have done to get rid of several perfectly good corpses? Would you have thrown them in the river?"

"No," I said. "I would have sold them to London Hospital or St. Bart's for vivisection."

"Exactly. It was all over those false certificates of virginity and the health records he provided. Would Miacca have suffered guilt? Not according to those letters or the souvenirs he took. He was proud of what he did. When the Carricks sent the notes to us and to Scotland Yard, they were thumbing their noses at Carrick's father and society in general. I have no doubt it was a delicious feeling until this evening when it all caught up with them."

"And it couldn't have been Stead because he was busy trying to force the bill through the House of Commons."

"Yes, but I must say you gave me a turn when you informed me he had purchased a child. I was guilty, lad, of thinking that the Fabians were incapable of producing men as high-minded as Stead. I disapprove of his actions, but I misjudged his motives and am glad to learn otherwise. It is a good thing to find someone of better character than one believed."

"What of Miss Hill, and Hesketh's belief that the socialists were involved in a conspiracy?"

"It went up in smoke, but it was not completely unfounded. As it happened, Stead did steal a child and had her conveyed to France. Hesketh did not know Gwendolyn De-Vere was a part of a larger scheme involving the murders of many children."

"To what extent were the Masons tied up in all this?"

"Hesketh is a Freemason and I'm certain Dashwood is as well. It's possible that they recruited members from the organization to join the Hellfire Club, but generally speaking the Masons attract high-minded individuals. Of course, there is rotten fruit in every barrel, and men like Hesketh join for the influence it gives them as well as for family tradition. I am certain he will sponsor his son in time. It is possible that Carrick himself may be a Mason. Joining would have been a good way to improve his business prospects. You would be surprised at how many members of the brotherhood there are in the British Empire. Aside from the police, there is the law and the military. Many towns have a lodge; but for the most part, they are benign, although I do not care for their theology."

"So you yourself are not a member, then."

Barker gave one of his wintry smiles, despite the sticking plaster on his face. "The question is moot. The first rule of any secret society is to deny being a member of one."

That wasn't an answer, I thought, but I let the matter rest. "Do you suppose Major DeVere will consider the case settled? That is, will he pay us? You did capture his daughter's killer, but she is dead and so is his wife."

"That is for DeVere to decide. We can but abide by whatever decision he makes."

"Speaking of services," I said, "I had better go to the C.O.S. and inform Miss Potter that hers are no longer required." I paused. "Wait. What about Joseph Chamberlain? How was he mixed up in all this? Was he a member of the Hellfire Club? As you pointed out, he, like the original founder, is a member of Parliament."

"To be truthful, lad, I'm not certain. He's not a libertine, so I doubt he was a Hellfire member. He's leader of the radical party, but not a socialist. I sent word to Pollock Forbes, asking if he would tell me whether the man was a Freemason, and he was not. He is a politician, of course, and shall have something to say about the new bill raising the age of consent, but he was not highborn, so I doubt he is one of Hesketh's cronies. The only connection he seems to have at all with the case is Miss Potter herself. Perhaps he is smitten with her. She is an attractive young lady and he a notable bachelor in town."

"But he must be twice her age."

"Some do not think that a liability. He is well established and popular. He may be prime minister one day. She could do worse."

I shivered. Just the thought of her married to the man with his gimlet stare, monocle, and sharp manner made my flesh crawl. It seemed like a sentence of death.

Just then there was a sound on the stair and a streak of black shot into the room. Barker's dog, Harm, had returned from his sojourn in the north of England. He ran circles about the room, between and around table legs and stuffed chairs, his black fur rippling. When he had gained enough momentum, he launched himself onto the high bed, walking up his master's limbs until he sat on the Guv's chest, sniffing at the iodine and plaster on his face.

"*Nee hau, Da Mo.*" He greeted the creature in Mandarin, the language in which the dog had been trained, and roughly patted him on the head with his bandaged fingers. The dog, like Barker himself, generally eschewed displays of affection, but had no trouble displaying them now. He rolled over onto his back in Barker's lap and began kicking his paws and gurgling like a baby.

The big man with his little dog looked about the room with its books stacked in piles and its furnishings and the red walls bristling with all manner of weapons and spoke. "It is good to be home, Thomas."

33

THE NEXT DAY, BETWEEN US, MAC AND I CONVINCED the Guv not to go to service. I told him he must heal, that his body had suffered a shock, and that he didn't realize how close he'd come to death, but it was only when Mac told him his appearance would frighten visitors away from the Baptist Tabernacle that he agreed not to go.

I went downstairs to my own bed. I'd had a most irregular schedule since the case had begun and needed rest myself. When one has been sleeping on a hard mattress on the floor for a week or so, a bed with crisp sheets, soft pillows, and a down counterpane is the closest thing to floating on a cloud. I tried reading MacDonald but fell asleep after the first few pages and dozed through lunch.

After another dinner brought in from the Elephant and Castle, I sat down at my small table and got out pencil and paper. I had a solemn duty ahead of me, one for which I did not feel equipped. I had decided to track down my late wife's resting place to give her a proper burial. I had a satisfactory bank balance now and could afford to give her the funeral she had deserved. The cost meant nothing to me, but finding her was another story. I didn't quite know where to begin other than to explore every cemetery in Oxfordshire. I would also have to go to Oxford, the place of my former disgrace, and speak with the very court system that had been responsible for my incarceration, as well as to hire a solicitor to search for Jenny's mother. She was an avaricious creature, and smelling the money, would place hazards and injunctions in my path until she was bought off. Who knew how long that would take? Then there was the coffin to buy, the exhumation that I would not be there to oversee, and the service. A simple Methodist service was what I would prefer, and I hoped her mother would not cause a tempest over that. There was so much to do and so little hope it would all go as planned, but that didn't matter. I would do it for Jenny. It was my duty. I only hoped Barker would not mind my taking a few days off.

After breakfast the next morning, I went upstairs, for Barker was not in his garden as usual. I found him at one of the tables in his garret with an open copy of the *Pall Mall Gazette* in his hand. This was the day Stead fired his salvo at the House of Commons. "The Maiden Tribute of Modern Babylon" screamed the headline. When I entered, the Guv motioned me into the chair and put the article into my hand before charging his thimble cup with another spoonful of tea.

I read. Stead admitted everything, which was the only way, really. He gave names of everyone involved, explained the depth to which the government had allowed this to go, and the numbers of the girls involved. He turned "white slave trade" into a phrase that everyone would use for the next several years and then forced it onto every breakfast table in the land between the toast rack and the Dundee marmalade.

"Good heavens," I said when I finally finished. "The government shall not be able to sidestep this or play it down."

"Precisely," Barker said. "Stead knows how to provoke people as well as any sermon writer in England, but Hesketh's people shall retaliate, you may be sure."

Barker and I went to our chambers that morning, but my employer spent his time in the office receiving messages and telephone calls about the coming crisis. It appeared all of London was in an uproar over the special edition. Some were calling Stead a monster, and others naming him a hero. The *Gazette* editor had pulled back the grate on a stinking cesspool, and now London would have to acknowledge it and clean it up. The children of the East End owed much to William T. Stead, but I had learned enough in Barker's employ to know what happened to those who pointed out the government's faults. They usually received nothing but punishment.

The Guv sent me off to the charity to have a private word with Miss Potter. I was going to tell her that the case was over and her services were no longer required but that she had acted admirably. I also had things to discuss with her of a more private nature.

She was not at the charity, as it turned out. Some of the volunteers were away, for it appeared the government was going to speak upon the matter of the white slave trade, convened by Chamberlain himself, at a building in White-chapel in Commercial Street. If I hurried, I could just make it. I sprinted out the door, thinking that perhaps now I could finally make sense of the connection between Beatrice Potter and Chamberlain.

When I arrived at the building, the meeting was already under way. The meeting hall was packed full of lower-class parents who had been upset by the morning's article, which must have been dispersed and read far and wide. Her Majesty's government must have been very concerned about Stead's article to convene a hasty meeting just hours after publication. Joseph Chamberlain had been dispatched to clamp a lid down on the problem.

"The dangers in the *Gazette* have been exaggerated," he told the crowd. "It was an incendiary headline produced solely to sell newspapers. The number of white slavers in England is very small, and they have always been caught and prosecuted."

"Then why has Mr. Stead barricaded himself in his offices?" a man asked from the audience.

"No doubt because the scandalmonger fears arrest from Scotland Yard."

I had to admire Chamberlain's fearlessness. The crowd could quite easily turn into a mob.

"Why hasn't there been a successful bill to raise the age of consent?" a woman asked. Her daughter was sitting beside her, obviously close to that age.

"We hope the bill will not be forced upon us," Chamberlain explained. "It is not that Her Majesty's government finds this unimportant. No one finds the slave trade more reprehensible than we. However, you must understand that there is a queue, and that bringing forward this bill shall push back badly needed funding or reform in other quarters."

They would not allow him to pontificate but peppered him with questions. I was impressed by his calm demeanor and logical mind. No subject was brought up on which he was not fully informed. Perhaps the government was capable of handling this, one could see them thinking, but there were still skeptics and angry mothers who remained unappeased.

I looked through the mass of people and saw Miss Levy sitting beside Miss Hill, but Beatrice Potter was not with them. Scanning the faces of the crowd, I looked for her light hair and lovely face before finally spotting her in the back, half hidden by a pillar. She leaned forward, looking mesmerized. Chamberlain's speech was not that enthralling. And then I realized what was happening. She and this man were lovers, despite the wide gap in their years. I had never stood a chance with her. When she had followed me from the British Museum, it had been merely to secure employment as a professional agent. I reached into my pocket for her check and, skirting the crowd, came up behind her. She started when I spoke.

"Good morning, Miss Potter," I said, raising my hat formally. "I realize this speech is important, but I would like to speak with you outside for a few moments."

She hesitated for a moment and then followed me out into Commercial Street, where the sunlight must have highlighted my burns.

"Oh, Thomas, your face."

"It will heal. I've gotten used to getting hurt in this line of work."

She understood my underlying irony, pursing her lips and looking down. "You found Gwendolyn's killer," she said at last. "It was Stephen Carrick. Inspector Swanson told us this morning. The charity is quite upset over it all, especially Miss Levy. She says it is yet another woman's life ruined by a rapacious husband."

I saw Rose Carrick in my mind's eye, flinging a pan of acid at me. I would hardly have called her a victim, but perhaps it was best to keep my own counsel. These girls had been her friends, after all, and perhaps the only semblance of normality she had known.

"I feel terrible that I never told you about Joseph," she continued. "I used you to make him jealous. I didn't plan to, but it happened anyway."

"Do the two of you plan to wed?"

"I'm not certain anymore. We have seen each other for a couple of years, but there has never been any formal announcement of engagement. We've broken it off twice. I felt free to speak with you and to invite you to hear Miss Lee speak, but I must admit I wanted to tweak Joseph's nose. You were a fine escort and I enjoyed our evening very much. More than I can say."

"Are you and Mr. Chamberlain together again?"

"We are at an impasse. I no longer believe he will marry me, and I refuse to be his mistress. Oh, I am wretched!" She held the palms of her hands to her eyes.

"I'm sorry," I said, and genuinely meant it. I didn't hold her actions against her, now that I knew more about them. She had already been punished more than I would wish.

"Mr. Barker asked me to give you this," I said, pulling an envelope from my pocket. "He encloses a bank draft for your services and a letter of recommendation. He sends you his compliments and says if you wish more work in the future, to speak with him again."

"Thank you," she said, taking the envelope. "I was very glad to help him, but I don't believe I shall be available for future work. This has been a rather trying time for me."

I pulled my handkerchief from my breast pocket and gave it to her. She wiped her eyes and held it to her lips, stifling a cry, before handing it back to me.

"I'd better get back in. Who knows what Joseph will promise the crowd." She attempted a smile. "I didn't want you to hate me, Thomas."

"Small chance of that, Beatrice, if I may call you that at our parting. I wish you only happiness."

"Thank you," she replied in a ragged voice.

I lifted my bowler and bowed, not daring to show how wretched I felt. "Good day, Miss Potter."

I whistled for a hansom, conscious of her scrutiny. Climbing into the cab, I waved, and then she walked into the hall and I never saw her again.

I was dispirited when I arrived back in Craig's Court. She had treated me poorly, so why did it feel as if it were the other way about? Beatrice was in a bad situation and all because of Chamberlain.

"Did you find Miss Potter?" the Guv asked when I returned.

"I did." Right then, I decided not to tell Barker about the relationship unless he continued to pursue Chamberlain's part in the case. "She said to thank you for the letter of recommendation."

"She deserved it," he said.

"Has the major communicated with you?"

"Not so far, though I sent him a note detailing all that we uncovered. He may be at his barracks."

"I hope so," I said. "I mean, I hope he hasn't gone back to the drinking."

"I would not worry over his lack of response. The poor fellow's got a lot to think over."

Jenkins came in with a new edition of *The Times*. I left the Guv alone to read it while beginning the process of preparing a bill. There was a weeks' worth of cab fares, Soho Vic's lads, the warehouse rental, and a half dozen other expenses. I wondered if I should expect a bill from Reverend McClain for his instruction, as well. Then another thought occurred to me.

"What shall become of little Esme, sir?"

"I'll send a message to Andrew to find a proper home for her, at least until her brother is released from the workhouse."

"Do you think he was angry about my losing the first boxing match?"

"If I know him, he'll say it was a typical example of the inadequacy of gloved boxing and your winning without them is proof. You needn't worry on that score."

"Has anything happened with Stead?"

"He is still in his office, refusing interviews. Vic reports that the Ratcliff Highway Boys have been gathering materials all day. Something is very definitely in the offing. *The Times* has been assessing public opinion all day and, I believe, shall come down in favor of a bill raising the age of consent to sixteen. I would hazard the bill is already being written by liberal members of the House of Commons.

The fight, however, shall be in the House of Lords, where Hesketh and his party votes. The latest editorials claim it shall pass, but not without some struggles."

"Are we going to the *Gazette* office then?"

"Oh, you may be sure of it."

After a dinner of haddock at the Northumberland Hotel, we proceeded to the *Pall Mall Gazette* building.

There was a large crowd in the street, and somewhere up ahead I heard the sound of breaking glass. I pushed my way through after my employer. When I finally reached the offices, everything looked so different from the last time we'd been there, I thought perhaps a bomb had gone off.

All the lower windows of the newspaper office were broken, and inside one could see a makeshift barricade of desks and filing cabinets. The upstairs windows were still intact, and now and again I could see the top of a man's head peer over the sill. In front of the building there were dozens of broken bottles, along with rotting vegetables, eggs, and fish offal, all glittering on the pavement. I lost sight of my employer but recognized the Ratcliff Highway Boys, with whom we had faced off in Bethnal Green. Lord Hesketh was keeping them very busy these days. Barker surfaced then, pushing his way through the crowd. He made his way to the door and knocked upon it through a hail of flying bottles, which he ignored.

The door opened quickly, and Barker stepped in but not before another volley of glass crashed into the office entranceway.

"Look, there's Barker's man," one of the gang members said, and I realized all of them were looking my way. Their leader stepped through the knot of them to get a look at me.

"It's him, all right," he said.

I wasn't sure whether they really meant mischief to me, but I was not about to take any chances. I thrust my hand into my pocket and raised my coat with my fingers around the butt of my Webley in its built-in holster. I gave it a gentle push until the muzzle poked through the eyelet hole sewn into the hem. Whatever happened, the leader of the Ratcliff boys was going down with me.

The leader shrugged his shoulders and raised his hands. "Keep your shirt on," he said. "You're a nervous little cove, aren't ye? No need to be a-fingerin' firearms. We're just 'avin' a bit o'fun."

Then they turned back and continued to pelt the door with bottles and food. They were yelling and joking and making a lot of noise, but if this was a siege, it looked like it would be a long one.

I assessed what strength the crowd might have. There were a dozen or so Ratcliff boys, and it looked as if the tumult had emptied every public house in the area. If they finally broke through the door, how much of this crowd would go with them, and what would happen then? Would they hang Stead from a nearby gas lamp? One could not tell what would happen when a crowd turned into a mob. *Where were the police?* I wondered. A Division was not so many streets away.

Barker slipped out again, and when the barrage of glass missiles came his way, he butted them away impatiently with the brass head of his walking stick.

"You!" he said, pointing to the leader as he walked to the center of the circle. The rough-hewn man met him there. I was not going to be left out; and as I stepped across, a fourth man, obviously his lieutenant, came as well. Our quartet met in the middle.

"How far are you prepared to take this?" Barker asked.

"As far as it need be," the young man jeered back.

"But how far are you contracted to go? Are you here to frighten Stead or to take him?"

"To take him."

"The damage is already done," the Guv said. "The article came out this morning."

"But Stead'll come out with another one tomorrow."

"If we let you come in and stop the press, will you let Stead alone?"

"Nah," he said flatly. "He is to be made an example of."

Barker crossed his burly arms and stood in thought. "There is a lot of give in that statement," he finally stated. "Do you intend to take his life?"

"I didn't say that, did I?"

"Break an arm or leg, then?"

"Hadn't thought that far. Are you tryin' to broker a compromise?"

"I did not say that, but it appears we are at an impasse. I'm certainly not going to recommend to him that he come out so you can break his head."

"He should have thought of that before he started making reckless remarks in the newspapers."

"I think it best," Barker said, addressing me, "if we went in and joined Stead."

Our quartet separated, and the bottles came flying again like arrows at a besieged castle. We squeezed sideways through the doorway, closed the door behind us, and listened as more glass shattered on it.

Most of the ground floor was deserted, but there was a brace of Salvation Army women at the door who seemed capable of taking on the entire crowd outside themselves and were not frightened by a little glass. In the back, there was a printing press going full blast, putting out another special edition for the next morning. Upstairs we found a couple of dozen employees watching anxiously out the windows. In Stead's office, the editor himself sat at his desk, while across from him, the stern but clear-cut features of General Bramwell Booth of the Salvation Army regarded us calmly. If the purpose of the crowd outside was to frighten the men into submission, they had chosen the wrong men. For all the cowering employees outside in the hall, these two acted as if it were any other evening.

"Their intent," Barker explained to the editor, "is to do you harm."

"I am prepared for that," Stead said coolly. "My subordinates have copy for the next two days, and if we are broken into and the press smashed, I have arranged with the *Standard* to borrow theirs for a limited run."

"How capable do you think they are of carrying out their threats?" Booth asked my employer.

"They are hirelings and only in it for the purse. I doubt there are many in the crowd genuinely perturbed over the 'Maiden Tribute' article. However, we cannot control the crowd. If they are agitated, we could have a riot on our hands. How well are you prepared for a siege?"

"We have food and water for a day or so," Stead said. "If they make a concerted effort to break in the door, we can push the press in front of it."

There was a crash of glass behind us, as one of the upper windows was shattered by a paving stone.

"Did you expect such a response?" I asked.

"Oh, yes," Stead said.

"They shall certainly have to force a bill in the House of Commons after today," Booth stated. "The edition has sold out. Half of London has read it."

"Shall you bring the child you purchased back to England now?" Barker asked.

"Soon," Stead replied.

Booth cleared his throat. "She's in a Salvation Army property we own in the north of France."

"Eliza is a smart little thing," the *Gazette* editor said, referring to the child in question. "She should do well if she is to speak at my trial."

"You believe it shall come to that?"

"It may, that is, if I survive this night."

There was a sudden thud at the outer door.

"Woodbury!" Stead called. "What is that racket?"

A young and frightened-looking clerk came shuffling into the room. "They've pulled a stout table from one of the pubs, sir, and are trying to use it as a ram."

There was a second crash against the door and a third. Barker looked over at me, as if to say it is only a matter of time now. Then suddenly, it stopped.

"What the deuce?" Barker asked.

Woodbury came shuffling in again.

"The police, sir! They've just arrived. It looks as if some of the crowd is going away."

"Thank heavens," Booth said, and Stead gave a sigh of relief.

Our celebration was premature, however. The Yard had not come to save W. T. Stead at all.

"Stead! Open this door and surrender yourself," a voice boomed from a speaking trumpet in one of the inspector's hands. "You are under arrest for transporting a child out of the country."

Stead drummed his fingers atop the blotter of his desk and rose. "I suppose that is it, then," he said. "You know what to do, Booth."

"I shall arrange counsel," the general said, shaking his hand. "God bless you, William."

"Thank you, Bram. Mr. Barker, they might have hanged me waiting for the police to arrive. I owe you a debt."

Booth's guardians at the front door allowed the police in, and soon we were all being questioned about the event of the evening, while Stead was put in darbies and escorted to Scotland Yard. The *Gazette* office was in complete disarray, and I did not envy the staff the tremendous work and expenditure necessary to get it looking as respectable as it once did, but I noticed that the press never stopped cranking out endless copies of the next edition. Booth took over Stead's chair and fired off messages and before we left, I noted that most of the staff was seated in front of typewriting machines, taking down the events they had witnessed firsthand that evening for the later edition.

By the time Barker and I left, the crowd had almost dispersed. People loitered about here and there, looking at broken brickbats and an inch-thick carpet of broken glass in front of the *Gazette*'s door. Of our friends, the Ratcliff Highway Boys, there was no sign.

34

I WAS LYING ON MY BED WITH MY ARM BEHIND MY head and a copy of *Donal Grant* in my hand. I wasn't doing MacDonald justice, idly turning pages, but then he was not the sort of author to read when one is feeling down. After another ten minutes, I tossed the book down on the bed and began counting the beams in the ceiling.

"Am I interrupting, sir?"

Mac had come in. I don't know what he puts on all the hinges in the house that all the doors open soundlessly, but it is faintly unnerving.

"I was working up a thought, but I don't believe I have the right equipment, and it hardly seems worth the effort. What do you want, Mac?"

"There is a young lady who wishes to speak to you."

Until I am dead, I shall always consider those to be agreeable words.

"Pretty?" I asked. For some reason, I've always considered Mac a fine judge of women.

"Yes, sir. Quite attractive."

"Did she give a name? Is it Miss Potter?"

"No, sir. Your visitor is Miss Amy Levy."

"Miss Levy?" I asked, putting my feet over the side of the bed and pulling on my first boot. "How extraordinary. I wonder what she wants. We cannot speak in the street. Show her into the garden and pick a flower for her, Mac. Recite poetry until I get there."

Mac rolled his eyes. "Very good, sir."

Lacing my other boot, I debated putting on a new pair of spats I'd recently purchased. Granted, I had no romantic plans for Miss Levy, considering her Israel Zangwill's girl; and, though she seemed rather sharp at times, how often does one find a girl at one's doorstep, delivered like a parcel? I straightened my tie before going downstairs.

Out in the garden, Miss Levy's petite form was turned away, surveying the miniature vistas in front of her. She wore a blue-gray dress with a white collar and seemed the kind of no-nonsense woman that eschewed artifice of any kind.

"Good day, Miss Levy."

She turned but did not smile, which was not a good sign.

"What an odd garden," she eventually said.

"It is Oriental."

"I know it is Oriental, Mr. Llewelyn. I am not ignorant. Tell me, does Mr. Barker enjoy torturing the trees?" She pointed to the corner where the Guv's *Pen-jing* trees stood on display.

"I think he rather does," I said, wondering if she had a reason for coming here other than to discuss Barker's trees.

She regarded me with her dark eyes. "I came here to slap your face for breaking Beatrice's heart, but it hardly seems worth the effort now. One hears how painful it is to be slapped, but nobody ever talks about how it hurts to slap someone. Why is that?"

"I scarce can say."

"My word, those are the ugliest spats I've ever seen."

We looked down at my boots. She was right. What had I been thinking?

"You cut me to the quick. I presume you have some information to impart, that is, if you've resolved one way or another whether you shall slap me."

"I'm still mulling it over. I came here with the express purpose of doing so, but something about being here has changed my mind."

"The garden does do that to people. Shall we go and sit in the pavilion?"

We crossed the little bridge that spans the brook and made our way up the rock steps to the pavilion where Barker spends of good deal of his time in fair weather. In the very center of it, Harm sat, mildly twitching his tail.

"And who is this?" Amy Levy asked.

"It is Harm, the guardian of the garden."

"He did not guard against me," she noted. "He never even left this spot."

"He likes women. It is men he attacks. He tried to bite Israel the one time he came out here."

"I've wanted to bite him myself once or twice. You are correct about the garden, by the way. It's very peaceful out here. I can hardly believe I'm in Newington. But that is not the reason I came here. I want to tell you about Beatrice."

I felt a tightening in my stomach. "What has happened to her?"

"She has had a nervous collapse, I'm afraid. She has given up her room and position at the Katherine Building and her volunteer work entirely and has gone back to live with her family."

"I am heartily sorry to hear that," I said, while inwardly a mantle of guilt fell about my shoulders. Perhaps I had been too forthright. I should have spoken to her more gently or stayed longer to see what she would do. Palmister Clay notwithstanding, I hate to inflict pain upon another human being, particularly one I genuinely liked. "Did she give any message to you for me or say anything about me?"

"That is a typical male response, Mr. Llewelyn," Miss Levy said coldly. "This is not about you. It is about her."

"Yes, yes, I know that. I'm sorry."

"She began planning her departure shortly after seeing you, from what I could gather. What exactly did you say to her?"

"I—wished her happiness."

She got up and walked across the lawn to the brook and watched it burble over the stones.

"I cannot understand it," she finally said. "Beatrice was so far above you. You are an ex-convict, working in an unsuitable occupation with limited prospects, while she is a brilliant young woman, attractive, from an excellent family, and she cared for you. And yet, you threw her over and broke her heart. Are you mad? Whatever made you do it?"

"Are you here on her behalf? Did she send you?"

"No, she did not send me. I rejoice in the breakup. You were unsuitable for her in every way. You were a disaster. I merely wanted to look you in the eye and to find out why you ended the relationship."

It was right there on the tip of my tongue. All I need do was spit it out, to say those few words. She loved another. It would have been so easy, particularly when faced by this angry young woman. But I couldn't. I don't claim to be a gentleman, but my father had taught me right from wrong; and it was wrong to reveal a young lady's confidences, even to her friend. Barker had reinforced the notion. With his strong views on Christian behavior and his more secular quotations from Confucius on how a gentleman should act, he had influenced me more strongly than I had realized. It gave me no defense in these actions. I knew what I had to do. I must take the blame.

"The fault was all mine, Miss Levy," I said. "I have issues of my own not related to her. I met her in the British Museum and found her charming. She offered to help us on the case, and I was taken with her. Before I knew it, we had begun a kind of courtship, but I was not ready for such a commitment. As you said, I am totally unsuitable for her, and what would I say when standing in front of a skeptical father, asking for her hand? I simply do not fit into good society."

Miss Levy bent down and picked up a pebble, tossing it into the brook. Then she took a slow walk about the garden, stepping across the boardwalk that skirted the pond, past the *Pen-jing* trees and through the standing rocks, over the bridge, and back to the pavilion. She sat down again.

"I was wrong," she began. "About the garden, I mean. It's not a regular garden, and it's rather austere, but it has something about it. It looks as if it's been here for hundreds of years."

"Barker works hard to make it look that way. He has a team of Chinese gardeners that work for him."

She looked me levelly in the eye. I believe she was a little nearsighted. It was unsettling.

"I was wrong about you, as well. Beatrice told me all about what happened with Joseph—well, about everything. I said you were unworthy of her and she defended you. I came, expecting you to reveal all her secrets. It's what most men in your position would have done. I can argue very well."

"I noticed that."

"I hoped to trip you up. But you took the blame yourself."

"The blame really is mine," I told her. "I'm still getting over various issues of my own. I lost my wife not two years ago, and much has happened since. Even had Miss Potter been free from any emotional encumbrance, our relationship would have been severely handicapped at best."

"That is . . . honest."

"I would not have you admiring me under false pretenses."

She smiled. "I have not said I admire you, Mr. Llewelyn."

"I imagine it would take a great deal to win your admiration, Miss Levy."

Just then I was looking at Amy Levy, and she was leaning toward me, a little too close for strict chasteness, perhaps, and I noticed something. I could detect the scent of powder. Despite the fact this young woman was being courted by my best friend in the world, for that one brief second, I desired her. I did the only proper thing: I moved to the other side of the pavilion for a respite and time to think.

"What is it?" Miss Levy asked, for she was quick and intelligent and nothing got by her much, I am certain.

"An epiphany," I said. "Something Barker said to me earlier just fell into place. It is a private enquiry agent's stock in trade."

Miss Levy stood. "I should be going. I must apologize to you, Mr. Llewelyn, for misjudging you. You aren't the opportunist I thought you were."

I gave her a grim smile. She knew me better than she realized, but it would do no good to tell her that. I walked her to the front door and dared shake her hand, which was dry and warm.

"When next you speak with Miss Potter, tell her I inquired after her, and that I am sorry I caused her any distress. It was not my intent to upset her life."

"I shall tell her, Mr. Llewelyn. Might I say that you are a true gentleman, one of the few I've met in London."

"I thank you, Miss Levy. That is high praise, indeed. Good day."

I found her a cab and saw her on her way, then went up to my room, feeling the irony of her last statement. A gentleman, me? I threw myself on the bed again and looked up at the beams overhead, all sixteen of them. Barker was one of the few men I knew who deserved the name.

I thought of the other meaning of "gentleman," the landed aristocracy. No doubt they considered themselves our betters. By rights, Palmister Clay was a gentleman, but not by my definition. A gentleman does not cheat on his wife or ruin a young girl. How can a man hold his head up knowing what he was doing to these women? I wanted to go back to the German Gymnasium and punch his face all over again.

I thought a lot about it over the next few hours and the

conclusion I came to was this: Man is capable of doing great harm, either in a single desperate act, or over a protracted period of time, out of neglect or selfishness or even laziness. But man can be more than a brute, and he should be. I shall even be optimistic enough to say he was designed to be more. Mind you, it is not easy, but it can be done.

I assumed that Barker would take a day or two to recover after his injury, but the next day, there we sat in our offices as if it were any other day. His short hair stood up on his head and with the red blotches on his face along his jawline and his bristling mustache half growing in again, he looked like nothing save a convict.

The Guv slid into his leather swivel chair, contemplated the stack of letters that had accumulated like snow on the side of the desk, and made a pronouncement, much as God himself did after creation.

"It is good to be back."

"Indeed."

Barker picked up the post and began looking through it. "There seems to have been an uncommonly large group of people in need of my services while I was recuperating," he noted.

"With your permission, sir, I'd like to recommend a client who might take top priority."

Barker turned his face toward me. I'd gotten his full attention.

"And who is this client?"

"It is I, sir."

"You?"

"Yes, sir."

"You wish to hire me?"

"I do not think I can make myself any plainer, sir. Yes, I wish to avail myself of your services. My bank account is now such that I can afford you, in a limited capacity, at least."

He turned his head to the side in a way I've seen Harm do when I'd done something that puzzled him. I suppose he was wondering about the ethics of taking on his assistant as a client. Finally he shrugged. "Very well."

"I need—"

Barker raised a hand, then gestured in front of him. "The client's chair," he said.

I got up from my desk and moved to the chair. It was the first time I had ever sat in it. From there, I had to say that Barker looked most imposing, even with his spiky hair.

The Guv lifted up the cigar box and opened it, offering it to me. I shook my head. He was enjoying this little masquerade.

"Very well, Mr. Llewelyn," he said, putting down the box and resting his thick fingers on the blotter. "What can I do for you today?"

"I wish you to locate the remains of my late wife, which are probably in Oxford, though I cannot be sure. I want to give her the burial she deserves." I reached into my pocket and took out a check, drawn of course on my private account. "This is to retain your services."

Barker looked at the check in his hand, read it over, and looked at me. Then he put it on the far edge of the desk, nearest my own, and sat back in his chair.

"I accept."

There was no other man in London I would trust with such a task. For that matter, there was no one else in the world.

ACKNOWLEDGMENTS

I would like to thank my editor, Amanda Patten, and my agent, Maria Carvainis, for their support and suggestions. I would also like to thank my daughters, Caitlin and Heather, who act as sounding boards, and my dear wife, Julia, who works tirelessly to help me with these novels because she believes in Barker and Llewelyn and most of all in me.

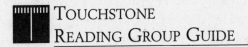
The Hellfire Conspiracy

1. *The Hellfire Conspiracy* opens with Major Trevor DeVere of Her Majesty's Horse Guard unceremoniously forcing his way into private inquiry agent Cyrus Barker's office. Why is the major upset? How does Barker get the major to shape up before he suffers a complete breakdown?

2. With what kind of tone does our narrator, Thomas Llewelyn, assistant to Cyrus Barker, describe the opening events? What does Llewelyn's tone reveal about him? What words would you use to describe him from the way he tells the story?

3. What is the meaning of "white slavery?" How does it differ from any other slavery? Discuss why this is or isn't a racist phrase in 1885.

4. When Llewelyn mentions the legal age of consent—13 years old—are you surprised? What does "legal age of

consent" mean? Does its present meaning differ today from that of 1885? What should the legal age of consent be? Why is it not 13 today?

5. What reason does Barker give when Llewelyn asks why the government doesn't put an end to white slavery? What does Barker's answer tell you about his beliefs regarding class and social justice?

6. William Stead, editor of the *Pall Mall Gazette,* is also investigating the disappearance of young girls. What is the goal of his investigation, and how does it differ from that of Barker and Llewelyn? From the goals of the police? What happens to Stead in the end?

7. How does the rivalry between Scotland Yard, the Thames Police, and the Metropolitan Police influence the plot? Do similar rivalries exist between governmental service groups today?

8. What is the common factor among the girls who have gone missing? How does this commonality lead Barker to the murderer? Are you surprised when you learn who the murderer is? Were clues provided prior to the revelation? If so, what were they?

9. Each installment in Will Thomas's series of books reveals a little more about Llewelyn's past. What new fact do we learn about his past in *The Hellfire Conspiracy?*

10. What do you think about journalism that has a social goal behind it—can it be unbiased, as journalism is supposed to strive to be? Does this type of journalism have a legitimate place in the greater arena of news reporting?

Book Club Tips

1. Visit willthomasauthor.com and share some of what you've learned about the author at a future meeting of your club.

2. Read the previous Barker and Llewelyn books chronologically, and discuss how the characters change and what keeps them interesting to you.

3. Sample Joseph Jacobs's *English Fairy Tales*, and compare and contrast the Mr. Miacca you find there with the character who appears in *The Hellfire Conspiracy*.

4. Discuss who should play each of the characters in the film version of *The Hellfire Conspiracy*, and why.

5. Find an English-style pub in your town and hold your meeting there.

A Conversation with Will Thomas

1. **Llewelyn and Barker continue to become more complementary to each other as partners (Llewelyn's book learning coupled with Barker's street smarts) in each succeeding novel. How do you envision their relationship in future stories? Will Llewelyn ever become Barker's equal? Or must Barker remain somewhat aloof and mysterious to Llewelyn in order to keep the interplay between the two characters interesting?**

   Eventually, most of Barker's secret past will tumble out. As Llewelyn moves from apprentice to journeyman agent, he will face increasing dangers and will grow. Both men must rely upon each other to survive and will go through trials and changes in their personal lives. Beyond that, Llewelyn hasn't told me yet.

2. **You write your books using pen and paper rather than a computer. Why? Do the pen and paper spark more creativity in you?**

   Pen and paper bind me closer to the characters. Sometimes I draw a character in the margin before I create a word portrait. In fact, the drawing left by Inspector Bainbridge in *The Limehouse Text* began as an actual sketch I made when I first plotted the novel.

3. **How much do the highly developed characters drive your story? What other factors help determine which plotline comes next?**

My characters provide good vehicles for moving the plot along, but ultimately it is social issues that drive my novels, such as anti-Semitism, terrorism, and child abuse, issues we are still struggling with today. At the same time, the entire series could be considered a bildungsroman about Thomas Llewelyn, as he grows from callow youth into full adulthood under Barker's tutelage.

4. **What was your inspiration for the plot of *The Hellfire Conspiracy*?**

I came across a quotation while researching *Some Danger Involved*, something about every Jewish mother in the East End fearing that her children would be snatched by white slavers. When something like that intrigues me, I always ask myself what the worst is that could happen. Then I throw that threat into Barker's lap.

5. **Is the character William Stead based upon a real person from history? If so, is he someone you admire?**

Stead's final moments were aboard the Titanic, helping women and children into the lifeboats, and calming those around him. He was a paradoxical mixture of socialist and Christian, as well as a newspaperman known for shocking headlines and hyperbolical expression. It was his efforts that finally produced a law against child prostitution. He was real, and yes, I admire him very much.

6. **In this exchange between Llewelyn and Barker, whose views do you sympathize with more, and why?**

> **Llewelyn:** "I thought this was a Christian country."

> **Barker:** "Then you are misinformed. We live on a mean, sinful planet, Thomas, and it shall only get worse if the Lord should tarry."

This question cuts close to the bone. Do I think we live on a mean, sinful planet which shall get worse before it gets better? Absolutely. But that doesn't mean we should stop trying to change it, or give up all hope that it can be improved.

7. **Why did you introduce Beatrice Potter into the story?**

When I first read of Miss Potter's thorny involvement with Joseph Chamberlain, I said to myself, here's another way to break Llewelyn's heart. I cannot recall another story in which a fictional character actually dates a historical figure, so I wanted to try it. Most of the characters in *The Hellfire Conspiracy* were real people, so it was a challenge to bring them into the story and yet render them faithfully.

Beatrice Potter (who should not be confused with children's author Beatrix Potter) eventually wed Sydney Webb, and the duo were famous political radicals during the 1880s and early 1900s, responsible for the passage of several laws on welfare and labor issues.

8. **The role of Jews in socialism and in many social causes is highlighted in _The Hellfire Conspiracy._ What inspired you to focus on this topic? What are some little-known aspects of social change or of the socialist movement in the late 1800s?**

Jews have a long tradition of doing good works for the community, both through donations to public works and through championing causes. The East End of the 1880s had severe social problems, such as poverty, crime, poor working conditions, and crowded tenements, and educated Jews worked to improve all of them. I chose to focus on this subject after studying the historical Jewish figures Israel Zangwill and Amy Levy. Also, most people don't know that Christian organizations were active in such causes, too—the Salvation Army, for example, was a militant participant in the socialist movement of that era.

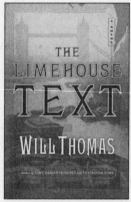